An Empire of Dreams

I0461061

LEWIS J JONES

LEWIS J JONES

DEDICATION

To Robert and Eileen.
This is for you.

LEWIS J JONES

ACKNOWLEDGMENTS

Thank you to everyone who asked how the book was going.
You gave me the strength and determination
to put pen to paper.

And thank you to you, for beginning this adventure.

AN EMPIRE OF DREAMS

— CHAPTER ONE —

The Fleeing Family

The dream of spring felt more distant than ever before. Summer had been a beautiful lie, autumn a blustery storm, and now the scathing hand of winter was at play. The once golden fields and thriving meadows of Merlow had been gradually transformed by the season's astonishing beauty. So tenderly the snow had fallen, dressing the endless patches of green in cloths of pristine white. The tops of ponds formed brittle shells, and curtains of woolly clouds slowly drew in overhead. Only then, when all was convinced of its cool innocence, did winter prevail with sullen brutality. A fierce tempest had grown over the course of a few days, drumming up arctic winds off the thunderous shoreline and hurling hurricanes down the streets. Hedges were stripped bare and loose windowpanes rattled and cracked in their frames whilst the shrinking days slowly sank into a favoured memory. Winter had never been so stunningly violent.

Alex sat at the window watching the fat flakes fall, mesmerised by their swift and daring dance. They topped the neat hedges and sprinkled the tall trees of the front garden he was surveilling, setting the scene as silent and absent of all life. Alex found his eyes tracing the reflection of his father's shadow, which stretched out over the snowy carpet. Despite his father standing in the stuffy heat of the hallway nearby, he was visibly shivering.

Two beams of light emerged at the road junction opposite, piercing the thick blizzard. Alex and his father watched together for a moment as the car drove cautiously down the street. Then the shadow swelled back into the warmth.

'He'll be here soon,' said Alex's mother to his father. 'It's not half past seven yet and he's always so punctual.'

His father gave a low hum. 'Yeah, I suppose he is.'

'It's going to be all right, you know. We get this done, we get tonight done, and you will feel the world better, trust me,' she said, her voice strong but soft. 'The world better . . .'

The past few weeks had been long and strange for the Priar family. It was out on an icy road, similar to the one Alex was now staring at, where his grandparents had tragically died. It was a car accident, he had been told, but a copy of last week's *Merlow Messenger* had told him considerably more. Their car had unexpectedly veered into oncoming traffic before crashing through the roadside barrier and skidding into a ditch towards the neighbouring village of Magralow. The sadness that hung over the family was like an oppressive cloud, painted even blacker by the fact that no one seemed to know just where his grandparents had been headed at eleven o'clock on an otherwise uneventful Sunday night.

A pinprick of light grew until a small red car came skidding out of the junction and bumped up the kerb outside Alex's house. The car's engine promptly stalled, a door slammed, and Alex could make out a slim figure battling its way through the snow and up the path through the front garden.

'That's him!' his father gasped.

Moving into the hall to welcome his uncle, Alex found his mother standing a few paces back from his father. A heavy stare of concern was locked upon her face, but as she spotted Alex her expression broke into a faint smile.

'Perfect timing. Uncle Abraham's just arrived,' she said, cuddling Alex at her side. 'Must have gotten caught up with the weather.' She looked down for a brief second, and Alex noticed tears welling in her bright blue eyes.

'Are you OK?' Alex said.

'Of course I'm OK,' she said with a sniff, rubbing his arm. 'I'm fine.'

Abraham climbed the steps and called out, 'William!' as he and Alex's father crashed into each other's arms. There was a moment of heartfelt mumbling between them, and when they separated Abraham rubbed his narrow, bony face. 'Brrr! So very cold! Sorry for being so late, the bleedin' car wouldn't start!' He wiped his eyes. 'Alex!' he then said with a gasp, rushing over to ruffle his hair.

'I'm glad you're here,' Alex said, looking up to his uncle with great admiration.

Leaning down, Abraham replied, 'Me too!' before brushing the snow from his slippers and turning to Meredith. 'Merry . . .' He sighed, squeezing her in a warm hug. 'How we've missed you. Maudlyn sends her love.'

'So glad you could make it. How are you?' As she took a step back, her gaze travelled down Abraham's tall body and then up again; beneath the weary, woolly shell of his cardigan he was hovering dangerously close to gauntness and ill-health. 'How are you both doing?'

'We are well—as well as we can be. I would have told Alex to come to ours but Maud said it'd be good for me to get out. I haven't left her side in weeks.' When Abraham noted the time, William and Meredith pulled on their coats and stepped out onto the icy top step. They each gave Alex a great hug and kissed him on the head before linking arms.

'I'm sorry you have to leave so soon,' Abraham said, his arm now cuddling Alex as they stood on the balmy border. 'How about you all come to ours for dinner? An evening next week? I know Maud would love to see you.'

'Of course we will. Sounds like a great idea,' Meredith said, tying her scarf.

'Love you, son,' William said.

'Love you,' Meredith added, and with that, they descended the steps through the white garden and moved out into the dark street. After one lasting wave they walked along out of sight.

By the time his parents had driven away, Alex had rushed off to set up the game of chess, his uncle's favourite game, in the lounge immediately off the hall. His uncle soon joined him on the thick rug, his nose burning as brightly as the handsome scarlet walls. The game stormed into play. Alex had long since learned, by letting his uncle win, he was guaranteed the treasured prize of his uncle's joy in return.

After the grandfather clock struck its eighth and final chime, the telephone abruptly screamed from the hall.

'Hello?' Alex said as he picked up the receiver.

'. . . Hello? Is that . . . ? Hel-hello?' The elderly woman's voice was crackly but not from the bad connection. 'Alex, is that?—It-it's your aunt. Is Abe there? I need him . . .'

Finding his uncle paralysed with fear at his side, Alex hastily passed him the phone.

'Maud, are you all right? What's wrong?'

Abraham fired his questions, and his eyes bulged behind his heavy glasses. Almost shrieking that he would be with her right away, he unintentionally slammed the phone on its hook. He launched back into his boots and had barely managed to say, 'I'll be right back!' before the door clanked shut behind him.

The small red car skidded away and Alex retired to the sofa to face the empty room. He was certain his uncle wouldn't be long. Maudlyn often needed Abraham's aid at the drop of a hat when he wasn't at her side. As his eyes became heavy, Alex allowed them gentle rest. He pushed back into the cushions and within no time felt himself drift from the cusp of wakefulness and plunge, dreamlessly, into the depths of sleep.

*

BANG! BANG! BANG!

Alex bolted upright and rubbed his face. The grandfather clock wore the expression of quarter past eight in the corner of the room. The door blew open the moment he pulled on the handle, but to Alex's surprise, the top step was empty.

BANG! BANG! BANG!

The three loud knocks rapped through the house from behind him. Battling the door shut and turning around, Alex felt as though his insides had slid into a bucket of ice: through the square glass panes of the back door he could see three dark figures. The shadows swayed in the brisk wind. Taking hesitant steps through the bright hall and into the gloomy kitchen, Alex could see their heads move in sync, following him.

'Hello!' The middle figure spoke abruptly in a loud, booming voice.

Alex stopped. His racing heart lurched within him. 'Hello,' he replied with a quiver.

'We are sorry to disturb you. So sorry,' said a woman in a calmer tone. 'We hope we haven't scared you. Our vehicle has faulted, er—broken, not far from here.' She pointed back to somewhere beyond the heavy snowfall.

A sharp gust of wind shot at the three figures, nearly knocking them over, so Alex hastily unlocked the door and offered them refuge, luring them into the brightness and warmth of the hall in order to see them better.

The central body emerged first, dressed in a long black cloak and propped up by a silver cane. Peering down at Alex through his thick bottle-end glasses, the man lifted the corners of his mouth, which was set in an aged, wise-looking face. 'Hello again. We can see each other now!' he announced in his lively voice. 'My name is Winton, and it is a great pleasure to meet you this evening.' His striped black suit and waistcoat were briefly exposed as he bowed over one arm.

As the shorter man and the woman joined him on either side, Winton guided them further into the house.

'This is Irwin here,' Winton said. The man had jet-black hair, a square-ish face and a particularly strong, short jawline. 'My son-in-law.'

Irwin shook Alex's hand firmly and nodded to him. 'A pleasure it is to meet you,' he said.

'And this is my daughter, Evelyn,' Winton continued, ushering her forward.

'Please, call me Evie,' she insisted.

Evie curtseyed, and her golden hair brushed her shoulder. When she rose again, Alex noted how remarkably similar to his mother she appeared; Evie too had a small, round face and bright eyes that gleamed like perfect gems, though hers were green, not blue.

Unsure whether to reciprocate with a bow himself or some grander gesture, Alex shyly offered, 'Hello, I'm Alex.'

The three strangers glanced to one another before Winton craned his neck around and commented on how beautiful the house was. But then the guests appeared quite lost. Evie continued to stare at Alex, wringing her hands in some state of concern.

'I must apologise again if we scared you. That was far from our intention,' she said. 'As we mentioned, our vehicle has broken and we wondered if we could possibly borrow your . . .' Evie's voice lowered before drawing to a halt. 'Your . . . er, the erm . . . a way to communicate, to speak to . . .'

'A telephone?' Alex suggested.

'Exactly, yes. Thank you,' Evie said, blushing.

Frowning with curiosity, Alex motioned to where it sat beneath the mirror.

Irwin picked up the receiver, and after examining it, held it the wrong way up against his ear while pressing seemingly random numbers. Winton smiled apologetically at Alex before moving to help Irwin. His cane clonked repeatedly against the floor as he shuffled.

After inviting Evie and Winton into the lounge, Alex filled up four glasses with water in the kitchen. Upon returning, he found them sitting where he had drifted off to sleep earlier. The space between seemed filled with secrets; their faces were mere inches apart, and words were slipping from the corners of their mouths.

'I feel quite the hypocrite wearing this,' Alex heard Winton say; he was stroking the silver watch on his wrist. But their conversation quickly turned to gratitude as Alex passed them their drinks, and the concerned looks on their faces subsided.

The embers in the fireplace were snoozing quietly as Alex sat down on the sofa nearby to feed on their warmth. Not knowing quite what to say, he began by asking where his guests were from.

'London. I grew up close to what was Mayfair,' Winton said.

'I know where Mayfair is. My uncle gave me a book about London before he took me to Hyde Park earlier this year,' Alex said. 'Where were you heading tonight?'

Winton glanced at Evie's jittering knee. 'To see a friend,' he replied. He paused. 'It has been terrible weather though, just terrible.'

'Are you home alone?' Evie asked with an undeniable clench in her voice.

'My uncle was here but he had to leave. It's my aunt—she isn't well.'

'I am most sorry to hear that,' Winton said sincerely.

Irwin set down the receiver and walked into the lounge. 'It is done,' he said, and in a gesture, he toasted to Alex before swiftly draining his glass.

Rising from beneath the faint screech of the wind outside, a dull humming emerged from somewhere in the room. It gradually rose above the grandfather clock's persistent ticking and the fire's waning crackles. In a swift movement, Evie set her bag on her legs, prised open its mouth and peered inside. Winton and Irwin leaned in closer around her as Alex watched on.

'What is it doing?' Irwin whispered.

'It hasn't done this before!' Evie said, sniffing nervously. 'Look! They're spinning!' she almost yelled, pointing to the concealed, resonating object within the bag.

'We barely know what it is capable of. We weren't told much about—'

'We weren't told anything!' Evie snapped.

Winton clambered to the window, unaided by his cane, but the closing storm meant that nothing but black sky and white earth was visible.

Evie was blinking rapidly now, and visibly panting. 'This isn't right! What are we going to do? We have to get back to the children! Imagine if we didn't, just *imagine!*'

'We'll be fine, don't worry,' Irwin said as he swooped his arm around her. 'It's getting stronger,' he called to Winton.

He's right, Alex thought; the humming sound was definitely escalating.

'It must be them, but how could they know we came here?' Winton asked. 'How could they have followed us back?' He turned away from the window. 'It didn't say specifically *why* we had to come; no more was said, was it?'

'*We don't even know why we are here!*' Evie said, her words strained through gritted teeth.

'What choice did we have?' Irwin said.

Alex noticed in the window behind them a flurry in the snowfall, a sharp gust of wind and then—

BOOM!

Everyone jolted as the red front door sailed recklessly through the hallway, ripping the telephone from the table in its stride. A ghostly wall of dust floated into the house. Figures shifted behind its veil. Before Alex could gasp for breath, red and green pulsating lights rained into the lounge. In a series of deafening explosions Alex dived to the floor, guided by instinct. Evie, Irwin and Winton crashed down around him as the house was plunged into a raging battle.

Rubble blasted through the room, cascading down upon Alex and his guests as shots ripped through the air. A particularly bright, pulsating light fizzled overhead and struck the grate in the fireplace. A huge fireball swelled into the room, it's heat almost blistering their skin, before oddly swallowing itself whole.

A glisten of silver caught Alex's attention: in Irwin's hand, a metallic device rapidly twisted and wrapped around itself until a weapon with a pointed, glowing tip formed, fitting his fingers like a glove. Irwin pushed to his feet, and with white shots screaming from his gun, he rushed defiantly into the war zone.

As the wall separating the hall from the lounge blew apart as though made of cards, Alex skidded onto the kitchen tiles, half crawling, half being pulled by Evie. A vivid green pulse struck the back door up ahead, shooting shards of glass in all directions. Winton threw out his arms, allowing his thick cloak to shield Alex and Evie.

'Under you get!' Evie demanded, shoving aside the kitchen chairs around the table and pushing her host beneath it. 'Stay here!' she shouted over the deafening battle. 'Don't move unless your life is in undeniable danger! Do you understand?'

Alex's mouth tried to form words but his voice failed him. He drew in his knees. Another earth-shuddering explosion boomed close by.

'You must stay here and keep quiet!' Evie yelled, and after forming a protective barrier around Alex with the chairs, she and Winton hurried away.

A violent flash of red light illuminated the kitchen. It sounded as if an angry giant was throwing a lifeless rag doll around the house. Alex gripped the hair around his temples as his world spun. Everything was beginning to slip away. Sounds were fading, colours were draining. He squeezed his eyes shut; his senses blurred into one another before they came crashing together. The pressure built, soared in his head, rose higher and higher, until—

BOOM!

Another explosion.

Alex opened his eyes. He continued to pant through the ensuing stillness. It felt as though a hefty hand was forcibly plunging down his throat and plucking out his precious gasps for air. One by one his senses returned and kindly began to piece together his surroundings. He could make out the muffled creaks of the splintered house and an irregular tapping noise somewhere nearby. There was a strong smell of burnt wood in the smoky air. When his vision cleared, it revealed chairs askew around the table as though an invisible monster had tried to seize him. After a quiet minute alone, and with no further sign of movement, Alex crawled out, heaved himself up and moved slowly into the hall.

The swinging chandelier caused lifeless shadows to dance all around Alex as he navigated his way through the destroyed room.

'Alex!'

Evie rushed towards him, visibly shaking. A trickle of blood flowed in a tiny river down her forehead. She latched on to him. 'Were you hit? Are you all right?'

All he could do was shake his head. Evie secured him under her arm. Vicious flames burned from holes stamped into the walls; furniture, snapped and splintered, was strewn across the fractured floor. With his glasses resting lopsidedly on his bloodied nose, Winton hurried them along, followed by Irwin, who had a bruise swelling on his right cheek.

A short distance from the front door Alex's feet drew to a halt. In the short corridor opposite the lounge were the bodies of two men. They were dressed in long black cloaks and lying on their backs. Their gaunt white faces suggested they were dead but their chests, which rose and fell very slightly, assured him otherwise.

'Almost there love, keep going,' Evie muttered over the whirling hum from her bag.

Alex and his guests had barely walked ten paces into the deserted street when a bright light swung over their shoulders. They turned to see a small red car crash up the kerb. In the drivers seat Alex could see Abraham, but it wasn't the Abraham who had left previously. The previous look of terror was now locked with a distinct sadness upon his face. He was trembling, shaking as much as Alex knew he himself should be having just experienced what he had. It was only after Abraham wiped his eyes that he glanced up to spot the four of them. Looking next to the doorless house barely visible through the blizzard, he leapt out of the car and yelled: 'WHAT THE HELL HAPPENED!'

Alex had never heard his uncle scream before; his bones quivered and his skin shrieked with goosebumps. Something was definitely not right. Abraham rushed over and grabbed Alex in an embrace that a boa constrictor would have been envious of, covering every inch of him with his protection.

'What happened?' Abraham panted, on the verge of sobbing. 'What the hell happened? Are you hurt? Are you—'

'I'm fine, I'm . . . all right,' Alex said, suffocating under his uncle's weight.

Abraham continued to mumble something, and when he came to stare at Alex, his wet eyes were bulging from his face. It was only as his uncle said it for the third time that Alex heard it clearly: 'We have to go.'

He found himself suddenly being pulled to the car by Abraham's iron grip and promptly smothered with a chequered blanket in the front seat. He said his uncle's name five times, and finally grasped his hand to get his attention.

'What's the matter? What's wrong?' Alex asked. 'Why were you crying?'

'You need to keep warm, that's what's the matter,' Abraham replied. 'It is very cold. I need to keep you warm. Keep you safe. You must be warm.' His preparations complete, Abraham closed the door and rushed off to inspect the broken house, not noticing the three visitors nearby.

There was a knock at the window, and Alex saw that his three guests were standing on the other side of the door.

'I'm afraid we must be leaving too,' Evie said, stooping down between her father and Irwin as Alex pushed open the door. Her words, however, were not followed by any others; suddenly, and once again, everyone seemed at a loss as to what to say. An apology? A 'nice to meet you'? A 'see you around someday'?

Winton cleared his throat before speaking in a slow and sorrowful voice. 'One day I truly hope you find it in your heart to forgive us for what has happened here on this rather . . .' He looked up, searching for the right word. '. . . betwixt night. I hope for that the very most.'

'I know not if I will ever forgive myself for what happened here tonight,' Evie began. 'I . . . I . . . I just wanted to say . . . I . . .' She lifted her head. 'I'm sorry for your loss.'

On the verge of tears, she turned away into Irwin's embrace.

'Take care, my friend,' Winton said, and he closed the door.

As quickly as they had arrived, the visitors had left, vanishing within the blizzard. Abraham entered and started the car some minutes later, seemingly too overcome to have noticed the guests. The vehicle rumbled to life and sped off back down the road from which it had come.

As the streets blurred by, Alex found that the only words in his head were the final ones Evie had said to him. Again and again he heard them, as if they were a colossal tidal wave washing away every other thought and feeling. Despite his attempts to elicit his memories, he could not recall whether he had mentioned his grandparents to the three mysterious people.

Abraham's muttering breaths kept rising and falling over the steering wheel. A spiderweb of wrinkles crinkled around his eyes as they squinted and strained. 'We have to go, get back,' he kept saying. 'Go back to Maud, yes . . . Get home, get back, sort it all through. It'll be fine!' He laughed with a sob before shaking his head.

'What is wrong?' Alex asked very quietly. 'Please, please tell me.'

'I know . . . I just know . . .'

'Know what? What aren't you telling me?'

'I know!' He slammed his hands upon the steering wheel, as if to persuade himself of this more than Alex. 'They are . . . they are . . .'

'Who is? Is it Maud? Is she all right?'

Confused and aggravated by his uncle's avoidance, Alex tried a different approach. 'Why did you come back so quickly to get me?'

Abraham's gaze did not move from the road ahead. 'I had to come and get you—had to know you were safe, keep you safe . . .'

Alex was exhausted. 'What has happened?' he asked wearily. 'Please tell me.'

Abraham did not respond. Instead, the car gained speed; the onslaught of snow consumed them further and further. They were nearly there.

Silence.

No words.

And then only one.

'Gone.'

Abraham finally turned to look Alex in the eye. The passing street lamps lit up the stream of tears upon his face. 'They are . . . they are gone.'

Dread dropped into Alex's stomach, and he felt himself sink deeper into his seat. The sensation of fear shooting through his body was breathtaking, spreading to every empty fibre between crown and toe. It felt almost as if something had fractured his body. 'Who is gone? G-gone where?'

'They are just . . . your parents . . . they won't be . . .' Abraham's words fell from his mouth. 'They are *gone*.' He faced the road again.

That was it: the sudden, stunning and lasting truth.

In the wing mirror beside Alex everything was fading away, draining into white, yet through the windscreen ahead a path was being thrown at him that he had no choice but to take; the unknown, swallowing them both up, was coming into sudden and immediate clarity from the darkness. Upon facing the wall of daggers before him, Alex felt the first sensation of warmth since leaving his house: a gentle tear rolling down his cheek.

And Alex didn't say a word because none came to him. And he didn't move an inch because he felt that if he did, his body would simply shatter as if it was made of the finest and purest glass in the world. But shatter it did nonetheless, and away he went.

— CHAPTER TWO —

When and Then

Alex was often woken by the eerie silence that settled into his bedroom around the midnight hour. The symphony of the rushing sea seemed so turbulent during the day, but when the cool night poured over the town, it brought with it a definitive stillness to all things. And this night in early July was no exception.

It had been a long time since 'that night', as Alex and his uncle called it. The night when everything changed. Alex, now nineteen years old, often spent the hours between twilight and dawn in an unbreakable limbo, with thoughts about what had happened and how little his life had changed since then swimming slowly through his head.

Right on time, things became too much to think about, and so, pushing the hungry questions into the corners of his mind, he turned over.

A sliver of moonlight broke through the curtains, like a thief in the night. It caught the edge of the photo frame on Alex's bedside table and spread down over the faces of his parents, sealed within it. Like beacons they shone, captured in a moment they could never depart from. Accepting that sleep was a world away, Alex pushed to his feet, slipped on his dressing gown and stepped out onto the balcony.

The sweeping beacon atop the lighthouse in which Alex now lived illuminated the tip of the tall, chapel-like building to his right. Perched on the rising cliff edge at the end of town, the Clockhaus stood with strong white walls, long stretching windows and a steeple so tall it often touched the clouds. Try as he might, Alex couldn't help but wince whenever he looked at the place; in this building he had spent almost all of his years. *Those long, long years*, Alex thought.

He turned back to the vast, open sea, watching its black mirrored body breaking over the rocks far below. The protracted quietness, so loud and so prevalent, had not left him since that night. It summed up all that he now was: empty, muted . . . nothingness. Being in such a small, quintessential seaside town, where the only event of mild interest was the high street market every Tuesday morning, the absence of anything remotely unexpected let the solitude of his existence prosper without discontent.

BWWAAARRRGGGGGNNNN!

The foghorn blasted out far away. Its violent echo swept through the town and into the shroud of the woodlands surrounding it. Piercing the curtains of night far in the distance, the bow of what grew to be a magnificent ship was revealed. Each sweep of the beacon above revealed a greater shadow; it was the length of a skyscraper and slicing through the water at frightening speed, heading right for the shore.

The horn bellowed again, like a long lick to Alex's quivering eardrums. The hull of the ship suddenly loomed over him, and he dived under his bed just as the sound of metal striking the shallow shores screeched beneath him. As if a bomb had been detonated, everything in his room was blasted from its place. Books flew from shelves, his wardrobe sailed across the room as if snapped from a slingshot and even the bed above him leapt as though flames had been ignited beneath its four feet. Alex threw his arms over his head as the foghorn blew one final time and the earth rumbled to a standstill.

He carefully slid himself out from his hiding place. *Is it them? Are they back?* Navigating the smothered floor, he raced downstairs. He threw on his coat as he fought with the lock, but before the air beyond could tempt or tease him, the front door flew open and a pair of bony hands plunged in.

'Are you all right? Are you hurt?' Abraham stammered, swiftly closing the door behind him.

'I'm fine . . . I wasn't hurt—'

'What if it's them? Do you think it could be?' Abraham asked, a crash of fear and madness in his expression.

'I don't know, it's probably just an accident, Abe,' Alex said. 'Just calm down for a minute.'

Watching his uncle rush to the small window overlooking the sea, Alex couldn't help but feel once again the almighty weight of the secret he had kept from him. Whilst Abraham had come to fear a night such as this, when those who had torn apart Alex's house could have returned, Alex had come to dream of it—a night when the three people he had met so briefly might make their way back into his life, and he might just be found again.

The words of truth about the three visitors that night again lined up on his tongue, always ready but always unspoken. He went to speak, but before he could utter a single syllable

Abraham had opened the back door and was guiding him out onto the wet stone platform.

'Watch your footing, be careful now,' Abraham instructed, forcing Alex along the thin edge of the cliff face. With their backs to the jagged rocks and the spraying sea before them, they progressed along the pathway and up into the Clockhaus' small garden. 'Have to get you safe, keep you hidden,' Abraham mumbled under his breath. He unlocked the back door and ushered Alex inside. 'Can't have people seeing, now can we?'

'No, couldn't have that,' Alex muttered sarcastically.

The overpowering stuffiness of the Clockhaus was immediate, but Alex didn't feel its true strength until he had moved through the narrow kitchen and up into the lounge. It was so intense that it knocked him back a step. Abraham often set the temperature so high that the big-leafed plant by the window wilted and drooped, the black sofas were difficult to remove oneself from and the crisp pages of the books lining the bookcases wrinkled and curled.

'Stay here, OK?' Abraham moved to peel open the front door only far enough for his thin frame to squeeze through. Receiving no response, he looked back to Alex.

'Yes, I won't go outside!' Alex said with a huff. After a lingering glance at his nephew, Abraham left.

Moving to his usual spot by the window, Alex sat down and prised open only the smallest gap in the curtains to watch the world beyond. One after another, people wandered sleepily into the cobbled street and made their way down to see the magnificent vessel. Having lost sight of his uncle amongst the growing throng of people, all still dressed in their nightclothes, Alex thought about just what someone would make of him if he was spotted. His hair had grown slightly longer and his freckles had at long last faded. His height now surpassed his uncle's, but he was far less weedy-looking. In many ways, without realising it, he had morphed into the image of his father in his younger years. His sea-blue eyes shone just like his mother's and father's in the few cherished photos he had of them.

And then, like a feather tickling some feeble part of his insides, a voice teased him. *It's night-time, no one would see you. No one would notice you in light of what has just arrived— who would even spot you joining them?* The voice was soothing, speaking in the same persuasive tongue that it had employed since 'that night'. However this time there was an opportunity for change. The three visitors could be out there; the events unfolding on the other side of the window could be because of them . . .

The idea possessed Alex so fully that before he could contemplate his actions, and more importantly their consequences, he left the safety of the Clockhaus and hurried down to join the stirring crowd. Suddenly, and most successfully, he had broken his old, withering promise to his uncle. Alex's heart was a sledgehammer thrashing in his chest —it had not acted in such a way for over seven years, lacking any worthy excitement or almighty fear.

Abraham's white wisps of hair became visible at the front of the group, and instantly Alex felt a sharp twist of doubt. He was about to turn back, but before he could move an onslaught of blinding flashes shot out into the crowd. Alex flinched, throwing his hands up over his face. Expecting devastation and destruction, the muscles in his body clenched. But nothing more than the grumbles and cursing of those around him filled the air. Lowering his hands to discover the local press responsible, taking photographs of the growing crowds, he turned back to the Clockhaus feeling somewhat foolish.

'*What are you doing here?*'

With a swift yank, Alex was immediately marched back to the Clockhaus by Abraham. Once inside, his uncle sealed each and every single lock upon the front door—at least half a dozen—and flipped around to face him.

In the seconds before his uncle's impending release, Alex was struck by just how haggard his uncle appeared. His face was shadowed, and his skin hung loosely upon his softening bones, giving him an air of sadness and regret beneath his rising anger. Despite the layers of clothing that padded his uncle, Alex knew that underneath was a walking skeleton with little apparent strength.

'WHAT DID YOU THINK YOU WERE DOING?' Abraham howled, now safe within their walls. 'What if that ship out there is them!'

'I wanted to see if . . . I wanted . . .' Alex sighed. 'I had to know if someone would—'

Abraham's scolding sigh cut through his words.

'You know, I try, I have tried for all this time to keep you here, to keep you safe. But . . .' Abraham screwed up his face and raised a fist before swinging it like a club back against the door. 'I can only do so much, Alex. What if someone saw you? All of this would have been for nothing! You can't do this, Alex. You can't!'

'I know, I am sorry, it's just, I never—'

'You know it's because I love you? Because I love you so damn much that I do this, that we do *all* of this?' Abraham looked at him with urgency. 'I understand, you've been kept away for all this time. I know—'

'But you don't know!' Alex roared as he marched forward. 'You don't know! You never "knew"—it's what you *believed* that led to all of this, but what if you were wrong? You already believe that ship is them, coming back again. And no other truth will persuade you otherwise!'

'I-I thought you believed the same!' What "other truth" could it possibly be, Alex?'

Alex shook the pictures of Evie, Irwin and Winton out of his mind before speaking again. 'I feel like I don't know what to believe now,' he grumbled. 'And I've had enough. I've had'—Alex caught his breath and expelled it gradually—'I just want to be a part of this world. I want to meet people, and have a friend again, a friend!' Alex gave an empty laugh. 'I mean, could you imagine such a thing? Can you imagine what that must feel like? Because I can't. I can't even begin to fathom it.'

Alex latched onto the back of one of the armchairs for support. Abraham wore a sympathetic expression; in the few feet between them was a great gulf of misunderstanding and secrets.

'I know we don't talk about what we have each been through over the years,' Abraham replied in a steady voice. 'All I know is what we, together, as a family, have been through, with . . . everything.'

'It's OK, I don't expect you to understand,' Alex mumbled as he moved directly towards the stairs.

'Alex please, please don't think I'm being cold.'

Impossible in this place, Alex thought, using the banister to hoist himself up. He knew his uncle would never truly understand what he felt, and at the moment, he was just too tired to care. 'It's OK,' he repeated unconvincingly. 'I'll see you in the morning.'

Crossing the landing, Alex walked into the bedroom he occasionally called his own, closed the door and fell onto the crisp bed sheets to escape.

*

The town was filled with an even larger group of bewildered onlookers the following morning. Those who had miraculously slept through the ship's arrival had stepped outside to find the typically quiet streets bustling with groups, most of which had ventured from villages and towns far and wide. Rivers of people flowed down to the shoreline to inspect the vessel and trickled away from it dumbfounded. Ten o'clock came and went and still there was no sign of anyone on board the ship.

After he'd showered and pulled on fresh although ill-fitting clothes from his wardrobe, Alex found his way back to the window with a steaming cup of tea and some toast. Between the pulled curtains he could see that the local police were attempting to tame the crowds, and barriers were gradually cornering off the shore. Despite the fierce downpour battering the crowd, Alex was able to spot a number of familiar faces.

Arthur Pemtril, a tall white-bearded gentleman dressed in a flat cap and his usual canary-yellow trench coat, paused to speak to various people before heading off down the high street. A stout and hunched old woman Alex had named Angelica drifted, to her apparent surprise, into the gathering of bodies. Shaking her head disapprovingly at the ship, she set her sights on the baker's shop and shuffled away through the crowds. Alex even spotted Herga Hyll, Abraham's greatest friend, dressed in a leopard-print coat and waving her arms exaggeratedly while talking to a neighbour.

With the arrival of the *Precipitous*, as Alex read it was named, timed perfectly with the printing of the *Merlow Messenger*, the week's edition was full of news about the ship, most of which Alex presumed to be either speculation or completely untrue. He glanced over the townspeople's accounts of their rude awakening the night before but couldn't help but feel that none came close to his own, and so cast the newspaper aside in favour of a new book from the shelf.

The day trudged on with the grisly onslaught of rain and occasional grumble of thunder. The wind picked up too, giving flight to a number of lucky umbrellas not held tightly enough. When five o'clock finally neared, Alex knew that Abraham would soon be home and they would exchange apologies, as was normal after one of their arguments. As he returned the newspaper to the table beside Abraham's armchair and slotted his book back on the shelf, through the window looking up to the woods Alex saw something that made him do a double take. Beneath the brooding clouds and through the wicked downpour, amongst the overweight trunks of Bedfellow Meadows' oak trees, Alex could make out a number of bodies. Between the streams of rain upon the window, there they were. Seven figures. Four adults and three children.

The tallest figure, who seemed to be directing the group, glanced towards the busy shore, and as he did so, Alex's heart leapt into his mouth. The man was wearing distinct bottle-end glasses, and a long stretch of silver propped up one of his hands.

It was Winton.

Alex's racing breath instantly fogged the window, and when he smeared it away the man and the six others were gone.

Could it have been him? Really? Alex thought. Precious seconds were falling, wasted and unused, like sand slipping between his fingers. Temptation was not calling now but mightily singing from the other side of the glass. Without another second of doubt, he threw on his coat, flicked up his hood and charged off down the path behind the row of old thatched shops. Passing behind the back of the post office, the fish-and-chip shop, the bakery and finally his uncle's clock shop, Alex quickly came to be beyond what he had ever been able to see from the Clockhaus.

The path before him was empty, and Alex slowed to a stop. He was imagining things, he knew it now, and his heart had drawn him from the warmth to the cold, from dream to disappointment. Imagining his uncle's reaction to his escape, he felt a swell of fear. Perhaps his wishing to see them again had led to his vision, but yet that did not explain why he had seen not three people but seven. *Seven.*

Alex shook his head; it was no use, there was nothing there to see.

But there was . . . There were footsteps! Footsteps dashing through the puddles, multiple feet pummelling the ground in haste. And as he turned back, peering through the relentless rain, Alex saw them. Shivers rippled through him just as the wind, like a howling banshee, carried words of warning:

'Quick! Don't just stand there!'

It was the voice he had longed to hear again; it was Evie. And as sinister shots rang out and the alleyway detonated as though filled with landmines, Alex scrambled amongst the group of people to run as fast as he could. Crackling spitfires of light shot around Alex's head. He ducked and swerved whilst dodging the bursting walls to either side of him.

An older lady—*Winton's wife?* Alex thought—was running beside him with a ghostly, fear-stricken expression.

'Haven't you missed this?' Winton shouted. White flashes behind them let Alex know that Irwin was returning vengeful fire.

'Missed what?'

'Being blindly terrified with little chance of survival?'

A row of bins up ahead exploded, spewing their flaming contents into the sky.

'Not exactly!' Alex shouted back.

The young boy leading the group swerved out into Haggowe Lane, the long road back to Alex's house, and they stampeded after him and into a side-street. Irwin held back to return fire using the same weapon Alex recalled from that night, but when the car beside him was struck and sent somersaulting across the street, he grabbed Evie's arm and charged on.

'There! Markle Woods!' Alex shouted, and the group swerved right, clambering over a fence and into the empty field on the other side. The soil was poisoned against their ambitions; it was soggy and stopped their feet from moving as quickly as possible. Evie swept up the youngest girl, who looked no older than about seven, into her arms and pleaded.

'Keep running, my loves! Don't look back now! We can never look back!'

Missiles of soil exploded up from the angry earth, chasing them up to the tree-line at the top of the hill and down the steep slope on its other side. Managing to keep his balance, the brave young boy skidded down into a deep trench difficult to see amongst the uneven ground and rocks, and one by one the group, apart from Irwin, who pressed back against a thick tree trunk, skidded down into hiding.

Neither a whisper nor a thought could afford to be spared; who knew quite what their assailants could detect? Evie, huddled at Alex's side, pulled in the boy and two girls and held on to them devotedly. At the opposite end of the trench, Winton pressed his and the elderly woman's hands together in prayer.

Is this it? I finally meet them again so we can die together? I rob Abraham of his last immediate relative? Alex thought. His decision to leave the Clockhaus, to leave his uncle, had come with consequences so colossal that Alex wished with all his being that he would make it through this for Abraham. As he glanced at Evie, who was staring back at him, she placed a finger carefully to her lips.

Unbearable waves of apprehension rose and fell. Dirt tumbled down upon Alex's shoulders, and he crushed himself deeper into the damp trench wall. They were there, somewhere above them: inspecting, waiting, scrutinising the scene. A gradual thumping sound grew louder and louder, followed by the appearance of a great glowing sphere. It soared overhead and burst like an igniting sun, throwing out a great web of light into the thick nest of branches above.

Through a small gully in the ground, Alex saw Irwin throw something, a stone possibly, in a different direction. It took a short while, but very gradually the footsteps moved on, snapping twigs at distances further and further away from them.

'*Pssst!*'

Irwin pointed in the opposite direction, and then leaned down and began to pull everyone up from the crevice. 'Keep safe, have faith!' he insisted, and so the troop, which now included Alex, rushed off through the woods.

They made their way wordlessly through the dips and troughs, following no path other than the one they were carving. The glowing orb dimmed, and the only sound remaining was that of bullets of rain hammering the leaves above, setting the woodlands alive with sound. Pausing every so often to inspect their surroundings, the eight finally emerged into a small enclosure where a fence blocked their path.

Treading carefully, Irwin, at the front of the group, stretched his hand forward. His fingers twitched. 'I can feel it,' he said. 'It's definitely here.'

And then Irwin disappeared.

Within a moment he had reappeared, and with him came a falling shimmery veil. Behind it, in the distance, was the same colourful field, in front of that the same fence, but now right before them a large vehicle was parked. Alex rubbed his eyes, and as he wondered whether he was only now beginning to imagine things, Evie ushered everyone inside before moving over to him.

Wearing the same red coat and troubled face as she had been that night, Evie had seemingly remained in a constant state of turmoil. Alex felt like he wanted to give her a reassuring hug.

'I'm afraid we need to leave at once,' she said hastily, 'but we cannot leave you here. We can get you home.' Evie lowered her head to meet Alex's stare. 'Do you trust us to do so?'

'Yes,' Alex replied immediately.

'Come on then, in you get.'

With Irwin and Evie taking the front seats, and the three children settled in the back, Alex took the free seat beside Winton in the central row of seats. The car grumbled to life and they slowly crawled up the hill.

Winton gasped. 'I am terribly sorry, Alex, how rude. This is my wife, Ambrose.' He leaned back, and the elderly woman on his other side finished checking on the children in the back seat and then turned to him.

'Hi, I'm Alex.'

'Oh, I've heard quite a lot about you,' Ambrose said affably. 'Beyond a pleasure to meet you, at long last.'

Ambrose had a kindly face and light, butter-smooth skin adequately fending off her true age. She had sincere and bright green eyes, like everyone else in her family, and her cheeks were perched high upon her face, so it seemed as though she was always smiling.

The car revved moodily as Irwin threw the gearstick around. 'Can't figure out . . . these . . . bloomin' . . . things,' he said with a huff before finally slotting it into gear.

Their destination, a place where they could hide, became the next topic of conversation. It was a discussion that, in total, took barely more than a minute of suggestions and one that culminated in a unanimous agreement: 'Your earlier suggestion, Dad', as Evie had put it.

Alex caught a glimpse of something silvery on Evie's lap in the wing mirror as the car crawled to the top of the hill and promptly stalled, not for Irwin's lack of skill. Overlooking Merlow and its distant shore, Alex saw the sizeable mass of the ship, domineering as it was, in the passing glare of his lighthouse.

The doors suddenly locked. Alex whipped round, confused.

'Hold on, everyone!' Evie squealed, causing Alex to clench his arms tight at his side, although he was completely unsure why.

There was a hissing noise, presumably from the device nestled in Evie's lap, and the car began to shudder as though protestors were stamping along its underbelly. Darkness shrouded the car in a hazy curtain, like the one from which it had appeared, and the vehicle suddenly lurched up from the ground. There was a sensation of simultaneous momentum and motionlessness; they were either moving incredibly fast or not at all, or quite possibly neither, or both.

Peering through the glass, Alex watched in wonder as seeds of blinding colours warped and waved and shot and whizzed and exploded all around them. So mesmerised, so completely enthralled was Alex that if he had been speechless in the woods he was now utterly breathless.

They were lifted right from their seats as they plummeted through layers of colours, which flicked past like pages of an infinite book. A cyclone of light lassoed the shaking vehicle, and now, somehow, their uncontrollable free fall had transformed into a spiralling ascension. As though with a gradual turning of gravity, they soared higher and higher, shooting through the panoramas of a million skies. And just as Alex's chest felt fit to burst, and he began to fear that they might not make it to morning, the colours connected and found their resting places around them, and they finally arrived.

— CHAPTER THREE —

The Day in the Night

Within the blink of an eye they were there. But quite where 'there' was, Alex was not particularly sure.

It was daytime; it appeared they had skipped morning completely. The red bricks of tall walls now stood to either side of them. The car shuddered to a standstill. With his head still spinning, Alex turned to his fellow travellers for an explanation.

'What happened? Where are we?'

'Somewhere entirely different!' Winton replied.

'*Somewhen* entirely new,' Irwin finished, turning back to see Alex's puzzled face. 'Yes, you heard me correctly.'

Alex stopped twisting around to focus on his thoughts, allowing his stomach a brief moment to swallow itself back into position. And then it hit him: they were wearing the same clothes they had been that night, the three of them, and their faces were unchanged. It was as if they had simply stepped between nights which were thousands of days apart, and Alex couldn't help but wonder whether they had stopped running since.

'Come on, let's see what all this hustle is about!'

Alex didn't know what Winton was talking about until he too stepped out into the narrow alleyway. The warm air was filled with the sounds of celebration, emanating from the far end of the alleyway, where a mass of bustling bodies was slowing passing.

Is this happening? Am I really here? Alex pressed his hands against the wall beside him as the questions hit him. He stroked its rough surface two, three times, up and down, but he still didn't know if it was real.

Ambrose slowly inched around to his side.

'OK are we dear?' she asked softly.

Alex finally nodded.

Ambrose gave a feathery laugh. 'Oh, I know. Was quite a shock for us too, but take your time with it, let it settle,' she replied as the two girls each took one of her hands.

'Why are the people so happy?' the older of the two girls asked, watching the people jumping around in their high spirits not far away.

'I would think they are very happy dear,' Ambrose said as she began guiding the girls towards the crowds, 'the Second World War has come to an end after six very long years.'

Alex jolted. *The Second World War?* The one he had read about in his history books?

His hands slid from the wall. *How can this possibly be?* Right at the end of the alleyway, a whole different lifetime waiting for him?

'The year is 1945, Alex,' Winton said, coming to stand beside him with a presiding grin. He pocketed a shrunken version of his cane in his inside pocket. 'Today is the 8th of May, 1945. To say that I have not imagined stepping foot into such a magnificent period of freedom would be a great injustice to such a time.'

The vehicle vanished just as quickly as it had appeared in the woods nearly sixty years from now. Everyone gathered somewhat apprehensively at the edge of the bustling, sunlit street. The family linked hands. 'Hold on, everyone!' Winton exclaimed, and they stepped out into the throng of revellers.

It was difficult not to be swept away by the euphoria surging through the crowd of hundreds, undoubtedly the largest volume of people Alex had ever seen. Men and women dressed in their service uniforms were accompanied by office workers in the swamped street, and people were waving from the windows of the stately buildings high above. Groups of comrades cheered and sang songs by Vera Lynn, as soldiers and old allies rekindled memories amongst the masses of waving flags; their celebration truly had no limit.

The sea of bobbing heads and shuffling bodies carried the group down into what Alex realised, to his amazement, was Piccadilly Circus. They steered past the halted buses and the central monument piled with revellers, stopping when they found a small, overcrowded pub in an adjoining street. Still hand in hand, the family and Alex, wormed their way through the cheering groups until Irwin found a table in the far back corner big enough for the eight of them. As they sat down a veteran jumped up on the bar and shouted, 'The war is over!' and the room erupted with an impromptu version of the national anthem.

When everyone was sitting closely around the table, Evie removed her coat, which had somehow turned a dusky grey, and leaned in. 'Alex, let me start by introducing our lovely children, Nora, Felicity and Daniel.'

Nora and Felicity had initially appeared identical, but as he studied them, Alex quickly identified a number of differences. Nora was older, and quite possibly the more confident of the two; her face was more developed, and seemingly prepared for stronger expressions than her sister's, whose face made a more neutral, innocent statement. Felicity was smaller, more petite, and had longer chestnut brown hair than her sister. As Alex waved to her, she tucked herself under her mother's arm to hide.

The young boy with a bobbed haircut who had bravely led them all through the rain rose from his seat opposite Alex. As he stretched out his hand, Alex realised that he was smaller than his sisters and undoubtedly the youngest member of the family. Taken aback but nonetheless impressed, Alex gladly shook his hand. 'It is nice to meet you,' Daniel said with a mature pleasantness to him.

'And you too,' Alex replied. 'It's nice to meet all of you.' He scanned the table with a smile.

'Well, it's a reacquaintance for some,' Winton said with a chuckle, observing his surroundings.

Just as things seemed ready to nose dive into the truth, they teetered on the edge again. The metallic beads upon Ambrose's shawl glistened in the dim light. In contrast to her previous terror, she now brandished a timid, gentle smile. 'We wanted to take you somewhere so that we could explain ourselves. We certainly owe you that much,' she said sheepishly. She sat back and tucked her hands neatly in her lap. It seemed she would not be the one to start explaining.

'So, where do we begin?' Evie said, glancing between Irwin and her parents.

'Well'—Winton leaned across the table—'we are the Evergreen family, and we are the "Wanted of the Law" and the "Unwanted of the People", as defined by the First Decree of the Great British Court. We are being pursued for the murders of two innocent people.' Winton reeled off honestly. 'Nice to meet you, again.'

Evie shifted nervously in her seat. 'Congratulations to my father for telling it how it is,' she said sarcastically, glaring at Winton. 'And for being rather too blunt.'

'You're . . . what? Sorry?' Alex spluttered.

'What my father means to say is that "when" we are from, we are wanted for a crime, a murder that we had neither part nor purpose in.'

'We were framed,' Irwin said, his firm voice tinged with sadness.

'Sorry, "*when*" you are from?' Alex said. 'So you are'—he shuffled his chair in closer—'you are from the future?'

'From your future, yes, Alex,' Winton replied.

Out of everything that had happened that night and the night he had just escaped from, Alex found this somewhat easy to accept. If anything, it certainly began to explain why everything seemed so out of this world when in the Evergreens' company. This led another, more pressing, thought into his head: out of all of where and all of when, everything that ever was or ever would be, the fact that this humble family had dropped out of the sky to him, twice now, was surely beyond coincidence.

Winton nodded, as though sensing the impending query. 'But our return to you was an unplanned decision of our time machine.'

Alex gasped. 'That thing brought you back to me?' he said, pointing to the glisten of silver within Evie's handbag, which she was clutching at her side.

'You appear to be the constant here, Alex,' Winton said mysteriously. 'We keep coming back to you.'

A deep frown forced itself over Alex's face as he sat back. 'Is it the police who are pursuing you?'

'Are the people hunting us down the police?' Irwin gave a short huff. 'No, they're far worse.'

'They are the people who framed us. Who imprisoned us,' Evie said.

'What do you mean imprisoned you? Are you—are you *convicts*?'

Waves of apprehension, revulsion and sadness swept over the Evergreens, and with this, their harrowing tale unfurled .

'It begins, I suppose, like every story does,' Evie said, staring into the distance. 'On a day just like any other.' However, the story Evie shared was not like any other Alex had ever heard. One day, out of nowhere, as the sun was yawning blindly into the morning, the Evergreens were framed for the murder of two people. The neighbourhood, the city, the whole nation was in uproar. It was an abhorrent crime! people said. To steal and sever a life—there is no act of higher disgrace or immoral doing! 'You see, we are from a time that respects and cherishes all life. There hadn't been a known murder in one hundred years, or ages as we refer to them,' Winton interjected. 'It is just something that does not happen, *did* not happen.'

Then Irwin took over, to deliver the tale of their escape. They were forced to run, and run and run and run they did. The family fled north, past every closing barrier and gathering force, to the Highlands. For months they hid beneath the floorboards and between the cellar walls of an abandoned house in a quiet, empty village, living off what they could fish, find or hunt. But after so long, eventually they decided they could not stay like that, could not live in that way for the rest of their lives, and so they did the bravest thing they could. 'The longer we stayed away from the world, the guiltier we became in the eyes of it. And so we did it—we went against the only advice we'd been given and we turned ourselves in,' Irwin said.

Ambrose reluctantly carried the tale on towards its finish, explaining their eventual capture, arrest and detainment by the most illiberal of authorities. They were interned in the prison chambers of the Tower of London, and as the world watched and waited for justice, upon their transfer to the Great Court for their first hearing, the Evergreen family were intercepted.

'Intercepted?' Alex replied, trying to drown out the singing at the neighbouring table.

'Someone broke us out. It wasn't the police—we were already in their custody,' Irwin said. 'It was those who had framed us.'

Ambrose sat back into her seat again, unable to restart her voice, prompting Winton to cast out the final details. Before he could begin, however, Evie had turned a sickly shade of green and Felicity and Nora had placed their hands over each other's ears.

Their destination was revealed to be a loathsome prison, riddled and rotting with the promise of eternal desolation. And they were not the only ones in it.

'It was buried so deep, that place. Like a tomb, to ensure that no one would ever find us . . .'

Winton's pause seemed to stretch on infinitely. But at long last it was filled by Felicity, who spoke three simple words: 'But someone did.'

Her words were an offering of such relief that everyone exhaled collectively.

'It was some three or four people who set us free,' Irwin added. 'We had never seen them before, but they saved our lives.'

The uplifting charm returned to Winton's voice as he completed the tale. 'So, we took what we had, that machine, and we did the impossible. And we were eventually led back to you, to the night we first met.'

At this, a warm, sparkling feeling, like hundreds of dancing pins, coursed through Alex's body. However, in spite of this most welcome sensation, Alex felt suddenly exhausted. Their story, had he lived through it himself, would have been more than enough to shatter him, and he doubted he would have had the strength to pick up the pieces of himself and carry on . . . again.

'All your friends, all the people you knew, who ever had a thought of you, everyone thinking you were . . .' Evie's words unfolded with such speed that she stumbled unintentionally into her emotions. 'Thinking you were these people who could do such a thing, *would choose* to do such a thing . . .'

Nora stretched out her hand and moulded it over her mother's on the table.

Evie sniffled, her eyelashes sprinkled with tears. 'Where are you supposed to go when the whole world is trying to find you?'

'All will be fair in the end,' Daniel said, reassuring her with a small toothy grin.

Alex paused for a moment, holding on to these words, and the atmosphere stilled. It was almost as if time had stopped beyond their conversation; the thrilling liveliness surrounding them not enough to penetrate this sincere and profound moment.

'I suppose it doesn't matter where you are, as long as you have someone. As long as you're together,' Ambrose mumbled, barely moving her mouth.

'Together you can survive the unthinkable,' Alex said, appreciating his words as much as hoped the Evergreens did.

The story had reached its end, and the Evergreens had emerged stranded at a crossroads pointing in a million different directions. They had been thrown back through time to a twelve-year-old boy in order to escape the terror they had lived through; where they were going now no one but Alex knew, for he found himself declaring, 'You are coming to stay with me.'

Ambrose appeared the most shocked. The others cast glances at each other. 'Don't make any promises for us, Alex,' Ambrose finally said. 'I doubt you want a group of people you barely know crashing into your life like this.'

'It's a bit too late for that, isn't it?' Alex laughed. 'You were sent to me for a reason, twice now! And we have to try to find out what that reason could be and how I can help you! And you can't possibly leave,' Alex said with certainty. 'It isn't coincidence that you came back to me.'

Winton ran his finger back and forth along his lips, nodding. 'No, it definitely isn't coincidence.'

'Plus, I don't want you to leave again,' Alex finished.

Looking to one another, it was clear that the Evergreens really didn't have a choice. They looked to each other again, and then checked three times over that he was certain before Alex finally insisted, 'Absolutely, yes!' The oppressive walls cornering them burst open and Alex was grabbed into handshakes and hugs all around the group. Even Daniel embraced Nora, causing her to squeal, 'Ew! Get off!'

'Our thanks will always be with you!' Evie cried, as they made their way through the singing crowds and back into the beautifully busy streets, inflating a feeling of joy so rich within Alex that he wondered whether he might just float away.

*

For Alex, the journey back to Merlow was just as spectacular as the trip out of it. Mesmerising and bodiless, the colours swam and coalesced through the nothingness around the vehicle until the thin spears of trees shot up, and Bedfellow Meadows and the twenty-first century were back at their feet again. It was only minutes after Alex had run away with the Evergreens through time, yet in their short absence, the sky had become overrun with dark, menacing clouds.

'Gets my stomach every time!' Winton exclaimed, rubbing it cheerfully as everyone disembarked.

Alex closed the door behind him and cleared his throat. 'Can I ask, how long has it been for you all since—'

'Since we first met?' Ambrose replied. 'It has been seven days.'

'Seven days?' Alex gasped, and he dropped his head slightly. 'It's been that many years for me.'

Hearing a scuffle behind him, Alex turned to find Irwin kneeling by the bonnet of the car. Between his outstretched finger and the ground, a green-faceted crystal was pirouetting. When he lifted his hand away it continued to spin upon its own invisible axis, weaving a silky shroud to encompass the vehicle, which slowly shimmered from view.

The prospect of a safe place to sleep had sparked excited chatter amongst the Evergreens as Alex led them through the woodlands to the far end of town. Knowing further danger could be lurking nearby, Alex walked at twice his usual pace, leading the group down to the rocky pathway between the Clockhaus and the lighthouse. Winton was required to overcome his terrible fear of heights and barely managed to shuffle, hand in hand with his wife, along the narrow pathway and down to the platform edge.

The lighthouse was cold and lifeless when they entered, but as the Evergreens pegged up their coats and slipped off their shoes, which had oddly undone themselves and fallen from their feet, it immediately began to transform in front of Alex's eyes. Never before had the lighthouse and everything trapped within its circular walls—himself included—had any purpose other than to simply exist. Time would whittle away and days would blur in and out in the same tired patterns, but always for nothing. Now the Evergreens were here and everything was being redefined; it all finally had a purpose; it was all for them.

The kitchen on the first floor was the shabbiest of all the rooms in the lighthouse. It was a plain and largely empty space with patchy pale walls and more empty cupboards than full ones. The adults congregated around the kitchen table, and with Alex's permission, the children moved into the adjoining lounge and slumped tiredly onto the sofa.

'Well, this is where I live,' Alex said. 'I used to stay up at the Clockhaus with my uncle but I mainly stay here now.'

The Evergreens were quiet as they surveyed the lounge, and Alex couldn't help but think how terribly boring the place must have looked to them. Apart from the sofa, small, unused television and small windows watching over the sea, the room whispered of a life half lived. Only a few ornaments, small things Alex clutched to from a seemingly previous existence, adorned the bookshelves and cabinets. Despite his having lived here for almost two years, there was little decoration to show for it.

'And a lovely place it is!' Winton said.

After serving up some fresh tea and toast, and then locating pillows and blankets for his guests, Alex finally persuaded Ambrose and Winton to take his bedroom, which he had rushed to restore to a respectable state. But as Alex was darting back down to the kitchen, he came to a halt on the stairwell. Out of the window to his side a figure was rushing across the wet, faintly moonlit stones of the high street.

'Abraham!'

Alex jumped into his shoes and shrugged on his coat as he called to his guests, 'I need to go! My uncle's heading back. I should make sure he doesn't know I was gone.' He rushed out the back door and along the path to the Clockhaus. Within sixty seconds Alex was in his favourite armchair—just as his uncle walked through the front door. As much as could be expected after one of their arguments, things appeared normal, and once Abraham had made his ritual jam sandwich, his most cherished meal, he dived straight into telling Alex all about his lively day.

With an unprecedented crowd of people swarming the town to see the new arrival, Abraham's shop had never been so busy, nor had business ever been so prosperous. He talked at length about the theories and cast doubt over the rumours regarding the ship's arrival, which his customers had twittered on about throughout the day. None of them, however, seemed able to explain why not a single passenger had been spotted aboard the ship.

His voice becoming dry and hoarse, Abraham fetched himself a glass of water from the kitchen and then lowered himself steadily into his seat opposite Alex again to drink it. As he did so, the awkwardness of their prior argument broke free, and swelled in the heat between them. Alex initiated the conversation with an apology. After staring at his nephew for a few seconds longer than would be considered normal, Abraham accepted before mumbling that Alex must never do it again. 'It's dangerous out there, Alex. Most dangerous.' And just like that things returned to how they ever were: quiet, reserved and unchanged.

Herga, who had swung past the shop around lunch, became the next item for discussion. She had confided that good news was on the way, although Abraham had not yet managed to wrangle out of her what this might be. But within only minutes of recounting the tale he had run out of steam, as though the rush of excitement was all too much for him, and he drifted into a gentle, sinking sleep. A faint smile was still etched on his face, as it was any time he spoke of his most admired friend.

Alex mused upon how his uncle would react to the news of the Evergreens having been there that night, and to the news of their return all these barren years later. It was a conversation that would require a considerable amount of planning and effort, for it was news, Alex was sure, that his uncle would not take well. It would no doubt refresh the idea that danger lurked beyond the insipid apricot walls of the Clockhaus. He thought again of the reason why he had chosen not to speak of the Evergreen's arrival seven years prior and found himself instinctively nodding. *I had to keep them a secret*, Alex reassured himself. *I couldn't tell him.*

Despite Abraham's slight, almost malnourished-looking frame, Alex struggled with his uncle's weight as he carried him to his bedroom under the stairs. He removed Abraham's glasses and tucked him into bed, and then kissed his uncle lightly on the head and smoothed his hair with his hand.

'I'm sorry for earlier, for leaving,' Alex whispered, staring down at his uncle's thin chest rising and falling with long, sweeping breaths. 'I hope you don't think I was abandoning you. I wasn't trying to run away—'

Alex paused, very uncertain as to the truth of his words. 'I'm sorry for leaving today,' he decided upon. 'I really am.'

When he crept back into the lighthouse he found Evie and Irwin still sitting at the table in the dim light of the kitchen. Their talking came to a halt as Alex slumped onto a chair beside them, unable to stifle a yawn.

It took Irwin a moment to lift his gaze to him. 'How did it go?'

'My uncle didn't know I'd left. I stayed with him until he fell asleep.'

'We were just discussing what could possibly have caused that ship to crash. You're very lucky it didn't take you out completely.'

'You mean that wasn't you?'

It had seemed obvious to Alex, now he knew of the Evergreens' return, that the *Precipitous* was their grand re-entrance into his small life, but the vacant looks upon Evie's and Irwin's faces told him otherwise.

'We like to be as subtle as possible,' Irwin said with a tired laugh.

Alex yawned again, stretching his arms out wide before lazily rubbing his face. 'I still can't believe it's been only a week for you all. I mean, a week! It's just been so long for me. It feels like i've taken the long way round to seeing you again.'

'I cannot begin to imagine,' Evie said sadly. 'But we are here now.'

Ensuring they had all that they needed, Alex wished them goodnight as they tiptoed around the children to make their beds on the lounge floor. He then set about making up the sofa-bed on the ground floor for himself. It was easy for Alex to accept that he might not get a comfortable night's sleep, for the pillows were awfully flat and the springs of the sofa like corkscrews, but he didn't care. It simply didn't matter.

They're here! They are actually here! The words looped through his fatigued mind as he gave up attempting to get comfortable. After all this time they had returned to him. They were here, only feet above him. They were safe—for now.

A blanket of chilling thoughts suddenly laid itself over Alex. He wondered how far away those pursuing the family were now. Any shadow could belong to them; their eyes could be pressing in amongst the gloom, their whispers sailing upon the wind. Just how long would it be until they found the Evergreens again?

A light flicked off somewhere above. Darkness flooded the lighthouse, and a final, lasting question came swimming through it: why had the Evergreens' time machine propelled them into the past, into the now, to him?

There was only one thing Alex could be sure of as he closed his eyes: in one way or another, time would surely tell.

— CHAPTER FOUR —

A Pensive Touch

'Pssst!'

'Is he awake?'

'I don't know. Go ask him.'

'Are you awake?'

'He isn't going to answer if he isn't awake, you dingbat!'

There was a giggly laugh and a quick scuffle.

'Shhh! Don't go waking him up, you three! Come up here, now!' And the three sets of feet scurried away.

Alex smiled and opened his eyes. It was a bright morning and unlike their journey through time it was one that he had not missed. The evening before, the kitchen had been its busiest to date, but when he climbed the stairs after getting up and washing his face, he found that it was now truly *busy*. All seven of the Evergreens were preparing breakfast; Winton was passing all the edible contents of the cupboards along the line formed by Felicity, Nora and Daniel, who began to sort out what was suitable for breakfast; Irwin was juggling various frying pans at the cooker and Evie was slicing up everything in the fruit bowl.

The family were wearing similar striped nightclothes, and each had rather fascinating bed hair. Winton's was almost entirely on end, as if he had stuck his fingers into a socket, and Ambrose's wavy grey locks had formed a large quiff. Evie had attempted to restrain hers in a plait, but frayed ends still broke free.

'Well, a jolly good morning to you!' Winton beamed, and a rush of morning wishes ensued.

Alex went to take a seat at the table but before he could, Ambrose rushed past him with a red sheet rolled up in her hands. Standing at the opposite end of the table, she met his gaze.

'You might want to stand back a little, dear. Just a few steps back. This has been known to go wrong before.' Ambrose glanced incriminatingly at Winton.

He shrugged and chuckled. 'I don't know what you're on about.'

Taking a moment to steady herself, Ambrose exhaled. 'OK, here we go.'

With a flick of her wrists the red sheet came rolling out through the air. It was over in a flash, but as the sheet unfurled before him, Alex spotted various things emerging upon it: white plates, shiny sets of cutlery, folded napkins and glasses, even tall candlestick holders in its centre. As the sheet settled, before them sat a perfectly laid table.

Alex gasped. 'Wow.' He blinked a few times to make sure he wasn't hallucinating.

The children applauded their grandmother, and she gave a slight curtsey.

'Show-off,' Winton muttered.

As though the whole affair had been timed to perfection, the table was suddenly swamped with food. Plates stacked with bacon, fried sausages and eggs and bowls of chopped-up fruit and yoghurt were set around platters of toast and dishes of porridge and seemingly every carton and jar from the kitchen cupboards, including jars of mustard, kidney beans and pickles.

On the sideboard, visible over Irwin's shoulder, sat an object that Alex's eyes kept gravitating to as everyone sat down and tucked in. Within two metallic rings was a masterfully complex series of bronzed cogs, steam pumps, ticking hands and mechanisms. Noting Alex's gaze, Winton brought the object over to the table for him to inspect more closely. He introduced it as 'the Evispen', the device that had returned the family to Alex. The individual elements of the time machine quietly hissed, whirring and singing to themselves like pieces of a complicated, moving jigsaw.

'We received it for my birthday last year—well, were left it, really,' Irwin said over his toast and honey marmalade. 'We don't know who left it, but it didn't reveal itself to us until the day we needed it.'

'Reveal itself?' Alex enquired.

'It was a present that could only open itself,' Winton continued. 'We could never get into it; there was no discernible *way* of getting into it. It presented itself the day it brought us back to you.'

'It was as though it had been waiting for us,' Evie said, fiddling with her plait. 'There was no return address so we couldn't have given it back even if we wanted to.'

'And why would we want to?' Winton said, gasping at the thought. 'Firstly, it saved our lives, and secondly, it's a time machine!'

On the Evispen's face, the current time flicked past in white numbers upon black tiles, and below it, in a similar fashion, the current date. The symphony of a thousand synchronised pieces, moving endlessly towards a common goal and unified purpose, was enough to bewitch Alex. So mesmerised by its power, prowess and, above all, subtle golden glint of mystery, Alex concluded that it embodied the very essence of the Evergreens in every possible way.

When Alex looked to the table once more he found the family again excelling in being exceptionally peculiar. One by one, everyone's menus began to take a turn towards the interesting. Ambrose scooped cranberry sauce into her warm porridge and swirled the contents. Daniel spooned some peanut butter out of a jar and spread it over his chopped-up banana, which he then covered in honey. Piling crispy bacon onto a bun, Winton sprinkled butterscotch sauce and, even more oddly, broccoli — both of which Alex had failed to spot previously — on top, squashed the bun halves together and took a big bite. 'Now I have missed this!' he mumbled between enthusiastic mouthfuls. Alex didn't know quite where to look.

'Can I ask what that is?' Alex asked a few minutes later, this time gesturing to a small metallic sphere with a short spout on the kitchen counter.

Winton almost choked on his food in his excitement. 'That's my Quottle!' He rushed to retrieve it. Picking it up, he gave it a stroke, and the spout emitted a puff of steam. 'Would anybody like a cup?'

'A cup of . . . ?' Alex asked.

'Anything you like! Well, within reason.'

Immediately, the group began making requests.

'A peppermint tea, please,' Irwin said.

'A mango tea for me, dear,' Ambrose said.

Evie was indecisive but eventually asked for a smoggy strawberry.

Topping the small sphere with water, Winton placed but a finger to it. There was a fiery bubble of water and a cough of red smoke, and then he poured the Quottle's smoggy contents into a mug and passed it to Evie. After pouring Irwin's and Ambrose's teas, Winton poured Alex and himself a 'good British brew!' as he had called it. As Alex took a sip and found that it did not disappoint.

When it was time to tidy up, Evie stopped Alex in his tracks. 'You needn't do anything,' she said.

The tablecloth rolled itself and its contents up at Ambrose's touch, and it was once again a small bundle of cloth. 'I'll give this a wash-through. It won't take two minutes!' Ambrose said, heading to the sink.

The children moved into the lounge, taking with them their warm atmosphere of laughter and play. Alex sat down with the remaining Evergreens at the empty table knowing, with a twisting feeling in his stomach, they now had to discuss much graver topics than time machines and strange kettles. Evie and Irwin linked hands.

'Please, ask what you need to,' Winton said, and so Alex dropped his voice low and asked why they had been framed in the first instance.

There was no immediate response, so Alex hesitantly continued.

'You were framed by these people, whoever they are, so they could capture you, but the police got there first,' Alex said methodically. 'So that's why they broke you out and then put you in their own prison. But . . . why? What was it all for? *Why did they frame you?*'

Ambrose sat down beside Winton and picked up her mug, which she held locked at her lips. She seemed very determined not to speak about such a traumatic experience.

Evie was about to speak, but her father half lifted his hand.

'They demanded that we tell them about something,' Winton said. 'Something called "the Heirloom".'

'But we don't know anything about it!' Evie cried out, unable to contain her defying distress. 'But they kept forcing their questions upon us every single day! They wore us down thinking we would give them what they demanded, but we couldn't give them anything because we *don't know anything*!' Her eyes welled with tears, prompting Irwin to pull her close.

'A woman'—Winton momentarily pressed his lips together —'she was known as an "Expellerant". She was very tall and emaciated, a true victim of age's old wills, as they used to say before our time, and looked'—he curled his fingers into his palms—'quite dead. She was named Dagatha Shrewm, but they called her "the Widower". She never said a word. Maybe she couldn't, but I remember her doing what she did with this rigid, lifeless look.' Winton's soft eyes squinted.

'What is an Expellerent?' Alex asked before taking a sip of his tea.

'Someone who serves to expel your memories,' Winton replied darkly. 'She would make you a widow of your most cherished remembrances.'

How such a thing was possible Alex did not know, nor did he want to know. The idea of what humanity had achieved in the future was deeply unsettling. What was worse was that Alex feared this might not be the limit of their oppressors' capabilities.

'The one she was with, who shepherded the woman, Amtrice, he was called,' Winton continued, 'he just kept on shouting. Over and over he would shout. Asking where it was, this thing, "the most coveted item in all of history".'

'Most coveted item in all of history,' Alex repeated.

'They presumed that we already knew what the Heirloom was,' Winton added.

'But I'm most afraid that we don't know what it could be,' Ambrose said, fiddling with the flower pendant of her necklace. 'Most afraid.'

'But if it's something so important and sought after then surely there's a record of it somewhere?' Alex said. 'Surely people would know of its existence.'

Irwin laughed lightly as he released Evie. 'Many secrets are passed throughout history unspoken to the common ear. You hear whispers, in the myths and legends that are told, stories passed through the bloodlines, but many secrets expire with those who lived them.'

The idea of such an artefact stuck in Alex's mind, lodging itself in his inability to fathom a way to possibly identify it. *Where are they to go next?* he wondered. *What's the logical step to take to begin such an unimaginable task—finding something in the entirety of history?*

Irwin drank the rest of his tea and set down his mug. 'We will start with those whispers,' he said with an air of confidence.

Without a second's notice, Alex's voice leapt from his throat. 'I want to help!' He looked at them eagerly.

Evie at long last broke her gloomy stare into the swirling mist of her drink and sighed. 'Oh Alex, does your kindness know no end?'

*

The sun had pulled itself higher into the morning sky when Alex and the Evergreens snuck out of the lighthouse, fully dressed and with their hair most certainly better tamed. They shuffled along the rocky path and darted back into the meadows, and within moments their chariot had reappeared.

Ambrose and Winton settled into the front two seats of the vehicle, the former holding the Evispen and taking instructions from the latter on how to use the device.

'Won't your uncle be wondering where you are?' Irwin said as he and Evie clambered in beside Alex after securing the children in the back.

'I only head over for dinner usually, and he's working at the shop today so I'll see him tonight.' Alex then watched as Ambrose closed her eyes and the top row of tiles on the Evispen, representing the current date, began to flick backwards one by one. 'Do you know how it works? I mean, how can a time machine possibly work?'

'It requires human interaction,' Irwin said. 'But like everything when we are from, it largely only thoughts and memories—a pensive touch, if you will.'

'Like everything?' Alex said.

'Knowledge is power, Alex,' Irwin replied. 'It's the mantra of our time, but you need not step foot in our time to understand that.'

Given what he had seen so far from the Evergreens, Alex supposed that this had to be the case.

'"Simplicity suffices and succeeds," as they say,' Irwin added.

Alex grabbed hold of his seatbelt, and they were sent rolling through the void of exploding colours once again. The trembling reached a final crescendo, the orchestra of colour curtained around them, and they stalled, having arrived somewhere new.

Weeds grabbed at their ankles as they disembarked and stepped into a wildly overgrown garden. A tall house towered at their side, its doors and windows haphazardly decorated with planks of wood to prevent anyone from entering.

'That was rather close, Amber!' Irwin exclaimed, shocked yet evidently impressed at how tightly they had landed in the back corner of the garden.

'You shouldn't mistake a carefully placed landing for a near miss,' Ambrose remarked.

Tucking away the Evispen, Evie looked at Irwin with a grin.

The car vanished from sight as the Evergreens and Alex climbed through the hole in the fence and made their way out onto a nearby street. As they walked the long, sloping road lined with terraced houses, Winton revealed that they were in the same year, or 'age', as he referred to it, as the one they had just left, 2001, and in a town called Pembletoe, not far from Colchester. It was difficult to imagine that the answer to the mystery involving the most coveted item in the entirety of history could be found in such a year and such a place, but Winton remained optimistically insistent that the answers they needed were ready and waiting at their destination.

After zigzagging through quiet streets and a series of alleyways between various parks and allotments, the group emerged onto a large open field surrounded by oak trees. On its other side was a great white temple-like building with tall stone pillars adorning its entrance. As they made their way towards it, Alex could see the words *Pembletoe Library* embellished in stark letters upon its apex.

The large wooden doors clanked shut behind Alex and the Evergreens as they entered the stately building. The echo continued through the rows of towering bookcases before them but was quickly superseded by Ambrose's trotting footsteps as she rushed ahead.

Alex called out to her. 'Do you need to ask where any—'

Ambrose threw her hands in the air. 'I know my way around a bookery!' she called back, and the group walked briskly after her.

'Mother works—worked—in a bookery . . . back home,' Evie said as they moved through the tunnels of books. 'Best to let her do her thing.'

After the group had claimed one of the long reading tables in the central reservation, underneath the cerulean ceiling adorned with gods and stars, Alex watched Ambrose set off in one direction and Winton and the children set off in another. The children returned first from the wooden labyrinth, clutching their choices. Then, from the other side, a tall column of books with legs approached the table. As Irwin unstacked the books, Ambrose's face appeared. 'I hope you like reading,' she said with a huff.

'Is that all of them? The entire movement?' Winton asked as everyone sat down.

'All ten, yes.'

After checking to make sure no other readers were nearby, Ambrose closed her eyes and placed a finger on each cumbersome book, one by one. The coiled borders printed upon each began to unwind, flowing in long golden strands to spell out the titles of each. Pulling in the one nearest to him, Irwin flicked through it. As he did so, the pages flooded with words and various hand-painted pictures and diagrams until, when he reached the glossary, the whole book was filled with content.

The book closest to Alex formed its title. He leaned forward to read the silky golden words:

The Movement of Bafflement and Eluding Presents:
Mysteries of Magnificence and Magnitude
Collection I - Mysteries of Cause

'So we're reading about all kinds of mysteries?' Alex asked.

Evie smiled apologetically. 'My father thinks there is only one way to solve a seemingly impossible mystery—'

'There is!' Winton eagerly assured them. 'You don't just look at one mystery. Elements of mysteries as great as this will echo through time; the tiniest details, spread throughout the chronicles, hidden in the folds between myth and legend, will give them away.'

'So are we to look for patterns?' Ambrose asked.

'Exactly,' Winton said. 'We must be very thorough. Many things won't make sense in these books—they are mysteries after all!' Winton flicked enthusiastically through his book before Evie retrieved small notepads and fountain pens from her bag and distributed them around the table.

'We must note anything that stands out or pricks our curiosity. Then, hopefully, figuring out this mystery will be far easier to achieve,' Winton said.

Alex peeled open the book before him. The contents page covered a range of historical events, from wars, assassinations and revolutions to explorations, inquests and discoveries. Each section had a vast number of chapters, but each chapter took up only a single page. Winton, spotting Alex's confusion, shuffled in close beside him and explained that each chapter was a single physical page, but within it were many subpages which would rise only upon his instruction.

'All up here, you see?' Winton said, tapping his temple. 'Let your thoughts navigate you. Think of the next subpage, or any specific page, and it will come to you. Go on, give it a try.'

Touching the page and pushing a thought, Alex was delighted to find it happened at once. The sentences melted into one thin line, from which a whole new subpage of text formed.

'I suppose they always did say one should read between the lines,' Alex said.

'Did they?' Winton replied cluelessly. 'Well, best get to it then!' He pulled closer his book, *Collection VII—Mysteries of the Long and Famously Dead*, and, along with everyone else, got to reading.

The first section, 'Waging Wars (Pt. One through Twenty-Three)' was the most mystifying and otherworldly piece of literature that Alex had ever read, and he had read a considerable amount of material in recent years. Each chapter followed the same structure: the initial story and full account of the event as it had been recorded—spanning anything from minutes to lifetimes—its deconstruction (including tiny details, reputed truths and certainties) and then, finally, the networks of theories and extraordinary ideas regarding why the event had transpired.

The few segments that Alex read long into the afternoon, only a sliver of the book's total contents, served as a history lesson in reverse. An event of particular interest was 'the Crowning Battle', more commonly known as 'the Crowning': a war between all seven continents of the world. Due to 'secressential governmental acts of deceit, distrust and disloyalty' and lies created to pit the continents against each other, all-out war had escalated in the world within only a matter of years.

According to the book, nowhere had been safe. Cities fell from the summer skies and towers toppled in the wintery capitals. Innocent people were murdered in the streets during the day and attacked in their beds at night; there were executions in the soundless playgrounds and the crowded centres for health and prosperity. It was a world sent spinning off its axis, set for self-destruction. Alex's mind burned bright with images of a world in ruin, a world of desolation and devastating loss.

After England, notably London—which had since been named the Illustrious Great City of London—halted all warfare, a global ceasefire was announced. An era of love, plenty, peace and truth began and an era of conquest, war, famine and death came to an end.

When Alex moved to write down a few points he found that the fountain pen leaked his thoughtful words upon the parchment the moment the two items touched. *I should have known better*, he thought.

Late in the afternoon, once all the books had been restored, or 'numbed', as Ambrose had put it, meaning their contents and abilities had been wiped with a single touch, the Evergreens and Alex left the library.

'There were some really strange things in the book I was reading,' Winton said as they walked back through the streets. 'Jack the Ripper, King Alfred Lewington—you know, the one who died face down in his soup at the Solstice? I remember reading about that when I was your age,' he said, glancing at Alex. 'And that Amelia Earhart. Oh, I came across . . . oh, what was it?' Winton screwed up his face slightly as he thought. 'Something like the Betramsa, no, the Berthesma Square?'

'It's the Bermuda Triangle,' Alex said with a laugh.

Winton shook his head, completely perplexed.

'I've been reading *Mysteries of Evading Escapades*,' Irwin said. 'I just can't get my head around how some of these people escaped. I mean, how do you escape from a prison buried deep beneath the Atlantic Ocean? Or from the Sliver Prisons of the Dremblar Dunes?' Irwin pursed his lips and frowned. 'It's beyond me.'

'What have you been reading?' Ambrose asked her daughter.

Evie cleared her throat and gripped Nora's hand more tightly. 'I've been reading about all kinds of wonders.

Mysteries of Mere Miracles, the book's called. Stories of people surviving some truly horrible things in this world.' Her gaze drifted to her feet as she finished with a tired voice. 'I suppose it gives hope for us all.'

— CHAPTER FIVE —

The Secrets We Keep

Alex's eyes flew open as thunder raged in his heart. It was the middle of the night, and darkness, like a waiting night-nurse, swept in to dress his eyes and drain away his surroundings. He sat upright, triggering the thick beads of sweat on his forehead to roll down his face. Hot and heavy came his breath. After taking a moment to remain still, he was finally able to ponder on the dream that had elicited such a reaction.

It was the first nightmare in what felt like a lifetime, but the same haunting scene he had spent years with. He was trapped, living within four inescapably high walls and in a constant chill. As he pursued possible exits while held by invisible shackles, his apprehension built and the temperature plummeted. Every time it would end the same. Upon his surrendering, the room would gradually morph into the octagonal orange walls and the insufferable heat of the Clockhaus' living room. His reality and nightmare had aligned so perfectly that he could easily step between them but could never escape either.

That is, until the Evergreens returned, for life had never been more exhilarating or more invigorating for Alex than it now was. It was in their walks to the meadows in the dazzling sunrises and their journeys from the library on moonlit nights; it was in the company of his seven companions with their otherworldly ways and magnificent and magical possessions; it was in their free falls through the colourful spectrum of time itself—it was in these things that Alex was freeing himself from the shackles that had bound his life.

A slow creak of a floorboard above told him he wasn't the only one awake. There was a squeal and a sniffling whimper, and then only the sound of his own creeping footsteps as Alex moved to crouch at the bottom of the stairs to listen.

Evie sat in the kitchen above, weeping.

'Ev-everytime I close my eyes, I c-can't help but see that place,' she sobbed. 'How can I block it out? What c-can I ever do to stop this . . . this torment?'

'It's all right, my love, we will get through this, we will pull through,' Irwin said, holding her close. 'We are here now, and we are all here for you.'

There was another set of footsteps, and Alex caught sight of Ambrose, hair askew, as she passed the top of the stairs.

'Is everything all—oh Evie, what's wrong, my petal?'

'It's the nightmares again. Could we get her a tissue please?' Irwin said.

It took Alex a few seconds to realise that Ambrose was hurrying in his direction. Throwing himself back beneath his blanket, he lay still as she fetched a handful of tissues from the bathroom and returned upstairs to soothe her daughter.

Whilst the weeping continued, Alex thought about the nightmares that still lingered with the Evergreens. Their worst nightmares had been reality too, he realised. The more he tried not to think of it, the stronger the image became in his tired mind. A savage, grisly corridor of rotting cells. Pleading hands shooting between the bars. Blood-curdling screams in the compressed, starving air. Hopelessness feasting on fear.

Alex turned over to face the wall. He could not bear to think of such a place let alone wonder what it must have been like to experience it for as long as the Evergreens had, against their will, against their rights. He closed his eyes again, knowing that sleep was now a world away.

*

Alex made sure that he saw his uncle at least once a day, not wanting to give him a reason to wander into the lighthouse and find seven strangers sitting around his kitchen table. In the evenings, when Abraham returned from work, Alex would be sitting in his usual locations in the Clockhaus, by the window or in the armchair, and they would talk and read as though nothing had changed.

The one thing more exhausting than Alex had expected was omitting the truth regarding his guests' existence. The problem with living with someone for so long and in such close quarters was that even the smallest change was the biggest difference, and Abraham had already noticed that something was not right.

'You're in a very good mood this evening,' Abraham had said on the third night after the Evergreens' return.

Alex set down his book. 'I can't be in a good mood?'

'Of course you can,' Abraham replied, flicking out his paper, drawing his gaze back to it. 'I just don't know what could have caused it.'

To say that Abraham did not like the unknown was an understatement that no one could make. His constant anxiety about Alex and their safety had driven him to the drastic lengths of protection he'd enforced over the years, and Alex believed it was this worrying that had given him his exhausted, almost ghostly, appearance.

Then again, two nights later, Abraham spotted something else amiss.

'Is everything all right?' he asked, having finished his jam sandwich. 'You seem . . . distracted.'

Alex realised that he had been staring off towards the lighthouse, letting his mind sail back to his furtive guests and that day's ever-peculiar readings. He nodded casually. 'Fine,' he replied. 'Everything's good.'

Every time Alex walked the rocky edge of the cliff to the Clockhaus that week, he'd fully intended on telling Abraham the whole and unadulterated truth. He'd set out the milestones of the conversation in his head; however, the second he'd sit down opposite his uncle and meet his eye, the planned conversation frayed apart in his mind.

'We all have our secrets and we all have our reasons,' Evie had said when Alex explained to the Evergreens that he was keeping them a secret from his uncle, and that he hadn't told him about his encounter with them that night. 'You can tell him about us, but only when you are ready. Only then,' she said reassuringly, helping to soothe the knot that tightened in Alex's stomach every time he thought about it.

And so when he was with Abraham, Alex would pretend that nothing had changed, when in fact his life had never been more different.

Since the introduction of the Quottle, which Alex had successfully mastered, many other ornaments and trinkets had come spilling from the Evergreens' mysterious trunk, now situated in the corner of the lounge. There were sets of glowing spheres which let the user deposit ideas within them, blank canvases which would paint scenes from one's imagination, sets of oddly shaped lightbulbs which lit up at one's instruction and tiny patterned cushions which puffed out to full size (and to Felicity's amusement) when in one's hands. And then there were other things, their purpose far more concealed, including frameless spectacles, an elaborate series of rustic cages and a box of tiny cocktail umbrellas which Alex presumed would expand to full size if so desired.

Things didn't stop there, however. Every item of clothing the Evergreens possessed could be manipulated at their will. Clothes would change colour, scarves wove themselves around their necks, hats grew themselves tall, blankets grew from tiny patches of material and shoes walked themselves onto their feet, as if all were under some kind of spell.

Adding to the vibrancy of his days spent with the Evergreens were the chapters of the *Bafflement* book, delivering its mystical stories of events throughout history and the future: the murder of JFK; the miles of carved tunnels found linking cities across England and Wales, the perplexing assassination of a lonesome astronaut on an abandoned space station; and sunken treasures hinting to the location of the fabled Atlantis: every story outshone the last. The second and third sections of the book—'Engaging in Explorations (Pt.

Twenty-Four through Thirty-Five)' and 'Assignments of Assassination (Pt. Thirty-Six through Fifty)'—were Alex's newly discovered fascination.

A few days later, as he finished his scribble of notes, Alex turned to the next chapter and sat back. It was nearing time to set off for lunch at the local cafe—Alex's treat, of course, considering he was the only one who had relevant money, albeit saved-up pocket money, to spend. Winton was not sitting beside him in the library as was usual, and it was a few minutes later, at the bottom of the stone steps overlooking the field they trekked across every day, that Alex found him.

Lowering himself down beside Winton, Alex saw that his eyes were closed and his head was drifting from side to side as though he were replaying a favourite song in his mind.

'Blimey!' Alex gasped, hand flying to his chest as Winton unexpectedly turned to him and flicked open his eyes. 'Talk about making me jump!'

'And you were the one sneaking up on me, young sir!' Winton said, tapping Alex on the knee. 'Doctors said I almost brought on my own demise when everyone'—he nodded back at the library—'arranged a party for my seventy-fifth. Invited all my friends they had, some whom I hadn't seen in over half a century, and I was so thrilled that I almost had a heart attack!' He chortled. 'One of my finest days . . .' Upon spotting a squirrel in the nearest tree, Winton paused for a moment to watch it jump between the thick branches. 'No matter how hard they tried in the prison they could never remove memories such as that. Some become so integral to who we are.'

The news that Winton was beyond the age of seventy-five was surprising to Alex, but his shock was superseded by the curious fact that the day he had almost died of surprise was one of Winton's happiest recollections. Something silver caught the light, causing Alex to enquire as to what it was.

'Oh this?' Winton said. 'It's my Ephemor.'

The faded coin, the size of Winton's palm, looked well handled. He elevated it in his hand. 'My one and only,' he added tenderly.

'What's an Ephemor?'

'This,' Winton said, clasping his fingers around it, 'is everything. Everything that's been before. All the good times.'

Confusion leaked over Alex's face.

'Ah, of course . . .' Winton said, recognising the novelty of such an item to Alex. 'Well, an Ephemor stores your memorandia, as we call it. Your memories. Everything in here is my life. Everything I can remember about my fondest times. All the memories, all the little ones you tend to forget throughout your life. When you get to an age like mine, it is your whole world within your world.'

Astonished at how one little thing could bring about all of that wonder, Alex happily accepted the coin from Winton's outstretched hand. It was heavy; cumbersome with the duty of bearing such precious recollections. A number of faded initials were engraved around its edge.

'All your favourite memories, right there in the palm of your hand. Relive them as you see fit.'

'What do you mean relive?'

'Well, you can relive them as everyone always has, in your head, albeit far more vividly, or . . .'

'What, like project them out?'

'Just like you're living them again!'

A sour idea made Alex squint slightly. 'But couldn't that also mean that your worst memories could be put into one of these, all your nightmares and all the things you try to forget?'

Winton's smile faltered for a moment. 'It is your choice what you put in there, as much as it is your choice what you wish to recall. Imagine,' Winton said with a surge of passion, scooting closer to Alex, 'just imagine! Being able to watch your precious memories all around you, reliving them as if you were there again!'

'Can you show me?' Alex asked with marked interest as he handed back the Ephemor.

Winton smiled appreciatively. 'Sometime soon. Very soon —I promise.' He tucked the coin into his blazer pocket and tapped it twice.

'I look forward to it,' Alex said.

*

With spaghetti bolognese bubbling on the stove and the Evergreen family either resting or, as Winton liked to do at the end of each day, analysing the group's collection of notes from that day, it was another quiet night at the lighthouse. Alex had just returned from visiting his uncle. When he entered the lounge, he found Felicity standing with a red book spread over her palms. It was an encyclopaedia about butterflies; each page flicking past revealed pictures of the tiny creatures and their dazzling patterns.

'Go on, Fliss, show him what it can do,' Ambrose said from the kitchen, and so Felicity closed her eyes and traced a finger over the open page as Alex drew in closer. A shiver ran down the book's spine. The pages stood up on end, creating an arch from cover to cover. A second later each page folded in on itself, over and over, until the book, flush with vibrant colours, was filled with a vast collection of intricate origami butterflies.

The creatures twitched and suddenly broke free from their bindings. Hundreds upon hundreds of butterflies came spiralling into the room, frantically fluttering their tiny wings, until around Felicity and Alex a calm cyclone of colour and patterns formed. Felicity plucked one of the creatures from the hurricane and placed it on her palm. It fanned its wings, which were a beautiful mix of orange, black and white, seemingly painted by the most skilled artist alive.

Alex lost himself for a moment. It was the most free he had ever felt, like the floating feeling he had experienced after offering the Evergreens a place to stay, but a thousand times stronger. This time he felt as though he might actually soar into the air himself.

The paper bodies came funnelling down to Felicity at her unspoken desire. Upon landing, each unfolded into a smooth page again until only a book, now empty, sat before her. She looked up to Alex, awaiting his response, but so amazed and so thrilled was he that it was difficult for him to provide one.

'Knew you'd like that,' Winton said, shooting Alex a wink from the kitchen table.

Similarly to everything Alex had experienced since the Evergreens moved in, the sense of fascination lingered, washing away the previous hold of sadness and emptiness over his life. The wonder of what the future with the Evergreens would hold was present every single day. It was in the Ephemor and the Evispen. It was in the Evergreens' faces as they welcomed him to breakfast each and every brilliant morning.

When it came time to leave the library the following evening, Alex stacked up the *Bafflement* books and followed Ambrose to hide them away. Whizzing down aisle after aisle, Alex hastened to keep up with her; she was deceivingly nimble for her age, darting between rows of shelves so quickly that Alex had twice gotten lost. On low shelves or ones only accessible by ladder, Alex hid their history all over the library, at Ambrose's instruction.

'Best to hide them in plain sight,' Ambrose said as Alex slotted away the final book.

Chasing after her once again, Alex questioned just how the books had come to be here and whether it was possible that someone else had also returned from their time.

'We were left a letter which listed each of these books and where to find them,' Ambrose replied, still moving swiftly. 'It directed us to this exact place, and told us the exact shelves to find each upon. The books aren't even registered with the library, someone has just used this place to hide them. The list was given to us with the Evispen, amongst a few other things which have yet to make their purpose known.' As she looked at Alex he saw in the blankness of her aged, yet predominantly youthful face, that her knowledge on the subject was just as thin as his. 'I'm afraid we do not know how the person who left us these things would know we needed them, or that they would be here, but here they are nonetheless, as promised.'

'So,' Alex said, jogging slightly to keep up with her, 'someone—out the blue—gives you this list, gives you the Evispen, and you just accept it? Just like that?'

Reaching the end of the aisle, Ambrose stopped at the sight of Evie and Irwin, who were pulling on their coats up ahead. She clutched the end of the bookcase, watching them intently as they fell into each other's arms and swayed as if dancing in the middle of an abandoned dance floor.

'When you have nothing, when there is nobody and nothing left except each other, and someone offers you help, you do not question it.' In a sorrowful voice, Ambrose had almost sung the pale words, and her hand placed itself over her mouth before she peeled it away one finger at a time. 'You take what you are able to . . . and we took the impossible.' And with that, she walked over to her daughter and son-in-law.

Being all too aware of the sacrifices that had to be made when all else faded away, Alex could very easily understand what she meant.

A thick drizzle descended over Alex, Evie, Irwin and Ambrose as they made their way through the alleyways, looking forward to dinner with Winton and the children who were back at the lighthouse. Lost in a bog of thoughts about how he was possibly going to explain everything to his uncle, Alex didn't notice that anything was wrong until he bumped into everyone gathered together in the alleyway.

'What's wrong?' he asked.

Irwin slapped a finger to his lips.

Now Alex heard them: the sound of distinct footsteps, back in the road they had just left. As they grew louder a figure suddenly darted into the alleyway. It slammed back against the wall, becoming completely immobile. From the dimly lit street, another set of footsteps continued to creep towards the alleyway, finally revealing the shadow of an incredibly tall and thin man. His head rotated, and a dagger-like pain stabbed at Alex's insides; he knew who the man was, if only from his malefic appearance.

Swathed in a black cloak, the man, easily conquering seven feet tall, had striking features. It was as if his face were made of a thousand shards of glass; he had an unusually jutting jaw, razor-edged cheekbones and cold black hair. His piercing stare hungered for the hiding figure, his head snaking and turning as he listened for any movement, any breath. This man was one who had been chasing the Evergreens the second time Alex met them.

With breath locked at the back of his throat, Alex could only stare at the shadowed man, waiting to see what would unfold. They were defenceless in the alleyway; if they were spotted, nothing would prevent their being captured. Alex hadn't seen Irwin carry his weapon since the night they'd met again, but he found himself running prayers back and forth in his head that Irwin had it with him tonight.

Thankfully, the shadowed man soon raced off down the street again. The figure peeled away from the wall, and after taking a moment, moved to the edge of the alleyway, peered guardedly into the street and slipped away out of sight.

'Wait!'

Alex could feel the pressure of Evie's gaze upon him with immediate effect.

'What have you done, Alex? You don't know who it could be!'

Ambrose gave a squeal and grabbed Irwin's hand tightly.

Very slowly, long fingers brushed along the wall, returning the stranger to the four of them. A woman's face peered through the gloom; the whites of her eyes shone like snowy moons in her dark face. She turned towards Alex.

'Hi,' Alex said with a nervous quiver. 'Can I ask . . . why was that man chasing after you?'

Evie's request that they leave came with a slowly pulling hand upon Alex's shoulder. 'No,' he said, moving out from under her grip and looking at the family. 'That man was chasing you all the second time we met!' He turned back to the woman. 'Was it because he wanted to take you back? Back to the prison?'

The pair of eyes widened but the woman did not reply.

'Why did you come back to this time?' Alex finally asked.

She moved slightly closer, and her voice was soothing.

'The fortunes of destiny.'

— CHAPTER SIX —

The Cabin, the Box and the Orb

Despite the lady having spoken only four words, Alex and the Evergreens were captivated by the curious being. She appeared to be levitating at their feet as she stared at them with a deep interest. The woman's body was thick and strong-looking, but Alex couldn't help but feel she had a certain mystical, ghost-like aura to her, as if her consciousness existed on a different plane entirely. Maybe it did. Anything was possible now.

'That's why he was looking for you, wasn't it? Because you're from the prison?' Alex asked.

'That man has been chasing me for a considerable amount of time. For months now,' she replied in the same soothing voice, calm and eloquent. She turned to Evie as if knowing she was about to speak next.

'You were there too?'

'I was.'

'And you came back when we all escaped, when we were freed?'

'I did.'

A befuddled look between Evie, Irwin and Ambrose was most telling; it seemed that none of them could fully recall the lady, at least without seeing her in a more generous light.

'I believe our introductions have been overlooked,' the lady said. An orange light, as strong as a thousand sparklers, suddenly burst from a device in her hand, carving a shadow all around her like a magnificent gown. Her dark skin and peaceful face glowed before them. She had full, blossoming lips, and the freckles decorating her cheeks were illuminated like maps of constellations. Her black frizzy hair was tied in a neat bun atop her head. 'You may call me Devetta,' she said.

Irwin introduced his family and Alex, prompting Devetta to curtsey. He then enquired as to how she had come to be in the same period of time that they were in.

Devetta looked at each of them before replying, 'I am afraid to declare that I feel no one could save the instrument which returned me to this decade. It is quite beyond repair.'

'Your time machine broke?' Alex said.

Devetta replied with only a long, slow blink.

'We could possibly have a look,' said Ambrose. 'You never know.'

Alex was glad to hear Ambrose make the offer; he too felt the desire to explore her mysteriousness a little further.

Thanking them, Devetta moved between Alex and the Evergreens and walked further down the alleyway. 'This way,' she said, and with her bulb-like device leaving a fine ribbon of light through the air in its wake, the group followed her into the open field beyond.

When Evie rushed ahead to speak with Devetta further, Alex moved to follow. But he had only gotten a few steps ahead when Irwin called his name and asked when he was planning to tell his uncle about everything that was happening. Alex slowed down, until he was back between Irwin and Ambrose, and told them the truth: that it would be soon, and he would tell his uncle as much as he knew he could handle.

Above all else, Alex knew that by keeping the secret from Abraham, he was being dishonest to everyone involved. He sighed and shook his head. 'Whenever I see him I have to pretend that I know nothing about you, and you don't deserve that. None of you do.'

'Don't worry about what we deserve, Alex. We have experienced far less than any person deserves,' Ambrose said with an attempt at a smile.

'Well that changes with me,' Alex said matter-of-factly.

Devetta peered back from further along the faint pathway they were following before nodding to Evie. Her bold plum dress blew out from her corset, giving the impression that she was a heavenly body gliding across the blades of grass towards the silhouette of houses in the distance. As she and Evie parted to welcome the others into the conversation, Alex asked whether they had all returned from the same time period.

'It would appear so, yes,' Evie replied.

'And so . . . we just happen to meet?' Alex looked to Irwin. 'Just like that?'

It was clear to Alex that something more than coincidence was on their side once again.

'That would appear to be the case,' Devetta said. Her tone remained void of any particular emotion as she went on to explain how after she had escaped from the prison, she, just like the Evergreens, had taken what she could. 'I took refuge in my box. The numbers of the device span—it whisked me away from then. I had faith it would deliver me where I needed to be.' She took a short look back at Alex and then the Evergreens. 'Quite enough said.'

'Sorry, your box?' Ambrose enquired as she playfully ran her fingers through the ribbon of light stemming from the device in Devetta's hand.

'Yes, I arrived here in it. The means by which I am here ceased to be shortly thereafter. I was searching for food this evening when Digwitch found me. I recall him vividly from the prison,' she said plainly. 'After everything they expelled, only desolate memories of those monsters are left.'

The gradient of the field levelled out as the group moved into the quiet streets of the neighbouring village of Pembletoe. The orange ribbon retracted into Devetta's bulb, and the group fell naturally into a greater state of awareness; every corner and opening was to be checked and double-checked before progressing. They could not afford to sacrifice a single element of their stealth.

'This is Hiddlestowe, where I have managed to hide since I was stranded,' Devetta said.

'May I ask how you came to possess your machine?' Irwin asked, before explaining how they had been gifted theirs.

Devetta's penetrating gaze was drawn to the bag over Evie's shoulder. She appeared intrigued, or very possibly amused, but it was difficult to glean any categorical emotion from her blank canvas of a face. Strangely, she replied that she had received hers in the same manner.

'*Really?*' Alex blurted out. 'Is someone just giving these things away?'

Devetta turned and escorted the group off the street and into a neighbourhood of thick wiry trees where, near a small lake, a lone cabin stood. Bruised wooden panels blocked the windows and doors, and the steps to the porch were splintered and broken. Removing the two planks of wood crossing the door, Devetta kindly gestured for them to enter.

The first thing to reach Alex's senses as he pushed open the door was the smell of damp. So potent was it that he felt as though he were wading through a stagnant river. He pinched his nose and made his way past the leather settee and deceased fireplace to his left to let everyone else in.

After closing the door behind them, Devetta wandered off into the adjoining room. 'I have been here for forty-two days' she said, her voice travelling around corners to find them. 'I searched for days, and this place found me.'

Catching her cracked reflection in a broken mirror, Ambrose complimented Devetta on how lovely the place was.

'Your mistruths are appreciated all the same,' Devetta replied, having reappeared in the corner of the room.

She was standing beside what Alex had presumed to be the curtain covering the window, but as he followed it up with his gaze he saw that it was hanging from the ceiling in a small circle, concealing something inside. Devetta pulled the nearby toggle and the thick drapes lifted away.

Amongst the cold mist which came crawling out over the floor was a white glowing mass, which Irwin and Alex knelt down to inspect. At the core of the ghostly sphere, fragments of clockwork pieces resembling the Evispen's were caught in slow, criss-crossing orbits.

'When moving in my belongings, I had set it upon the mantel ledge there,' Devetta said, motioning to the fireplace. 'But it became unsettled.'

'Unsettled?' Alex said.

'It began to shake, entirely of its own accord.'

The Evergreens exchanged glances. Evie, who had moved down to examine the mass too, looked up to Devetta and cocked her head. 'That is what happened to ours previously.' She glanced briefly at Alex. 'It was only moments before they found us again.'

'They may have been close, but they never found the location of my hiding,' Devetta said.

Layers of clouds glided away, revealing a set of broken fragments at the very centre of the sphere that weren't moving.

'Time has fractured at its very core,' Devetta said, confirming Irwin's question before it had even formed on his tongue. 'I believe it is healing. It has condensed in size with each passing day. But even if it does heal itself, I know only too well that it will not be one coherent piece again.'

It was evident from the blank looks on Evie's and Irwin's faces that they would not be able to fix the device, and so Devetta moved to draw the curtain down. Before she did so, she stared down into the misty orb. It was a most dire, despondent stare. As the material swept down, Alex realised that the motion brought with it the end of her travels. Once again, he found himself speaking before he knew it.

'You are coming to stay with us.'

Devetta blinked only once in what was presumed to be shock, but when he repeated his offer, going on to explain at length that he believed there was a reason for their meeting as they had, she accepted, curtsied and swept away to gather her belongings. A minute later Devetta returned, completely empty-handed. 'I am ready,' she said.

Alex and the Evergreens looked at one another and then back at her.

'Got *everything*?' Alex said.

With a single nod, Devetta retrieved a tiny dark wooden box from a slit in her dress and held it out. 'Everything I need is here, in my Elongress.'

'Your what, dear?' Ambrose replied.

'The box, I presume?' Alex said.

Devetta raised her eyebrows as though to ensure they were paying attention. She set the box down behind the torn sofa, and with the touch of her finger and to the surprise of them all, the box grew before her. After it had surpassed them in height, the two halves of the Elongress peeled apart and a light flicked on inside.

Beyond the columns of drawers, gorgeous dark leather lined the Elongress' deceivingly spacious halves. A spectacular collection of frilled dresses hung from a rail on one side, and on the other a number of random items were stored, including an oversized umbrella, boxes of crystal baubles and collections of necklace pendants and rings. Upon the back wall Alex spotted a number of pendulums, all swinging out of time to one another, and even more oddly, in the far back corner, a tower of antique typewriters.

Fetching a large book wrapped in a folded leather skin from somewhere in the cabin, and depositing it in one of the bottom drawers, Devetta welcomed everyone aboard. As everyone climbed inside, she explained that the Elongress was her wardrobe, trunk, conduit for travel, and any other useful item that it saw fit to be.

'Your father will love this!' Irwin exclaimed to Evie as they followed Alex and Ambrose inside. Devetta then nodded to the cabin as if thanking it for housing her during her transition. She slotted in beside Irwin, and the two halves of the Elongress clamped together, bringing the five of them face to face.

The walls of their new vehicle shuddered from bottom to top, making the various items hanging from them quiver and rattle. The Evispen, held tight within Evie's hands, whirled in a flurry of life as the numbers of the current date began to spin, one by one.

Suddenly, they were yanked backwards as the Elongress began to spin rapidly. Their bodies were forced flat against the padded walls. There was a heavy sound, a tumbling noise, as if gravity were reeling, corkscrewing out of control around them. Evie was squinting, her hands white as she gripped the Evispen with all her might. The typewriters frantically typed of their own accord as Alex dug his fingers into the thick leather wall to hold on. At last there was a final whirling scream from the Evispen and everyone except Devetta was thrown to the floor.

The Elongress unsealed itself and gradually opened. Evie shrieked - all around them was the crushed wooden frame of Alex's bed.

'Oh, Alex! I'm so sorry! I was trying to land us in the kitchen but I got distracted!'

'It's OK, at least no one was hurt.'

'I once landed on the grand piano of King Malverick Orvander,' Devetta said as they stepped down off the bed. 'An introduction, nonetheless.' Placing the tip of her finger to the box there was a small *pop!* and the Elongress instantly shrank to pocket size.

As if anyone needed any further surprises, the bedroom door flew open to reveal Winton holding a rolling pin above his head. The children peered around his quaking knees.

'No need to look so frightened, it's only us.' Evie moved forward and kissed her father on the cheek.

As they all moved down to the kitchen, Alex introduced Winton and the children to the new guest. Daniel was rather transfixed by Devetta's giant figure, and couldn't take his eyes from her. 'You are very tall!' he exclaimed.

Devetta captured his hand with a generous handshake. 'You are rather small, down there.'

'No I'm not, I'm quite tall for my age!' Daniel said, his pride slightly wounded.

At Alex's request, Devetta took the lone armchair in the corner of the lounge, and to her captivated audience told of her terrifying ordeal to date. Having been captured following the framing of the Evergreens, she too had been dragged, silent but unyielding, to the prison to which they had all fallen victim. The purging of a lifetime's most cherished memories; the starvation; the sleep deprivation and subsequent prying open of her dreams—all the physical and mental torture she survived was for the purpose of aiding her assailants in trying to locate the mysterious and elusive Heirloom. Despite her oppressors' believing that those they had imprisoned knew what the item was, Devetta assured her audience that she, like the Evergreens, knew not of its origins, location or purpose.

Devetta, too, had been framed for a crime, but quite some time after she had been locked away in the prison.

'That's likely so that if you escaped, you wouldn't last long out in the world again,' Evie said dolefully. 'Well, you wouldn't if you were framed for what we were.'

'What were you framed for?' Alex asked Devetta.

'Ephemorical desecration.'

'What is that?' Alex said, and the group turned to Irwin, who was standing by the kitchen.

Irwin dipped his head reservedly. 'It is the forceful purging of memories from within an Ephemor—memories of someone living or otherwise' he said. 'It is a cruel, sadistic act. It, too, like . . . murder, had not been committed in one hundred ages. Nothing bad like that had ever occurred since the Crowning. Desecration of another's memories warrants a life sentence, and rightfully so—what right or privilege does one ever have to tamper with, *destroy*, another's memories?'

Sat between the pillars of her parents, Evie spoke in a voice that was vacant, if not utterly forlorn. 'I do not believe that those chasing us would simply stop if we gave them what they wanted, what they locked us away for. Too much has happened. To them we are loose ends now. It doesn't matter why they think we have the Heirloom; it will not change a thing.' She cuddled Felicity tighter on her lap. 'They will be searching for us for the rest of our lives.'

The words Alex had said sixty years previously, in 1940s London, echoed back to him, and it became crystal clear how the Evergreens had clung to life for so long: *Together you can survive the unthinkable.*

When Irwin and Winton offered to collect fish and chips from the high street for dinner, Alex explained to them once more the difference between pounds and pence and set them in the right direction. From the window he watched them leave. Despite the night, which was slowly drifting in across the sea and pressing down from the sky, the Clockhaus gleamed, acerbic pearly white, at the edge of town. Its many windows remained plated with fabric—the curtains were always shut, even on the sunniest of summer days—but around their edges Alex could see light: Abraham was home. Alex contemplated sharing with him the truth tonight, but his head was already shaking from side to side.

Devetta was also Alex's guest now, the eighth who had taken up his offer of a place to stay, and, in his eyes, at least some minor form of protection. *Just how long will it continue?* The voice within him questioned his instinctual actions so very discourteously. 'There are a lot of us here now, and he has to know,' Alex said as he heard footsteps behind him. 'I can't keep hiding this, hiding you all from him.'

'I know,' Ambrose said. 'It is an incredibly gracious thing you did today . . . again. Although I will soon have to question where you'll be keeping people if you invite many more to stay.' She laughed as she walked to the head of the table, red tablecloth in hand. 'After dinner, how about we have a talk through what you'd like to say to your uncle?'

Alex thanked her and watched as she shook the tablecloth out in the air. It landed, perfectly set and ready, over the kitchen table.

The high street was dark and lifeless when Alex looked out at it again, but high up towards the meadows he spotted a faint white light whizzing about. He leaned closer to the window to inspect it, but it was only upon hearing the children giggle behind him that he checked over his shoulder to find what appeared to be a small white bird flying around the room. It was joined by two other creatures, one grey and one black.

As he moved closer to them, Alex saw that all three were small paper origami animals, each evidently powered by the children's guiding thoughts. Daniel's had taken the shape of a small penguin, Nora's a grey scrub hare with long flapping ears and Felicity's a pure white horse with broad, robust wings —Pegasus. The Halpens, as Daniel introduced them, stayed with the children, following them around and landing upon them before flying away again.

After chasing one another in circles, the Halpens landed on the table beside Alex. Up close the creatures were astonishing. Thousands of tiny paper feathers made up Daniel's penguin's black wings and Pegasus' queenly mane. The lively hare even blinked its stone-like eyes.

It was Daniel who knowledgeably responded when Alex asked how the Halpens appeared to act by themselves. He explained that a bond, a *thread*, could link one's thoughts to basic artefacts, and when they weren't being controlled, these artefacts could act on a series of simple thoughts themselves. To Alex it went some way in explaining why he had awoken a few days ago to find Daniel's penguin tap-dancing on his face for its own presumed enjoyment.

'What is it like, when you come from?' Alex asked when the Halpens flew away, their commanders following them. 'I keep trying to picture what it could be like but I can't seem to imagine it.'

Ambrose and Evie grew visibly mindful. The Halpens flew to the far corner of the lounge, where Devetta was searching through her Elongress. Ambrose finally found the words.

'Well, when we are from, everything just . . . flows.'

'What do you mean? Flows from what?'

'Flows from you,' she replied. 'Your thoughts are the key to everything. You have seen that for yourself, but it is much bigger than that. It is the foundation of our time.'

Alex sat down and shuffled his chair in closer, an eagerness drawing him in.

'It's a place where your imagination is not bound by scribe or speech. A place where we share memories as a common courtesy to friends and family, where the memorandia we hold lives on after we pass.' Ambrose took Evie's hand and held on to it tightly. 'It is a place where your dreams grow from you as you sleep.'

The tingly feeling, like a flock of sparkles, coursed through him with a surge of excitement. His eyes widened beneath his loaded cheeks.

And then Evie finished the conversation simply. 'It's a place unlike anything you could ever imagine.'

*

The persistent white fog that had swamped the town of Merlow had provided Alex with safe passage up to the Clockhaus on the morning he finally told Abraham the truth. Since its arrival in the days previously, rolling off the choppy sea as a drooling mist, it had fermented menacingly through the streets until the entire town was lost to it. Alex had never felt so closed off from the world beyond.

Despite knowing how small the cobbled area between the Clockhaus and the lighthouse was, in the company of such weather it became an infinite nether-space between past and future, and ultimately, between restraint and freedom. The crowds had since fallen away under the forceful fog, and Alex came to stand at one of the recently erected fences staring up at the black hull of the *Precipitous*, quite alone.

Over the three days since Devetta arrived, Alex had woven his secret of her and the Evergreens into a chain of unbreakable words. What he had told Abraham was admittedly not the full truth he had hoped he would be able to share. With several key time-travelling and convict-related elements omitted, it was to Alex's great surprise that his uncle had given a response, and finally an offer, that he could never have foreseen him making.

The children were sitting on what Alex was coming to call his bed when he eventually returned to the lighthouse and hung up his coat. Felicity was reading about the fashions and times of the fifties, whilst Daniel was as equally consumed by *The Witches of the Well: The Pembletoeish Tales*, which Nora, who was playing with her Halpen, had told him she saw little worth in.

Alex held back giving any definitive answers to everyone's questions as he walked up into the kitchen, instead inviting them to take a seat at the table so that he could explain what had happened. Devetta was the last to join them, setting down her adopted book, *Mysteries of Transition*, and taking the final seat opposite Alex.

Alex looked at those with whom he now sat—people who had survived the incredible and the unbelievable. And although he could not claim to have had his memories ripped from him, or to have been exiled and on the run, and thankfully so, he realised that in many ways, he too was a survivor, and it was finally time to explain why. Building up a dam within him and steadying his emotions behind it, Alex cleared his throat.

'It's time you knew the truth about me,' he said, taking a long, deep breath. 'It's time you knew about my life since "that night."'

— CHAPTER SEVEN —

Ephemor

'"That night", the night we met,' Alex slowly began, looking to Evie and Irwin on his left, and to Winton on his right, 'that was the night my parents vanished, never to be seen again.'

Everyone but Devetta jolted. Evie gasped. Irwin was looking around, seemingly confused but already beginning to connect the dots.

'Nothing was ever found of where they went, or . . . or what happened to them.'

'I am very sorry to hear that.' Ambrose sniffled, her eyes becoming small and wet. 'I am so very sorry.'

Alex could feel tears filling his own eyes too. His breath wobbled on its rapid journey in and out, but he forced out its quivers, swallowed, and continued.

'When Abraham picked me up, because I hadn't told him about the three of you being there . . . and he hadn't seen you . . .'

'Oh n-no,' Evie stuttered.

'He told me that those men coming after you, those men who came to my house, were there for my parents, and for me.'

'Your uncle thought that?' Irwin said, almost pleading that it was not so.

Alex nodded glumly. His uncle had always believed this, and had always maintained that William and Meredith's failure to return was visible proof.

'It isn't a coincidence they vanish the same night those men turn up, Alex!' his uncle would always say during their arguments. 'It isn't, it isn't, it isn't!' Although Alex agreed with his uncle on this one point, it was for an entirely different reason: it was the Evergreens, this mysterious family on the run, who were the actual prey of this unknowable force; they were the reason why the two men swaddled in black had come to his house—not him, and not his parents.

'I see it in his eyes every day,' Alex continued. 'He is an incredibly stubborn man. He believes that those men were there for me and my parents, and nothing is ever going to change that. Even if I had told him about you being there that night he would have said you were strangers who were at the right place at the right time, or made up some excuse to maintain what he believes.'

'And what do you believe Alex?' Winton said, waiting worriedly.

Alex believed what he knew to be the truth—that neither he nor his parents had been in any danger that night, and there was a light sigh of relief from the Evergreens as he told them this; unlike his uncle, Alex had believed the right thing.

'The weapons you had and they had . . . you'd been there only ten minutes when they came. It was obvious—it *is* obvious. They're trying to find you.'

From some suppressed corner of his memory came his uncle's maddened, swivelling eyes accompanied by a war of words, and Alex flinched. 'No,' he mumbled, his fingers tracing the cracks in the wooden table. 'I remember seeing it in his eyes. He knew he had to do what he did.'

Devetta had not removed her gaze from Alex across the length of the table.

'What do you mean?' Winton asked, a quiver in his voice.

Alex remained silent. His mapping fingers stopped.

Evie shuffled in her chair. 'Alex, what do you mean? What did your uncle have to do?'

'Believing what he did, it was the only way for him to keep me safe . . . to know that no one would find me. He . . . he hid me from the world so they wouldn't find me again.'

The truth. At last, it had been said.

In an instant Evie grabbed her face and began sobbing uncontrollably. 'Oh *God* . . .' she cried over and over, finally pushing away from the table and rushing into the lounge. The children started running after her but Ambrose called them to her as Irwin moved to console Evie, trying his best to shield Alex from her raw emotion.

'He kept me away,' Alex mumbled, mind wandering and voice failing. 'Locked me away.'

'For all this time? All those years since we saw you last?' Winton asked with pain in his voice.

Alex slowly and conclusively turned over his palms. The action spoke the obvious: of his secluded, concealed life, a life spent kept away and scurrying along the thin path between where they sat now and the Clockhaus; of why his uncle worried so; of why he had seen only a small portion the high street; of why there were so many hooded coats by the back door. Endless years watching out the window. His life since that night was perfectly summed up by no words at all.

Poisoned feelings continued to flow through each of the Evergreens. From what Alex understood, had they not arrived that night, their oppressors would not have followed them back, Abraham would not have incorrectly believed what he had, and Alex would not have been locked away.

Every word Alex gave in an attempt to unburden the Evergreens felt almost like begging. He found himself promising that he had been taught all that he needed to be; that his uncle's shop had given them a slight but steady income with which to enjoy life. He told them of Abraham's dear friend Herga, who had been of great comfort over the lonely years and as much an aunt to him as Maudlyn had been. He told them that above all else, he was loved. Finally Alex sat back and crossed his arms. Trying to prove that he had lived some kind of worthwhile existence since they last met was incredibly draining.

Alex fetched a glass of water, drank it dry and then hurried down another. Upon reclaiming his seat, Evie did so too under Irwin's protective wing, and Alex shared the news of his visit with his uncle that morning.

As rehearsed, Alex had told Abraham a story which encompassed equal doses of fact and fiction. Where possible, he'd stuck to the truth. He told of how he had offered shelter to the family when their car broke down in the snow, and how they had kept him safe when they came under attack. What pained Alex the most was having to play into his uncle's mistaken belief that he was in danger. He'd kept his voice calm and collected as he pretended, again, that the men who were in fact hunting down the Evergreens had been there to take him away, like his parents. After revealing that the family had come knocking at the Clockhaus the day after the ship crashed, with nowhere left to go and nowhere to stay, Alex realised that the entire conversation needn't have been practised at all.

'The moment after I said that you were there "that night", that you protected me, he just . . . switched off,' Alex said. 'He should have been furious, thinking I'd endangered myself by allowing you to find me. But there was nothing. Inviting you to stay with me went against everything he has done to keep me safe.' Alex frowned, thinking of his uncle's non-explosive response. 'I promised that I wasn't in danger, but he didn't say a word until he finally made'—Alex huffed, not knowing quite what to make of it—'an offer.'

The Evergreens shifted in their places around the unwavering column that was Devetta, listening dutifully.

'He offered that we all move in with him, in the Clockhaus.'

Evie emerged from behind her hands, which had been covering her tear-stained face. Daniel lent in to brush away the wet drops that remained, but Evie gently caught his hand and squeezed him in close. 'He said that?' She sniffled. 'He really offered us that?'

'He did. And I think we are wise to do accept his offer. It's a far better place for you all, lots more space, and he's got a pantry full of food there—'

Alex stopped quite abruptly. The idea of the dungeon-like pantry sent an uncomfortable twitch to his stomach.

It was Felicity's giggle, at the hand of her sister, that signified Alex's tale had come to a close. The tense atmosphere began to dissipate, the mood lightened and the group shook hands with Alex and hugged him, as if he had been introduced to them anew. Winton poured each of them a welcome serving from the Quottle, and upon finishing his own drink, a mug filled with whirling purple fluid and hints of lime glowing like fireflies, he twirled around from the counter and remarked, 'Right! Who wants to see something bloomin' amazing?'

'Meeee!' the children chorused.

The kitchen became fit as a stage for Winton's performance as all got to their feet and helped to move the table and chairs to the edge of the room.

'What shall we see then? Suggestions, please!' Winton called out.

'Grandma Imelda's party!' Nora shouted.

'The Nightingate Revival!' Daniel squealed.

Winton rocked about like a jester. A glisten of silver caught the light between his hands.

'The painted cliffs of Dover!' Evie said, already on the road to recovery.

'Our first.'

Ambrose's request suddenly toppled the pile of recommendations.

'The day we met. Our first together,' she said.

Everyone looked between Winton and Ambrose, clearly confused.

'We haven't seen that before,' Evie said, still sniffling. 'Why haven't we seen that before?'

Ambrose claimed Winton's hand, and he smiled affectionately to her. 'I keep that memory close because it is one of my most precious. But share it with you all I shall,' he said. 'Everyone ready?'

With his Ephemor gripped tight in his remaining hand, Winton closed his eyes. From every direction and to every point, waves of silky light swept forward. It was like aurora borealis painted by the most accomplished hands. Alex swung his head around to capture and savour as much awe as his limited senses could absorb. Within only seconds, dark olive walls were stretching around them, and the aromas of spices and herbs were pinching at their noses. As the final pieces fell into definition, the audience came to be standing in the aisle of a handsome green-tinted bistro.

Alex didn't know where to look; there was so much to see. The plush booths and busy tables surrounding them were filled with chattering, smartly dressed business people, each with a Victorian-esque yet modern twist to his or her dress. Aproned waitresses carrying overflowing trays were whizzing around the course of the cafe, and long windows revealed all kinds of antique-looking shops buried in the cliff face opposite.

The group moved over to a booth by the window, where young Ambrose sat, watching the hundreds of passers-by swarming the rocky street. She was wearing a long dress the soft shade of forget-me-nots, and her curls of auburn hair were perched upon her narrow shoulders. The young woman had the same small face, with a thin nose and prominent, rounded cheeks, as the elder one stood opposite her.

'I look so young!' Ambrose said, simpering.

'You look beautiful, Mum,' Evie said.

Young Ambrose pressed her finger to a painting of a small teacup on the wall. It glowed, and steam twisted away from it. A minute later a bustling waitress came racing up to her side.

'There you are, my lady, as requested: one mango marshmallow.' The flamboyant waitress gasped as she looked up at Ambrose from behind her overflowing tray. 'Oh! Well don't you look the epitome of elegance!'

'I am meeting someone.'

'A gentleman? *A date?*' the waitress asked. Ambrose nodded excitedly. 'Well I do wish you all the best—not that you shall need it!' The waitress gasped again before flying away.

Ambrose turned back to the window, but no less than thirty seconds later—

'Greatly begging your pardon, ma'am.' The young voice, confident and assured, contained a note of wisdom now so familiar to Alex. The group shuffled aside to reveal a man in a slick tailcoat, a triangular bow-tie and familiar bottle-end glasses. Alex could have spotted who it was a mile away.

'Oooo! Check you out!' Evie giggled, looking to her father.

'I am sorry to trouble you, but I have been watching you from the booth over there,' young Winton said as he took a keen step forward. 'And I was just so taken with you that I—'

Winton's words were cut short as blinding flashing lights shot from his glasses. 'Oh! I! Ahh!' The lights flickered on and off, over and over, until they finally shorted out with a fizzle of smoke.

The children howled with laughter, and the gentlemen in the nearby booth sniggered. Young Winton found himself at a loss for words. 'I'm terribly sorry,' he said at last, pushing the frames back up his long nose. 'I've been blinded by some misfortune with these glasses—'

'*You've* been blinded?' Young Ambrose laughed, rubbing her eyes.

'Well done, Winton,' he said, throwing his hands on his hips and tutting to himself. 'Blind her before you even know her name!'

There was a moment's pause, and he turned bright red.

'My name is Amber . . . Ambrose.' Winton did a double take. 'Would you like to try that again?' she offered.

Without hesitating, Winton gave a long bow and introduced himself afresh. 'I have come over to ask you whether you would like to accompany—'

'Yes,' Ambrose replied, the green in her eyes glowing with exhilaration. 'Yes, I would like that very much.'

'—accompany my pet pheasant to the Deveaux Gardens,' Winton continued casually. 'He is somewhat belligerent, hasn't been walked for weeks now, mind you, and he keeps trying to eat my hat.'

Ambrose's expression rose with surprise for a brief moment, and Alex couldn't help but grin. 'Of course, yes, that is—hmm.' Ambrose stopped rambling to sip her drink, and Winton's face burst into a smirk. 'Please tell me you don't have a pheasant!' Ambrose snorted, laughing as if she had known the man a lifetime.

'No, no pheasant I'm afraid. Not with me, anyway.' Winton snickered. 'So how about it? The Gardens? No pheasant, I assure.'

'I would like that,' Ambrose replied. Taking Winton's outstretched hand, she rose to her feet and curtseyed, and they moved away into the shimmery edge of the memory together.

The colours around the group glowed like fiery embers before slowly fading, returning them all to the confines of the far less fascinating kitchen.

'And I've been blinded by your love ever since,' Ambrose said, and with that she planted a tender, lasting kiss upon Winton. 'I'll never know who the gentleman I was supposed to meet was, but I'm so glad you found me first.'

In the centre of the kitchen, the Evergreens came together. Their arms spread around each other as they nestled their bodies close. Alex could now see above all else how a memory so cherished and savoured could bring a family together in the face of such adversity, and he found himself wishing for nothing more than to follow the endlessly young Ambrose and Winton on their first date into the Deveaux Gardens.

After witnessing such a wondrous memory, and still adjusting to the fantastical way that the Evergreens lived their lives, Alex instantly saw the Ephemor's benefits over his earlier suspected doubts.

*

The final glimmers of sunset drained from the sky as evening settled and the Evergreens, Alex and Devetta finished their supper. The table was loud with kept thoughts. The silence was finally broken by Evie, who was paddling the watery remains of her soup with her spoon.

'May I ask about something you mentioned earlier, Alex?' she quietly asked, her gaze fixed on her bowl.

'I know what you're going to say,' Alex said; he too was stuck in the cognitive bog of the day's revelations. 'You're wondering why I didn't tell my uncle today that those men were really there for you that night.'

Devetta spoke up unexpectedly. 'I understand most clearly. To confess would be to admit that you were in no danger, had not been for all this time. Therefore, Abraham would know that for the past seven years he has been stealing a life that has not required collection.'

'The guilt of knowing he locked me away for no reason would kill him,' Alex said in agreement, looking sadly to the Evergreens. 'And if I had told him today that these men are after you and you are living with me, it would have refreshed his fear anew.'

Evie hung her head. 'That's not what I was going to ask, actually.'

Alex smiled invitingly.

'As far as we know, those men came to your house to find us that night we met. And you could have been killed, Alex.' Evie's voice was tired but incredibly serious. 'As a result, your uncle kept you away all this time. Seeing that if it hadn't been for us then none of this would be the case, I, we—we wondered whether . . . whether you blame us?'

Alex waited until Evie finally met his gaze again before he resolutely replied. 'No. Not at all.'

'Why not? Why would you ever want us in your life again after that? It is because of us that you were locked away for all these years.'

The remaining Evergreens looked apprehensively to Alex; this had clearly been on all of their minds.

'For all these years I didn't tell Abraham that you were there that night. I kept it a secret, kept *you* three a secret,' he said, looking to Winton and Irwin, beside Evie.

'Yes, you said, but—'

'*My* secret,' Alex said slowly. 'I think you forget that the night we met was when I lost everything . . . my parents. It was the night my life changed completely. You are one of the lasting memories of that night, something to hold on to. After all this time, I never quite let go of you.'

A look of relief rushed over the Evergreens, but over none more so than Evie.

'You were there when I lost it all, and you became my secret, one that I clung to. I wished that I would one day meet you all again. Because after all those searches for me, after all those years, no one found me again like you did that night.'

The Evergreens were visibly touched by his heartfelt words. Even Irwin, one who kept his emotions under a tighter rein, struggled to remain composed.

'I have always considered you to be my friends, and I think of you this way still,' Alex continued. 'That's why I want to help you. I think the more fitting question is: why would I not want you back in my life?'

Overwhelmed once again, Evie wished Alex and Devetta goodnight and headed for bed. The rest of the Evergreens followed her, and Devetta ventured downstairs to where she now slept—at her insistence—in the rickety rocking chair by the back door. Now alone, Alex found himself lost in a most familiar place.

The dusty old cupboard at the edge of the kitchen was just tall enough to allow Alex to see out of the window facing the town, and just wide enough to allow him to draw his knees into his chest; the perfect place for him to sort through his muddled head. The light from the Aglow, as Devetta had named it, was casting a fading halo around the kitchen, lighting up the quietness of the room. Alex found his gaze slowly following its circumference until another golden light caught his attention. It was the Evispen, resting on the nearby cabinet like an out-of-place ornament.

How has it led them to me twice now? Alex squeezed his thoughts like petals in a flower press, trying to extract some stronger scent or understanding from them. Turning back to the window, he rubbed its condensed face with the cuff of his jumper. Not much could be distinguished amongst the thick fog, but Alex looked out dedicatedly all the same.

Was it that his wish for his friends to return to him had been granted? Was that why they had come journeying back to him through time and space, after all their fear-filled heartache and pleas for redemption? Had he wished so very hard that, somehow, his dreams had echoed through to the Evergreens so many millions of miles of untold time away? Then, if so, why had his most deeply rooted desire not yet been answered?

The moonlit mist swirled, listening to his thoughts.

Will you ever come back to me? Alex said, his thoughts speechlessly forming into prayer at his mouth. *The night you both leave, the night they arrive?* His mind alive with memories of his parents, Alex passed a lengthy glance behind him. *But if those who came to my house weren't there for you and for me but for the Evergreens, then what happened to you? Where did you go?*

'When will you come back to me?' Alex finally found himself whisper, staring back out to the landscape again.

The swirling mists sailed on, refusing to tell of what had come to pass and what was yet to come.

— CHAPTER EIGHT —

Heading Home

The coastal breeze brandished iron fists and threw salty sprays at Alex, Devetta and the Evergreens as they stood on the back doorstep of the Clockhaus, anticipating how they would be received. Alex was rather impressed by everyone's efforts to dress as smartly as affordable, except, as usual, for the indifferent Devetta. He had only just finished warning the group of his uncle's nervous disposition when Evie spotted the frogs on Daniel's shirt leaping around him.

'Now we must respect the era we are in, please,' Evie said, glancing expectantly at each member of her family. At her words Daniel's frogs stopped leaping, the butterfly hairpins in Felicity's and Nora's hair stopped fluttering and Winton's tie stopped dancing indecisively between stripes and checks. The children's Halpens unfolded into creaseless scrolls of creamy parchment, and Irwin picked up the trunk.

With his heart a storm in his chest, Alex slowly unlocked the door and stepped inside. This had to go well.

The group waited in the kitchen as Alex climbed the few steps up into the stifling lounge. Abraham was standing in the middle of the room, and as he turned around, Alex was immediately impressed; his shirt was smooth and uncreased, and done up to the top button beneath his dark cardigan, his hair was combed and his ratty slippers had been switched for shiny shoes, which shuffled and tapped about the floor.

'Everyone is here then?' Abraham said. His voice was dry and slightly higher pitched than normal.

'Yes. And they're very excited to meet you.'

'Really?' Abraham sounded honestly shocked. He stood up a little straighter.

'They're going to love you.'

Whisking his trembling hands behind his back, Abraham flattened his foot to the ground and pushed a smile onto his face. Alex watched him anxiously as Ambrose stepped first from the kitchen.

'Why hello. It is *good morning*, I believe?' she said.

'Is—is it is a good morning?' Abraham stuttered. 'I—I don't know. I haven't been outside today.'

Ambrose giggled. 'I can assure you that it is a good morning. Somewhat windy but otherwise quite pleasant. My name is Ambrose—'

Before she had finished her courtesy, Winton galloped up the stairs. 'Hello, dear sir!' He shook Abraham's hand vigorously. 'I am Winton! Great, *great* pleasure to meet you!'

In his inability to produce an equally igniting introduction, Abraham appeared to swing between shock and concern.

'I am terribly eager to get to know you more!' Winton finished. Standing aside with Ambrose while Abraham gave a gentle welcome to the children and a timid nod to their parents as they entered the lounge, Winton pointed to the vinyl player on a nearby table and gasped. 'Oh look! He's got a victrola! That's a genuine relic in our time!'

Devetta's interstellar presence finally came to occupy the room. Her arms swept out gracefully as she curtseyed, and her layered gown spread in a pool of material around her. 'It is a magnificence to meet you,' she said.

Fearing that Abraham was already overwhelmed, Alex went to lead everyone away.

'Before you take your belongings upstairs I want to say something,' Abraham said stiffly, halting their departure. He gave a long sniff. Alex gulped. 'I have to say thank you to the three of you who were there, who saved my nephew, my boy. I don't know where I would be if those people had taken him, too.' Abraham's hands wrung with agitation in front of him, and he was shaking like a leaf before flight in a gusty wind.

'He'—Irwin looked at Alex—'and you'—he smiled at Abraham, 'are most welcome.'

And then it happened. Abraham's eyes met Alex's and they held contact for a moment. It was brief but telling. Devetta and the Evergreens' presence was substantial for him, that much Alex knew, but there was more; Abraham could barely look at any of them. He expected at least something from his uncle, be it a faint smile, or some word of approval, but none came. Abraham's gaze fell, and he walked off to the kitchen.

With an awkwardness growing behind and an optimism dying within him, Alex invited everyone to follow him to their rooms.

The bedroom Alex sometimes slept in on the first floor, with its crisp white bed sheets and light stripy walls, was collectively claimed by Evie, Irwin and the children. Winton and Ambrose settled into the dark-panelled spare room next to it, and so Alex continued with Devetta up to the second floor. 'This is the last place we have left, I'm afraid,' he said to her as they climbed the creaky stairwell.

To Alex, the attic had always felt like a cathedral sitting on top of the Clockhaus, albeit only in size; there were no gloriously painted windows, sounds of heavenly choirs or tall carved arches above, no matter how high up in the clouds they were. Only old wooden beams and mismatched floorboards defined the chilly, abandoned space.

'You're probably wondering why that's there?' Alex said, gesturing to the mountainous heap of dusty furniture to their side that ran the length of the room. It consisted of hundreds of old cabinets, doors, tables, stools, chairs and chests all interlocked and orderly stacked.

'No,' Devetta replied, paying it only the slightest interest in her inspection. 'Your uncle has an eye for antiquities. Obsessive, one could say. It seems Winton shares quite a similar fascination.'

Reaching the other end of the attic, where a set of neglected French doors opened to a tiny balcony that overlooked the whole of Merlow beyond, Devetta brought the Elongress to size before them. Its halves opened and the chambers inside the doors swung out over and over until it spanned nearly the width of the room. The layers of drawers split apart like fanning fingers at each end revealing many locked chambers no doubt containing all manner of enigmas and impossibilities.

'Everything I need is within, but thank you,' Devetta said, somehow sensing Alex's impending offer of anything she might need, and with that he wandered back downstairs to unpack.

The final habitable space was on the first-floor landing. The small area had provided no purpose whatsoever over the years and now contained only a dilapidated teak wardrobe full of Abraham's oldest clothes, which told of another age altogether. The walls were covered in insipid wallpaper, distressfully patterned and stained, resulting in Alex falling onto the mattress set out for him and unpacking his bag through half-shut eyes.

From the centre of the tiny space Alex could reach every wall, and so his task of setting out his few belongings took only minutes. As he did so, Abraham's frigid introduction replayed in his head. The great gratitude Alex knew his uncle truly felt towards Evie, Irwin and Winton, though based on an entirely incorrect assumption, had not been expressed as it should have been. His uncle's instinctual reaction should have been to latch on to each one of them in wild, uncontrollable appreciation and declare himself forever in their debt. But he hadn't, and that meant something was definitely not right. Setting out his alarm clock, which had never received so much use as it had recently, Alex vowed to keep an even closer eye fixed upon his uncle for the foreseeable future.

The final item in Alex's bag was his most cherished photograph. He did not assign it a position right away. Instead, he let the frame rest in his hands. There they were again, as always, watching him from the other side of the glass. As Alex opened his eyes a little more, he felt his mind being pulled away—through the window overlooking Bedfellow Meadows, out across the tips of the pine trees and down past the stumps of their trunks, out through the back alleys and into the street and, finally, back to his childhood home again. It was so close yet so very far away. Then Alex thought of the Evispen, the impossible machine, and he realised that no distance was too far to travel. Not Merlow, not London, not yesterday nor yesteryear. It was only a thought and a quick spin through the emptiness to get there. That was all it would take.

He placed the frame down at the top of his mattress and placed the pillow upon it. Hopefully, if he was lucky, his parents would find him in his dreams.

Dinner that evening was met by very large appetites. Whether it had been their uncertainty over how Abraham would take their arrival or their long afternoon reading in the attic together that had caused such hunger no one seemed to know, but as soon as Alex served up the large dish of shepherd's pie on the makeshift table in the lounge, everyone dived in without question. Before Alex joined, his head still toying with the idea of returning home, he went to Abraham's bedroom door. It opened before he could knock, and Abraham squeezed into the lounge.

'Oh!' he said with a gasp, appearing to suddenly remember that he had guests.

'We've just cooked up your favourite if you'd like to join us? It was a group effort,' Alex said.

There were murmurs of how delicious it was, and everyone shuffled to make room. Abraham's watery gaze flicked between his slippers and the group before straying to the front door.

'I'm good, good th-thank you. I'm eating at Herga's tonight,' he mumbled. 'Lock the door after me,' he said to Alex, and he grabbed his coat from the stand and swiftly departed.

His appetite suddenly squashed, Alex took his seat at the table just as Winton said that he had a terribly serious question for him.

'Very important question. Now, back home, we heard stories, odd stories, of fish . . . with *fingers*.' Alex let out a snort. 'Can you confirm such nonsense? I mean fish! With fingers!'

Alex tried to keep a straight face as he explained what fish fingers were.

'Oh!' Winton bent over the table as he guffawed. When he lifted his head, a blob of shepherd's pie sat upon his nose. His eyes crossed as he looked at it, and he let out a shriek. Everyone around the table, except for Devetta, burst into laughter. 'Been having nightmares of these fish with . . .' Winton waggled his fingers and squirmed. 'Never mind,' he said, wiping his nose clean.

The next morning Abraham had left before anyone else had awoken. The more Alex thought about it throughout breakfast, the more he wondered whether his uncle had even returned the previous night. He thought of asking Herga about him and his behaviour, but he didn't know when he would see her next. As Irwin led everyone back to the attic, Alex tried to focus on the thought that it might just take some time for his uncle to warm to the additional faces. Possibly . . . eventually . . . hopefully.

Having covered 'Clues & Crypts (Pt. Fifty-One through Seventy-Two)', which told of the elusive codes, riddles and puzzles scribed in various forms across the world, from the Egyptian hieroglyphics to the riddles found in the hidden chambers beneath Stonehenge, Alex excitedly delved into the next section. Each story in 'Perplexing Prophecies (Pt.

Seventy-Three through Ninety-Nine)' proved to be just as tantalising. The fourth entry particularly piqued his interest, leading him to read it twice. The mystery told of the Prophets of the Crucible, who, in the decades leading up to the Crowning Battle, had envisioned its slow forging through the cracks between the continents. The passages detailed the Ollipitha trials, which held each to account for their long lists of crimes and grievances, followed by the bursting success of the Crowning which tore through every land, street and city on earth.

Alex was penning some scruffy notes on the section when an almighty screech interrupted his thoughts.

'I've found something!'

Winton was waving around a handful of papers. The many words he wanted to say came forth in a jumble of sound.

'Simple words, Dad. What is it? What have you found?'

'There's something! A connection. Look. Look!' He held the pages still and traced the top one with a hurried finger. 'It talks here about a hamlet whose seventy-six residents all suffered the same nightmare one autumn evening, and'—he pulled another paper forward—'here! It says . . . ah! All six hundred and thirty-two passengers of a ferry ship were found floating dead in the English Channel from an evening journey from Dover to somewhere called Calais.'

'Who wrote about these?' Alex asked.

Irwin slowly raised his hand, confessing to writing about the drowned passengers. 'It was in *Mysteries of Evading Escapades*,' he said. 'They were all presumed to have abandoned the ship but it was never known why. The last records show that the ship was in working order and making good time, and there was no sign of a fire or anything that would explain the passengers' behaviour. And there was one body that was not found,' he corrected, as though just to add further to the mystery. 'The only conclusion made was that these people threw themselves into the freezing water for no reason whatsoever.' Irwin, visibly bothered by such a twisted idea, leaned against the mountain of furniture and folded his arms tightly.

'I wrote about the dreams,' Ambrose said in her usual quiet voice. 'It was in *Mysteries of the Unnatural.*'

'How can everyone have the same dream?' Alex said. 'I'm guessing that's not possible where—sorry, when—you come from?'

'It most certainly isn't,' Winton said gravely. 'Considered to be a most unnatural thing if there ever were one!' Winton was still looking at everyone as though this finding was the answer to their problems.

'Why do you think these two things are connected?' Irwin asked.

'Isn't it possible that some power was being exerted over the people in these two tales? Someone, somehow, pushing dreams through people's heads or making them lifelessly throw themselves overboard?' Winton shrugged. 'People don't just come to a decision, especially not one that would most definitely result in death, without either sufficient motivation or momentous influence, and I doubt it was the evening's menu that sent everyone overboard!'

'These stories have been tales and myth for years,' Irwin said. 'Who is to know if any part of them could possibly be true?'

'Do you forget how we came to be here?'

Evie shot her father a startled look.

'Are these tales any more of a madness than the Evispen?'

Irwin gave Winton a sulky glance; he was right.

Alex agreed with Irwin, though. The idea that they were talking about, something controlling living people, was preposterous. However, upon spotting the Evispen on its newfound cabinet in the corner of the room, Alex bit his tongue.

'That's all these books are—stories passed down and told throughout the ages,' Ambrose said. 'But who is to say what's true?'

'We are all stories passed down in the end,' Devetta mystically concluded as she returned to her book. There was no conclusion on Winton's findings, and as everyone else followed Devetta's lead and returned to plundering the books, Alex wondered how much stranger the mysteries would get, the Evergreens and Devetta included.

*

There was another Abraham-shaped hole at the end of the table during dinner that night, and thankfully so, for Alex was finally able to declare his intentions to the group. His desire was met with understanding and not the vicious scolding it would have received had he informed his uncle of the same news. And just as he had imagined over the many years since that night, the next morning he came to be standing on the corner of the road opposite his childhood home.

The yard's once green grass was now thick clumps of weeds, and its wild hedges were browned and bare. The property was a stark contrast to the flourishing gardens neighbouring it. The only property worse off than the Priar's was the abandoned house opposite which was utterly derelict and overthrown in gloominess.

Leading Devetta across the road and up the path, Alex found that at least the front door had been replaced, its beaten descendant having vacated the premises long ago. A sound nearby snatched their attention: through the thinning hedge beside them, Alex could see Mrs Boteley, a wilting old lady with crooked shoulders and strings of grey and white hair tied at the nape of her neck, step outside to look at the purple pansies and yellow daffodils of her garden. She had been Alex's friendly next-door neighbour for years; his throat lurched. He wanted to speak, just to say hello, but he immediately thought better of it. With the key, which he'd managed to find hidden in Abraham's room that morning, trembling in his hand, he unlocked the door and followed Devetta inside.

The house before them was not the one Alex remembered from that night, and his stomach dropped in disappointment. If the outside had reflected an undoubtable change since Alex had last seen it, then the inside delivered the exact same effect. The hallway, the kitchen and in fact the entire house—everything was completely immaculate. There were no burning holes in the walls, no rubble or bricks scattered over the floor, not a scrape nor scratch upon any surface; in fact, all the furniture had seemingly reformed and returned to their posts. Skirting the edge of the hall and caressing the unblemished walls, Alex reached the table beneath the mirror, where he had answered Maudlyn's call that night. The *ching!* of the telephone rippled through the chasms in his memory.

There was a strong nip to the air in the living room, and Alex wondered whether that was why the grandfather clock's face had frozen, its hands settled at quarter past eight.

'It's like nothing ever happened. It's like . . . nothing changed,' Alex mumbled to himself.

Absorbing the details of the room, Devetta crossed the thick rug. She lifted her eyes to the painting above the fireplace. 'I applaud such skill,' she said. 'Did you paint this?'

'Me?' Alex asked incredulously. Devetta looked at him, her question remaining. 'No, no I didn't. Did you honestly think I could have?'

With a soft blink Devetta turned back to the painting. 'We are all capable of so much.'

Moving to examine its flawless details, Alex had almost forgotten how much he adored his favourite painting. 'My grandmother painted it, actually,' he said. The painting bowing down over the room told a picturesque tale from within its resplendent golden border, one of a rugged woodland. Many animals and other hidden details, waiting to be found upon a closer look, were tucked away within its robust foliage, rocky structures and flowing spring waters.

Devetta moved away, and Alex sank into the familiar seat by the window, unsure how to feel. Had he found the house just as he had left it, he knew he would have felt that it didn't reflect the change in his life, but to see everything the same as it had been before he met the Evergreens, close to being *exactly* the same, it almost delivered the same crushing disappointment. It was as if it had all been covered up and forgotten about. At either extreme, nothing could accurately reflect just how upside down his life had become.

'It is safe,' Devetta informed upon her return a few minutes later. 'We are alone.'

'Did you expect to find anyone?'

Although Devetta did not reply at once, Alex somehow got the impression that she wanted to ask him the same question. 'This was the last place the Evergreens were witnessed, aside from in the high street,' she said. 'It would make sense for these people to return to the familiar to locate them.'

'You sound like my uncle,' Alex huffed.

He continued to explore the house and found it to be just how he'd recalled it. Upstairs, his parents' bedroom, which he lingered in for some time, still breathed their fragrances. The dusty spare room was still stacked with piles and piles of his father's paperwork. As he pushed open the door to the final room on the landing, his bedroom, Alex felt as if he were receiving enormous applause. Everything had shown up for his return. His favourite books sat waiting and ready on his bedside table; the various figurines and toys that joined him in adventures stood in formation on the carpet; and the white pages of colouring books were anticipating his craft and creativity.

Although he wasn't searching for anything in particular, Alex began to look in every drawer and cabinet around the room. He realised that to someone else, it would look as if he were searching for his past, as if it were hiding in the space between spaces. When he eventually retired to his bed, his feet hanging over the end, he closed his eyes and tried to remember what life was like before all of this had begun. Before the Evergreens, before his parents left that cold, snowy night. But try as he might, his memory was blighted by the past seven years and everything that had not happened.

'What drew you back to this place?'

Alex sat up to find Devetta standing by the window with her hands interlocked behind her. Still presuming she knew everything without needing to ask, a sense he had garnered from the very first instance he met her, Alex figured that she had only voiced the question to get *him* to understand why.

'My uncle never wanted me to come back here. He never spoke about this place again after he took me away, but I knew that he returned. I would see the keys hanging by the door every day,' Alex said. 'I've often thought about running away to home, to here, just to really see it again.'

His voice fell away. Devetta turned ever so slightly towards him.

'Accept my apologies, but I believe there is more to your answer,' she said, her tone pacifying.

Alex had not expected her to reply in such a way. He stood up and watched her as she moved to the nearby cabinet and picked up a photograph of Alex as a baby. The way she stared into his printed eyes made Alex think she was searching for something herself.

'I don't know . . .' Alex said, struggling to understand his own motivations.

'You said before that you regularly think about this place. That, it would appear, you had not stopped thinking about it,' Devetta remarked, placing the photograph back on the cabinet. 'You did not have to return here to think further about what has been with you for all these years.'

Alex felt Devetta's unbiased words attempting to dig at the inner truth as she moved over to him, but the harder he thought, the less clear the answer became.

'I—' Alex sighed. 'I would picture, just think about . . . imagine . . .'

'Imagine what?'

'Everything that happened.'

'You do not need to imagine what already transpired. We imagine the impossible. We dream of things to come. We do not imagine our past, we remember and relive.'

'I . . . I . . . I don't know.'

'You know,' Devetta stated, tenacious in her search.

'I don't! Not unless you do?'

'What drew you back here? Why not wish this place farewell and be done?'

'I can't,' Alex replied firmly. 'I can't let go of this place.'

'Why not?'

'Because I will . . .'

'Yes?'

'Because I will always hope!'

Devetta inhaled. 'Hope,' she finally replied, seemingly satisfied.

Just then, the doorbell rang.

— CHAPTER NINE —

A Familiar Place, a New Face

Devetta turned her head slightly towards the sound while keeping her gaze upon Alex. 'Expecting?'

Alex shook his head. 'Ideas?'

'None pleasant.'

Devetta flew from the room with such swiftness that by the time Alex had reached the landing she was already at the bottom of the stairs.

The doorbell rang again.

The perfect candidate for a body guard, Devetta held out a hand, flattening Alex against the wall in the hallway, out of sight. A second later, she eked open the front door.

'Hello, madam,' said a slick male voice. 'I am looking for William and Meredith. Do they still live here?'

'I am afraid they do not have residence here anymore,' Devetta replied, her words dry and steely.

Alex edged in closer.

'Oh, right. I presume they have moved.' There was a pause. 'Would you happen to know where to?'

Devetta gave no reply.

'I'm sorry, my name is Thomas and this is my wife Stephanie,' the man said, hoping to ignite a similar introduction from Devetta, however she remained silent.

The names were distantly familiar to Alex, that much he knew, but who the couple were or how they fitted into his past he could not recall.

Stephanie cleared her throat. 'We were good friends with William and Meredith, but we moved away you see, to America, about a good ten years ago now. We've only recently moved back into the area and thought it would be nice to see them again,' she said sweetly. 'We've been knocking every other day but there's been no answer. It seems they have moved on.'

'We're sorry to have disturbed you,' Thomas said, and the couple presumably went to leave.

In an instant their surname flashed before his eyes, and Alex heard his voice shout, 'What's your last name?'

Devetta repeated the question immediately.

'Roberts. I'm Thomas Roberts.'

'I know them,' Alex whispered. Feeding the desire to connect with some element of his old life, he crept out from his hiding place and opened the door more generously.

It was clear that Thomas and Stephanie were no longer people who fitted in with Merlow. A sharp side parting, broad shoulders and shiny pointed shoes made Thomas come across as a powerful man held in high regard by many. Huddled under his arm, Stephanie was a much less imposing figure. She had a small heart-shaped face and auburn hair tied back behind her head. Her dazzling blue eyes looked Alex up and down.

'Alex? Is that . . . ?' The small pigeonhole of her mouth grew wider. Thomas quickly realised too. 'Oh my—you may not recognise us, but we were friends of your parents! How you've grown!' She beamed.

Devetta appeared unconvinced, but Alex took charge and quickly invited them inside. It was only as Stephanie squeezed past him that Alex realised she was pregnant. Her stomach bulged out massively beneath her red blouse, and she stroked it with both hands as she waddled into the lounge after Thomas and slowly sat down by the window. She looked around the room, astonished by her surroundings, and to Alex's surprise, she began to recall the dozens of times she had been to his house when he was a child. What was more surprising, however, was what she said next.

'Your mother and I met, of all places, at a hospital,' Stephanie said. 'Bravemear Hospital it was, not far from here. We were put in the same ward after both of us gave birth on the same day. I had just given birth to our two children and your mother had given birth to you,' she said with a beautiful smile, her perfect white teeth gleaming as she smiled. She looked down to her unborn child, her hands gliding over the circumference of her stomach. 'They've got a sibling on the way now.'

'So where have your parents gotten to?' Thomas asked, before mumbling to Stephanie, 'You know, I wouldn't be surprised if they went up Elgapham way, they always liked it there.' He straightened his shirt collar, almost as if to assure himself of how different he now was.

Alex reluctantly told Stephanie and Thomas of his parents' disappearance, and instantly, Devetta picked up the end of the truth and ushered it into lies. She presented herself as a family friend who had taken care of Alex in the years since, and who often returned with him to his home in the hope of finding them there, waiting for him again.

Thomas and Stephanie looked at one another with dumbfounded expressions slapped upon their faces. They began their questions as Alex had expected them to, but as he had no possible answers to them he could only shake his head.

'I'm so sorry to hear—'

'Thank you,' Alex said, cutting over Stephanie. He gave a brief, fleeting smile and she seemed to understand that he couldn't bear to relive the loss all over again in their conversation. There was a long pause, and then, latching to any possible distraction, Alex asked, 'When is your child due?'

Stephanie's hand drew Thomas' to her swollen mass, the diamonds of their matching rings twinkling together.

'It won't be long now,' Stephanie said, 'but I do often dread to think the size I'll become.' She rolled the beads of her pearl necklace between her fingers. 'We'll have to finally agree on a name soon.'

'Well we don't know if it's going to be boy or a girl,' Thomas said.

'But that's part of the fun!' Stephanie said, laughing as she rolled her eyes. 'Oh—before I forget, have you heard in the news? Those people on the loose? Are you making sure all your windows are locked? I remember hearing there were some robberies around this area some time ago.'

Alex remained quiet as his stomach tightened.

'It was on the news, don't know how you haven't managed to hear about it! It was some family,' Stephanie continued, and Alex's stomach contorted. 'They were spotted in the area and are wanted for, oh, what was it?'

'*Murder,*' Thomas finished with a sinister undertone.

Having kept a constant eye upon the newspapers that Abraham picked up daily, Alex knew that there hadn't been anything in the news about the Evergreens. Devetta had progressed to the edge of her seat, seemingly ready to strike their guests down if it was required of her.

'No, I haven't heard anything,' Alex finally replied.

'Oh! He kicked! Feel it, feel here!' Stephanie gasped, and she moved Thomas' hand to the northern hemisphere of her stomach. There was a brief and uncomfortable pause. And then Stephanie spoke in a cold and deprived voice. '. . . Are you sure?'

With a flick of Thomas' arm, a dark, life-sucking pulse had blasted Devetta across the room and sent her crashing into the wall. She slumped at the foot of the grandfather clock, which guiltlessly observed the interaction.

'I felt it!' Thomas gasped. He hadn't moved his focus from Stephanie's mass.

'Are you sure they aren't with you, Alex?' Stephanie said, looking up to him with a chilling stare.

Standing up to help Devetta, Alex suddenly found a weapon pointed at his perspiring face. 'Hold it!' Thomas screamed. As he governed Stephanie to her unsteady feet, it was clear that Thomas had transformed into another person entirely. The slimy but charismatic charm left his eyes like a sharp breath over an infant flame, and his face was furrowed, pushing down through disgust and into bitter resentment. He now took on a dominant, almost hellion presence.

'Sick of this stupid *STUFF!* Stephanie screeched as she ripped the necklace from her body and beads were sent flying through the room. 'Bloody . . . things!' She tore the clip out of her hair, unleashing fiery red down upon her shoulders. 'Keep it on the boy!' she howled at Thomas.

Alex was terrified, but his anger at the couple for what they had done to Devetta instantly shot words from his mouth. 'I'm not a boy!' he screamed.

'Man, boy, child. All the same,' Stephanie spat. She removed her weapon, and it formed around her hand like Thomas' had. She pushed it firmly against Alex's chest. 'God, I hate children.'

Every ounce of respect that Alex had for her evaporated in that instance. 'You don't deserve to be bearing that child,' Alex said angrily.

Stephanie wiped her lipstick-covered mouth on her free hand, and her lips curled into a snarl. 'It doesn't deserve me,' she replied sinisterly, and her hand grazed her stomach in some kind of sick affection for what lay within.

Hate glowed in Thomas' eyes. 'Do you know why they're here? Why the Evergreens came back to this offensive time, to you? Do you *even know?*'

The whipping hands of the wind outside thrust a cloud of early autumn leaves at the window, and there was an almighty *CRASH!* as the front door blasted open. Stephanie screamed and Thomas snapped his head back towards the hall. A figure strode in behind Stephanie, out of Alex's sight, and a long-barrelled weapon pushed against the back of her head. An unyielding hand gripped her shoulder, locking her in position.

'Drop it,' a male voice commanded.

Thomas' face was boiling with anger. 'Arvaeneous, faultless timing, as always.'

The man, whose brown mane brimmed Stephanie's crown of red, was wearing a long midnight-blue cloak and polished, although recently muddied, black boots. His words were resolute—he didn't need to shout as Thomas had. Instead, he exuded a calm demand for respect. Leaning to one side, he winked a vibrant blue eye at Alex.

Stephanie finally threw her weapon to the ground.

'Do it or I will end her,' Arvaeneous said, now directing his demand to Thomas.

When Thomas' weapon finally devolved into black metal around his knuckles and was discarded, Arvaeneous smiled at him. 'Thank you,' he said, and then with the barrel of his weapon he struck Thomas around the head.

Stephanie screamed as he hit the ground. Immediately, Alex rushed over to Devetta and helped her to her feet.

'Into the street - now! There could be more of them coming!' Arvaeneous yelled.

Racing down the steps and into the street, Alex, Devetta and Arvaeneous ran as fast they could. They had only reached five houses down however when there was a loud blast behind them. The road quaked as if someone had ripped the carpet out from under their feet, and they crashed to the floor.

Thomas wasn't letting them get away alive.

'Get up! Go!' Arvaeneous shouted, and they pushed back to their feet.

The fir trees in the front garden up ahead burst into a hail of wooden bullets as Thomas bolted down the street after them, firing erratically. Crackles of fierce red light ripped through hedges and cracked the pavement beneath them. As debris bounced across their path, Arvaeneous whipped around and returned fire. Dodging a crumbling lamppost, Alex diverted, ducking down an alleyway to their side and pulling the dazed Devetta along with him.

After a short distance, Devetta skidded to a halt. 'The Evispen!' she said, panting. 'We do not have it! We cannot leave it there!' Demanding that Alex return to the Evergreens immediately, Devetta raced off down an adjoining alleyway, back towards the house.

Whatever Devetta had thrown to Alex as she departed he had somehow managed to catch. Just then, Thomas came crashing into the alleyway after Arvaeneous, sending shock waves along the wall that blasted bricks all around them, and Arvaeneous dragged Alex onwards into the courtyard to their right.

'That one there!' Arvaeneous shouted, pointing to a garage door up ahead and throwing Alex the key.

Hastening to unlock the rusty door, Alex heard a loud, regurgitating groan from Arvaeneous' triple-barrelled weapon. With a gruff mechanical cough thousands of lights suddenly spurted from its tip. The lights swam through the air before detonating like the core of a nuclear bomb, blowing Arvaeneous and Thomas in opposite directions to the ground.

Pushing back to his feet, Arvaeneous ducked into the garage, and Alex slammed the door behind him. With no time to spare Arvaeneous was off, searching for something amongst the stacks of stale cardboard boxes and workshop tools crowding the space. The edges of the garage door began to buckle and curl as Thomas attempted to blast his way inside.

Alex expanded the Elongress, throwing white light into the dingy room just as Arvaeneous emerged from the back of the garage with a briefcase in his hand.

'What the heavens—'

'I don't have time to explain! Get in!' Alex screamed; the door behind them was only seconds from buckling entirely.

Their carriage snapped shut around them, and Arvaeneous opened his briefcase, revealing a machine that appeared strikingly similar to the Evispen. The second his skin touched the metal, they were off. The Elongress plunged through the floor, instantly spinning so fast that Alex felt as though his innards were being squeezed out through the pores of his skin. A deep revving roar screamed into his ears as the force of their free fall tore his breath away.

'Hold on!' Arvaeneous yelled over the spiralling roar, not daring to let go of the machine.

Alex's fingers tried to grip the sides of the Elongress but he was slipping, the humming noise was growing, the bulb above them was flickering, and then they were gulped into darkness.

*

The flourishing field of corn appeared endless as it waved, ignited by the bright, wide-eyed sun. A coastal breeze fell, and very gradually a stillness swept over the field like a drifting fever. A distant sound grew louder, a whirling whine that culminated in a soft *boom* as a wooden box appeared in the air. Plummeting at magnificent speed, the spinning box crashed to the ground, hurling two bodies from its protective clutch amongst a plume of papers.

Lazily brushing off the corn imprinted upon his face, Alex rolled over and slowly pushed himself back to his feet.

'You all right over there?' Arvaeneous called out, wobbling slightly as he too stood up. 'You seem a little—phew—a little dizzy, no?' Pulling his velvet waistcoat tight, Arvaeneous touched the hem of his shirtsleeve and immediately his cloak flew up over his body and disappeared beneath his collar. He wiped his hand across his forehead and studied the blood on his fingers. 'Oh . . .' He took a step forward and crashed back to the bed of corn.

'*You* all right over there?' Alex asked somewhat anxiously.

Arvaeneous pushed to his feet with a giddy grin. 'All fine over here. Sorry about the trip—can be a bit bumpy when you're in a rush. How are you, please?'

'Better now that I'm away from those people.'

'Aren't we all!' Arvaeneous replied with a glum laugh as he made his way to Alex. 'I'm afraid to tell you that everything they will have told you is a lie, Alex.'

'They were impersonating friends of my parents?' Alex said. 'I couldn't remember their faces. The last time I saw them I was only a child. I honestly thought it was them.'

Arvaeneous gave a thoughtful hum. 'Yes, we must be careful now, you cannot trust anyone.'

The man, who could have been only eight or so years older than Alex, and who boasted particularly prominent cheekbones on his youthful face, appeared vitalised with determination. Alex felt at ease; there was something familiar about him, as though he were a long-lost friend.

Arvaeneous jogged back to the Elongress. 'Lots to do, much to be done,' he said. 'Now are they with you? The Evergreens?' He began collecting the papers scattered on the ground, but when he received no response, he came to a stop and looked back at Alex. 'The Evergreens? Evelyn Evergreen, Winton Evergreen, Eleanor "Nora" Ever—'

'Yes, I know them, but how do you?'

'I know them, but they do not know me. Not yet, at least.'

Alex helped Arvaeneous gather the final pages and slot them into the central part of the briefcase, followed the device which had led them to their curious location. The two halves of the briefcase then flew up and snapped shut around the handle. The moment Arvaeneous touched the Elongress, it also snapped shut, and subsequently shrunk with incredible speed. 'I can't imagine this is yours?' he said, passing the now tiny, weightless box to Alex, who shook his head.

Alex then watched as Arvaeneous slipped the long-barrelled weapon into his holster. 'What kind of gun is that?' he asked.

'One that gets the job done,' Arvaeneous said with a chuckle. 'It's called a Thunderstruck. I couldn't tell you how it got the name . . .' he said, smiling as he made his way towards the canopy of trees nearby.

'Just so you know, Merlow is likely a *really* long walk from . . . wherever we are, no doubt,' Alex said, following him.

'Merlow, eh? So that's where you've been hiding? We're not far from Dorset at the moment. Lovely place.'

'How do you know about me?' Alex then asked.

'I know about the Evergreens, and I knew that if I found you I would find them.'

They entered the shade, and the air's sweltering pressure lessened. Catching up to Arvaeneous, Alex studied him carefully, wondering why he wanted to find the Evergreens and whether he wanted to take them back to the injustice forced upon them. All Alex could be sure of was that if this was so, Arvaeneous would not get within one hundred miles of them.

'Why did you rescue me? How did you know that Stephanie and Thomas would be at my house?'

'There is one thing you should know and must always remember about me, Alex: I am always here to help.' Arvaeneous' face reflected how perfectly resolute and unreservedly proud he was of this statement. There seemed a sense of nobility to his offer too, as if it was more a living duty than just words. 'Let me complete my welcome. Yes, introductions, they are key, I remember. Well, I am Arvaeneous and I am a lawman.'

'A lawman? You work for the police?'

'I uphold the Law of the People—from my understanding it's the same thing as a policeman in this time.'

It was a moment before Arvaeneous realised that Alex was no longer at his side. When he turned around he found Alex standing ten paces back.

'If you're working for the Law then you want to take them back, don't you? Send them to the courts where they'll be found guilty for a crime they didn't commit?' Alex said. He shuffled his feet deeper into the dirt. 'No. I'm not taking you to them if you're going to send them back.'

A tiny flicker passed over Arvaeneous' mouth, and he shook his head slightly. 'They told you about the prison, I presume?'

Alex slowly nodded.

'Harlow Penitentiary, where they were locked away?' Arvaeneous waited for him to nod again. 'I set them free from that horrible place.'

'That was you?' Alex exclaimed.

'I was one of them, yes, and memorandia will be my proof, as will be my word.' Arvaeneous walked on and Alex quickly caught up to him. 'You have to see, Alex, once everyone was set free from that place, the Evergreens vanished completely. Using their house as a means of escape, which I must frankly applaud them for doing, they fled their time. The people who kept them locked away, however, who framed them for such a disgraceful act of inhumanity, chased them. Two of them were the people in your house just now. I'm not sure how they knew where to go, but they went all the way back to your years—the twenty-first century, was it?'

'Yes, 2001, but I first met them seven years before that,' Alex said, and as they made their way beneath the canopy, he shared with Arvaeneous everything that had unfolded since that night.

'You were kept away for all that time? How did you not go mad?' Arvaeneous finally gasped. 'Well, when the Evergreens escaped from the prison I didn't know where they had gone, had no idea that they could have left that period of time at all. I resorted to following those who are pursuing them. I just had to pray that when they found them, I could get to the family before they did. I had been following Stephanie and Thomas'—Arvaeneous shuddered at the mention of their names—'for weeks. I heard them say that your house was one of the last places the Evergreens had been seen, and they were patrolling the area waiting to see if they would return.'

'You know why they want the Evergreens too, then? What they were imprisoned for?' Alex asked.

This time Arvaeneous stopped in his tracks. 'You know?' he said, staring at Alex.

'Of course, this Heirloom, the most coveted item of all time, or whatever,' Alex replied. 'They imprisoned the Evergreens thinking they knew where it was. How it made its way through history without being found though we have yet to find out.'

'So *that's* what they were imprisoned for? That's what he *really* wants?' Arvaeneous said quietly, walking back to Alex.

'He?'

Arvaeneous shook his head and gave a droning hum. 'He, yes. Whitsnare.'

Despite the fierce heat, a cold feeling shivered through Alex's bones.

'Whitsnare wants the Evergreens. He thinks they know where the Heirloom is. He had them, once, finally, in that prison, and then he lost them. He lost them to me,' Arvaeneous said, an edge of delight in his voice. 'There's no proof that Whitsnare constructed that prison, but it was him. Oh, I know it. But now he wants them back, the Evergreens,' Arvaeneous said darkly. 'He wants them back *so* much.'

Grabbing a fistful of corn, Arvaeneous let the kernels drift from his palm as he explained how he would lay out everything as soon as he met the family. Above all, he promised that he could help them to freedom. 'I can always do better,' he said reassuringly as they exited the canopy of trees. 'In this briefcase is their freedom. Well, the beginnings of it.' He gave it a small shake in his hand. 'There is much to be done.'

The shape of civilisation shimmered in the distance. Appearing satisfied, Arvaeneous jumped ahead to a spot indifferent from any other around it. 'I think here will do,' he proclaimed.

'To do what?'

'Return. For you to take us to the Evergreens.'

'Right here?' *Anywhere along this path would surely have sufficed*, Alex thought.

As he enlarged the Elongress, Alex held back for the slightest of moments to let his thoughts take him one step further. In Alex's eyes Arvaeneous was a true knight. Armed with his distinctive weapon and deft determination, he had already saved the Evergreens and Alex from scenarios, aeons apart, that would have undoubtedly ended in death. Alex felt very certain in his belief that leading Arvaeneous to his guests was the right decision—that it would lead to their rightful freedom.

'Right here,' Arvaeneous confirmed. 'I had to be sure too, you see. Right! In you get.'

Again the briefcase unfolded and Alex was handed the fragile time machine. It looked similar to the Evispen, the only difference being that there were no numbered black tiles upon its front spelling out the current time and date. Its face was defined by only the tiny clockwork pieces and interconnecting mechanical parts, which were quietly hissing and ticking. It must have been obvious that Alex had never used one before because Arvaeneous began giving instructions straight away.

'Picture it clearly, the time and the place,' Arvaeneous said. 'Relive it in your mind, but let your feelings, your *feelings*, pull you there.'

Being the first time he had ever used a time machine, Alex realised that right in his very hands was the object that could fulfil his greatest desire. A stream of scenarios—where and when his parents would be, waiting and willing, young yet unknowing—rode in on higher and higher waves in his mind. Knowing this wasn't the right time to go searching for them though, he finally settled the tide and closed his eyes.

Drawing forward the attic, with its chilly air and long walls, and focussing on the emptiness and restraint he felt whenever he thought of the Clockhaus, Alex felt the Elongress lift, gravity looped, and they returned to it safely. After the dull thud of their arrival, footsteps charged over to them, and Alex was pulled from the Elongress into the sea of overjoyed faces.

'Thank the heavens! Thank them all!' Evie gasped, flinging her arms around Alex's neck.

Nora and Felicity were jumping around in excitement, and Daniel waved to him.

Alex spotted Devetta in the crowd too and he breathed a sigh of relief.

'How are you back, young sir? How?' Winton called out.

The hubbub of cheering sank away as hands gripped the edges of the slightly parted Elongress and Arvaeneous stepped down into their company.

— CHAPTER TEN —

Ghosts in a Memory

The welcome of a newcomer to the group had called for Alex to share, to everyone's great concern, the ordeal of his return. At first no one recognised Arvaeneous, and he appeared hurt though not surprised by this. Winton did, however, sense something familiar about him and with this Arvaeneous' past was revealed.

Allowing their guest to make his own reintroductions, Alex journeyed down to the kitchen to make everyone a drink. As he gathered the mugs he thought again of how big the group had become. In light of Abraham's ambivalence towards Devetta and the Evergreens, Alex knew Arvaeneous would have to remain hidden; Abraham would not likely be able to withstand the announcement that someone else was living under his roof.

There was a shuffle of slippers and Abraham stepped down into the kitchen, talking animatedly about what he was going to buy Herga for her upcoming birthday. Alex poured out enough drinks for everyone, and for a few minutes it was almost as if it were just the two of them again. Alex's mind, however, couldn't help but peel away from their conversation and wander to those above. Arvaeneous could help greatly in their efforts to free Devetta and the Evergreens. Working for the Law, he would know lots of things that they didn't, surely. He was beginning to work out where in the Clockhaus Arvaeneous could stay when—

'So you think she'd like it?'

'. . . Yes,' Alex said, unconvincingly.

'You don't even know what I was suggesting, do you?' Abraham said, disappointment heavy in his voice.

'Sorry, it's been a long day.'

'It's not even eleven o'clock in the morning!'

Abraham huffed, his smile faltering, and he loudly stacked the plates into the cupboard. Without looking, Alex knew his uncle wanted to glance up to those above them. Their guests were sitting heavily on both of their minds, a connection over the canyon between them. Thankfully a helpful idea dropped into Alex's head, and he suggested the 'outlandish-looking handbag' Abraham had mentioned spotting a few weeks ago at the market. After agreeing that the 'outlandish handbag' was ideal for Herga, Abraham turned to rush away but bumped straight into the solid mass that was Devetta.

With a short yelp Abraham jumped back and then, dipping his head, squeezed past her into the lounge.

'Is there a fire?' Alex joked as Abraham hurled his feet into his shoes with such speed he almost fell over.

'Must get to Herga's, she's cooking us a big lunch,' he said, shoving his thin arms into the thick sleeves of his coat. 'Helping her to sort through some boxes of her mother's things. Will be back before late.' He smoothed down his collar, squashed on an old cap and, with a crooked smile at Alex, swiftly left.

As he prepared the drinks, Devetta told briefly of her own journey back. Thankfully Stephanie had already departed by the time she had gotten back to the house, and the Evispen, which Devetta had stored safely during their visit, was untouched. Despite having been almost killed by Thomas, Devetta was a picture of health.

Arvaeneous and the Evergreens were standing at the far back of the attic when Alex and Devetta joined them with a tray of drinks.

'Ar-vay-nee-us,' Ambrose said, pronouncing his name with difficulty, 'has memorandia that requires our immediate attention.' The family looked as though they had been dangled over the edge of a cliff, and it was only when Ambrose explained further that Alex understood why. 'The prison . . .' she said gravely. 'We have to go back.'

'I want to prove to you all that I was involved in your release from that place,' Arvaeneous said, 'and then we can begin to discuss your incredibly overdue freedom.' Irwin nodded reservedly on behalf of them all.

From the black pyramid that Arvaeneous held tight at his chest, shafts of dark light seeped into the air like wisps of inky tentacles. The attic began to darken as the memory was gradually brought to life. The scene that evolved around them took the form of a hilltop overlooking the busy skyline of London. A grassy carpet rolled out beneath their feet, and at once Arvaeneous lowered his voice.

'This is the night I first met Whit . . . the man who framed you. He requested that I meet him here, in the Fields of Ablipeux.'

Amongst the silky darkness, a tall figure sat on a bench facing the sloping plain. A rigid spine kept him sitting perfectly upright; the black of his cloak loosely defined the contours of his body.

The full moon fell into place high above them, completing the memory.

'He'd requested my expertise within the legal sector of Ingenium, considering my background,' Arvaeneous said, wandering along the blurry edge of the memory.

'Your background as a lawman?' Ambrose asked.

Arvaeneous gave a nod and watched Irwin bravely circle around to face the man.

A second Arvaeneous, cloaked in grey, stepped into the memory. He was visibly unchanged from his slightly older self standing opposite him. He fastened the halves of his tailcoat into a single piece with only a touch and moved towards Whitsnare.

'This is a special place. I have brought you to a very special place, here,' Whitsnare said, having sensed Arvaeneous' warmth. He continued to face forward. 'I did so because, in short, I have a degree of respect for you. I think you are worthy of witnessing this place that I hold very close in my memories. But worthy of stepping foot within it in daylight, you are not.'

The younger Arvaeneous perched lightly at the end of the bench, and Whitsnare's face crystallised. Skin of frosty white, low, pointed nose and a rigid, bony skeleton pressing through his flesh; Whitsnare was a terrifying subject to behold. The dead holes that were his eye sockets sat above flat cheeks like bottomless pits, and his lips were thin like razor blades. With his slicked-back hair and a tie just visible around his neck, he looked like a businessman. But at the heart of him, Alex knew that Whitsnare was nothing more than the manipulating nucleus of an evil, remorseless cancer.

'You are to work for me at Ingenium.'

'If I may ask, why me?' Arvaeneous bravely but cautiously asked.

'I know your talents,' Whitsnare said, his gaze unmoving from the city. 'Your legal expertise, knowledge and practice within Pensivital Anamnesis and Ephemorical Legislation is like no other. It would be of considerable value to keeping Ingenium a rich and persevering organisation that pushes the boundaries of apperception and greatness.'

Arvaeneous remained silent for a moment, his warm breath forming clouds before them. 'Thank you for your offer. I will think on my privileges.' And with that, the memory began to drain away.

'This was after Holverson, the previous director of Ingenium, was outed,' Arvaeneous explained to the group. 'Whitsnare was taking Ingenium onwards, and the intelligence we had received suggested that Whitsnare had far too many deep, dark secrets for anyone's good,' he said. 'I had been briefed and prepared by the Prisidium to join Ingenium and work undercover to find out what they were.'

'How were you prepared?' Irwin asked.

'The Prisidium constructed my record as being one of succinct, but subtle, notoriety. They believed Holverson had not been solely to blame for his . . . corporate indecencies. Their prediction that I would catch Whitsnare's attention once I was provided with enough criminal boastings was correct.'

'The Law made you into a criminal?' Evie gasped. 'And you agreed?'

Arvaeneous confirmed this, even going as far as to list the corporate espionage and other treasonous, secretive charges he had been labelled with. Most curiously, he then reported that there was not a single record available on Whitsnare; it was as though he had 'just slipped into existence one day.' This revelation prompted questions from the Evergreens as to whether Whitsnare was even from their time at all.

After drinking down his tea, Arvaeneous saw to continuing his story. Dark colours spread from his Ephemor once again, causing the room to shift and evolve with the changing memory. Through the colours came a busy office scene. Rows of stately desks populated the fresh new floor, each topped with peculiar circular typewriters which typed upon funnels of parchment growing high towards the ceiling. The noise of the room was distorted, as though being listened to through a wall.

'This is a long time later, the day I found out about the penitentiary,' the remembering Arvaeneous said, causing Evie to pull the children in even closer, and he stepped back to watch the memory with the group.

Still suited in his supple grey tailcoat and pointy leather shoes, the memorialised Arvaeneous stood facing a tall window. Upon hearing his name, he turned around to find three gentlemen emerge before him. Dressed in navy and green suits, the men had matching almond eyes and chestnut-coloured hair.

'What can I do for you gentlemen?' Arvaeneous said as he moved the few steps to his desk to organise his papers.

'We do not have time to talk of comforts I am afraid,' the central figure said.

'Well that sounds rather ominous. Please, do share.'

The rightmost brother stroked his light beard and rolled his eyes. 'Please forgive Lamond. He can come across rather more frank than he would like to, but I am afraid in this instance the news cannot wait.' The man stepped forward. 'My name is Filligus, this is my brother Lamond'—he gestured to the tall, serious man beside him—'and my youngest brother, Mogum' he said, gesturing to the man on Lamond's left. 'We are the Haipstring brothers.'

'Mogum,' Nora snickered, and the man from the memory looked around as though her giggles had distantly reached him.

'We are in desperate need of your help, Arvaeneous,' Lamond insisted. 'You see, we know who you are. We know your truth because . . .' He inched closer. 'Because it is our truth too.'

Arvaeneous casually dismissed knowing anything about any such secret while flicking through hundreds of inky subpages of the book before him, prompting the observing Arvaeneous to comment, 'I never was a particularly good liar.'

Lamond continued, revealing that they had found a secret. 'A secret that could bring him down, truly *finish* him.'

'His greatest truth,' Filligus said, 'so heavily concealed that all have become blind to its possibility. The clandestine confinement of all those people who have vanished—a penitentiary.'

The Arvaeneous from the memory mouthed the final word to himself.

'We need you to come with us. We know its location,' Mogum remarked, somewhat sheepishly.

'We have him, Arvaeneous, right in our hands!' Filligus exclaimed in a compressed whisper. 'You can free them all!' He handed Arvaeneous a small envelope containing details of where to meet them that evening, and then the brothers nodded graciously and made their way through the maze of desks and away.

'The Haipstring brothers were from another delegation of the Prisidium,' Arvaeneous explained. 'Under orders to search for the forty-eight missing people—'

'There were forty-eight people in that prison?' Alex choked out the words.

Arvaeneous ran his hand through his hair and sadly nodded. 'The brothers' search for them led to their discovery of the prison, but how, I do not know.

'The Prisidium is the confluence of all layers of the Law,' he explained with a recognisable undertone of pride. 'When we are from it is embodied by a gigantic black glass pyramid in the Concordium District of London.'

A clap of thunder initiated the beginning of the next memory. At a city intersection, a grey car, wheel-less and floating, glided to a stop. As the Evergreen children jumped in the unresponsive puddles, the memorialised Arvaeneous climbed aboard the rustic vehicle with the brothers and sailed away. The streets then rolled out into a seamless patchwork of colourful fields, and on the thin road weaving between them the car emerged again before stopping outside the remains of a derelict brick building.

'This is the place,' Filligus said as they exited the vehicle to examine the many billboards and banners spelling warnings of quarantine and unsafe structures.

The memory spun, and Arvaeneous and the brothers, and the watching audience, came to be standing in the dark interior of the ruins. Claimed by the deathly grip of overgrowth, most of the boarded windows had buckled, letting splintering light strike the filth corrupting the room. Amongst the thick weeds and vines, Lamond quickly discovered a door and called over the others. It was difficult to see amongst the rubble, but as Filligus moved his hand through it and mentioned something about a 'twist of perception', they walked through the door and down a series of steps, causing the memory to change once again.

This time a long white corridor lined with doors stretched out through the attic. Alex stepped aside as the memory of the four men passed through the Evergreens, weapons gripped firmly in their hands. In a startling bombardment of noise, the doors all around them began flapping open and shut. Everyone stopped in their tracks, but after only a few seconds each lost its energy and drifted shut again.

'Likely some kind of deterrent,' Filligus said as they pressed on.

At the far end of the corridor was a lone red door, which Lamond hastily unlocked and held open. Arvaeneous, the brothers and the nine ghosts hurried through into the square room beyond, which was only twice the size of Alex's new bedroom. Apart from a small staircase in the corner of the room, every wall around them, and even the ceiling, was filled with filing cabinets. A white Halpen fluttered against a long window to their right, luring the quartet over. At once, without a second's hesitation or warning, the Arvaeneous in the memory charged down the stairwell, causing the memory to turn one final time.

This time came the prison itself. Rotting cells closed in around the Evergreens again. Cowering people pleaded, sobbed and screamed in shrill, broken voices. Their lifeless arms could not extend towards their saviours, nor could their malnourished bodies crawl.

Evie was now white and shaking with fear. 'I don't think I can do this,' she whimpered. As if by instinct, the children linked arms with their mother and together they withdrew from the memory. Ambrose stood paralysed with terror, and now Alex could understand why she had been unable to speak a word of the prison at their first breakfast together.

Prisoners began to inch forward in their cells having noticed the four men. Their discoloured hands slithered over the metal bars, grabbing for them.

'Save us! Please say you are here to free us! *PLEASE!*' A woman called out from further down the corridor and she began to yank upon the bars in insanity. The droning voices quickly grew in intensity, and soon the room was filled with pleas for freedom.

Beside another red door at the very end of the aisle was a rusty electrical box which Filligus immediately ran to. He threw various levers about until there was a loud buzzing sound and the cell doors grudgingly dragged open. The almost lifeless bodies came falling out into the corridor.

'You need to get up, start running, don't stop running! Up through there!' Filligus beckoned as Lamond and Mogum began to shuttle the slow swarm of people towards the long fermented idea of freedom.

'Please g-g-get me out of here!' A woman in torn rags wept as she fell onto Mogum.

'BAGGIE!' Arvaeneous screamed, making the colours of the memory temporarily flare, and he came skidding to the woman's side. He seized her frail hands and brushed the matted grey hair from her face. She gazed dozily up at him.

Other survivors scurried past, and Alex spotted the observing Winton with his hand over his mouth, staring down at Baggie. *Did her know her?* Alex thought.

'Is . . . is that, you?' Baggie cawed, her hands reaching for Arvaeneous' face. 'You said . . . you said you w-would come.'

'I said I'd always be here for you,' he replied. 'If you're going to make me out as some kind of a hero then you make sure you keep my words as they were.'

A skinny figure swooped down as the final hustle of bodies raced past, and Winton's pinched face peered in from the memory. 'Is she okay? Do you need help?' he said as the other Evergreens rushed past them, fleeing from the prison.

A hand fell onto Arvaeneous' shoulder. 'You can't go yet, Arv,' Lamond said from behind him. 'There is more to be done.'

Baggie was helped to her feet and carried away by the escaping Winton. 'I—I will find you!' Arvaeneous shouted after her. 'I'll find you . . .'

Baggie's head rolled to one side, but her gaze stayed fixed on the tearful Arvaeneous. 'You always keep your promises,' she wheezed, and she was transported away.

This time the memory faded entirely, revealing the attic that they had been standing in all along. One by one each fell into a seat by the French doors. Evie and the children eventually returned, but just like the others could only sit in silence.

Although he did not want to ask, Alex thought that now might be the most appropriate time. 'Can I ask, were all forty-eight of those people in the prison framed for a crime?'

'Only the eight of you were,' Arvaeneous replied, glancing to Devetta and then the Evergreens.

There were no gasps, but the befuddled looks between the Evergreens clearly said that they had not known this.

Evie looked as though she was particularly struggling with the revelation. 'When we were on our way to the court and Whitsnare kidnapped us and took us to that . . . prison, the world must have thought we were still out there?' That we had broken ourselves out and were on the run again?'

'Yes,' Arvaeneous said. A series of agonised sighs followed. 'I'm afraid so. You have to remember that Whitsnare is always a step ahead. Always. He took precautions to ensure that if you somehow escaped from that prison, everyone would be terrified of you; your words, your memories, none of it would be trusted. With the whole world against you there was never going to *be* an escape, what with the evidence seemingly undeniable. He must have believed with certainty that you had what he wanted.'

'The Heirloom?' Irwin said.

Arvaeneous glanced at the ground. 'It looks like it, yes.'

Devetta paced back and forth. She appeared to be processing every syllable of every word that had been spoken. 'Seem,' she said. 'You declared that the evidence would *seem* undeniable.'

'Exactly! Just you wait, because I can do it,' Arvaeneous said with incredible joy as hopeful gazes watched on. 'I can make you free once again.'

*

The chatter continued throughout the afternoon and into dinner, alive with the increasingly brighter idea of freedom which defined each of Devetta's and the Evergreen's hopes and dreams. No one was surprised that Arvaeneous fell asleep the second he made up the bed at the back of the attic; he had been awake for days searching for the family. Leaving him to rest, the Evergreens and Alex settled at the opposite end of the attic. Devetta, however, stood alone further along the mound of furniture as though waiting for someone.

'Everything OK?' Alex said as he approached her.

'Most certainly. I was hoping to speak with you regarding an item I came across whilst at your home,' Devetta replied.

She brought her arms out from behind her and offered Alex a small red book. 'My understanding is that it is what people used to refer to as—'

'A diary,' Alex answered, puzzled by his feelings as he took the thin book into his hands. 'It's . . . it's my father's. Thank you.'

'You are most welcome.'

The diary entranced Alex as he wandered down to his bedroom. Kneeling on the mattress, almost automatically, as if he had rehearsed the event a hundred times over, he pulled open the bottommost drawer of the shabby chest. He lifted up the pile of Abraham's old shirts until he created a space just big enough for the diary, and right there, he set it down.

Although he did not yet understand his feelings about the discovery of the diary, he knew exactly what he thought about it. After pressing down one of Abraham's old jumpers over it, and then another, burying it layer after layer, Alex finally, for the time being at least, closed the drawer.

— CHAPTER ELEVEN —

Freedom

There was not a single pair of eyes fixed on anything but the slightly bruised black briefcase when Arvaeneous placed it before them all the next morning in the lounge. 'In here are the beginnings of our journey,' he stated. The concept of its contents already met the requirements of being granted a chapter within the *Bafflement* series; the idea of evidence that could prove their innocence took no shape and held no weight in the farthest stretches of anyone's imagination. When Arvaeneous touched its handle, the briefcase began to slowly winch itself up on two rickety springs. Upon reaching ten feet, its halves unclasped and unfolded over and over down each side, revealing many slots of stored parchment.

'Awesome!' Daniel gasped.

Arvaeneous slipped out a wedge of parchment and sat down amongst the group. 'Before we start, you must understand the nature in which your crime took place.' He swallowed loudly. 'Well, the thing is, it isn't known *how* you were framed as such, but you were framed because you *did* the crime.'

The silence that followed was thick with confusion.

'But we didn't!' Evie cried. 'We were nowhere near them when . . . we don't even know where they live!'

'Perhaps *did* is the wrong word. But you were there,' Arvaeneous said. 'That is how they framed you—they *placed* you there. All seven of you, at the place where and when the crime happened.'

Arvaeneous went on to explain in detail the terrifyingly inhumane crime that the Evergreens had been framed for. The family had visited an elderly couple, who worked at the Prisidium, for evening dinner. Gathered at the Whittingham's house, around the banquet table the nine of them dined. It was a feast of courses: platters and trays loaded with all delights, and bottles of costly wine and elegant desserts to be fancied and craved and devoured. However it transpired that for the entire evening the couple, Florence and Bartholomew, had been dead. Traces of the deadly poison was found in both of their soups, but not in any of Evergreen's, meaning that the family had sat with them both, eating, joking, screaming in laughter and delight, for hours after the hosts' lungs had expired and their eyes had glazed over.

The Evergreens hung their heads; the crime they had been framed for was incredibly twisted.

Arvaeneous explained that he had experienced the memory from the person who had witnessed them around the table—whose memory had condemned them. The Prisidium had deconstructed every single fragment of it to ensure that the Evergreens were not memories themselves, and it was confirmed that each had had physical presence. Each had actually been there, eating food and drinking wine, and as

Arvaeneous reluctantly summarised: 'Memories can't interact with things in the real world.'

'How could they possibly do that?' Alex remarked. 'How could they actually be there when they weren't?'

The idea that it was actually a future version of the Evergreens sat around that table left Alex's head as quickly as it had entered, and he was glad to hear Arvaeneous voice the same reasoning.

'I do not believe, nor will I ever believe, that you would ever commit such a crime,' Arvaeneous said to the family. 'I am not even going to entertain the thought. You see, to show that you didn't do the crime we need to prove that Whitsnare *did*. Whitsnare is stringently meticulous, he will have planned the crime he framed you for to excruciating detail, and there will be a trail of that. There's always a trail, and that is what we need to be able to prove. And combined with Whitsnare's motive of believing you have the Heirloom - the reason why he framed you in the first place - we stand a chance at proving your innocence and Whitsnare's guilt,' Arvaeneous said. 'That is what we need. Now, I have to mention of a possibility, a strong possibility of something that you likely won't have considered so far. So,' he said, clapping his hands together as he looked around the group, 'are we ready?'

Arvaeneous was wearing a brave smile, trying to instil confidence in his audience. The Evergreens glanced at one another, clueless as to what was about to follow.

'There is a likelihood that the evidence we need is hidden somewhere—somewhere in time.'

'In time?' Irwin repeated, frowning.

'It makes sense, does it not?' Winton said knowledgeably. 'Hide it in a different time when the people don't exist and the crime hasn't taken place, and then the evidence can do no good nor harm. It just wouldn't make sense if it was ever found.'

Devetta looked at Winton as though she had made the same deduction.

'Good, you're getting the hang of it,' Arvaeneous said. 'Some time, some place, yes—the evidence is out there. Knowing Whitsnare, he will have buried it somewhere in history, and buried it well. I am certain that the answer to where it lies will be found somewhere in these papers,' he flicked their edges in his lap, 'and the ones in there,' he pointed to the briefcase. Arvaeneous slotted the bundle of parchment back into the briefcase, which then folded itself up and lowered to the ground in slow, tired movements. He moved to pick it up but abruptly stopped.

'What's wrong?' Alex asked.

Arvaeneous finally picked up the briefcase. 'You know, Lamond gave the evidence we need to find a very specific name. He called it "the Versidges".'

Winton sighed.

'What does that mean?' Alex asked.

'It's derived from the word *versidgeous*,' Winton said in a voice lacking its usual joy. 'It means "to disgrace". It is the most disgraceful act that one could commit.'

Alex wished he hadn't asked.

*

After a hurried breakfast and a short spin in the Elongress, the group walked across the open field towards the library. Having just had a riveting conversation with Winton about the concept of 'elevensies'—'Do people in this time feel the need to eat eleven things before eleven o'clock each morning?'—Alex jogged ahead to talk with Ambrose.

Not believing his uncle could accept another guest without becoming incredibly suspicious, Alex was forced to admit to Ambrose that Arvaeneous would have to remain hidden for the time being. As Alex thought about the practicalities of such a task, he was taken for a minute by the small growing heads of chrysanthemums upon Ambrose's cardigan, which were shying from their bloom. The idea of keeping a guest locked away reminded Alex of his own experience over the years. His concern must have been obvious as Ambrose touched his arm and gave him an imploring look.

'It's just, I'm keeping so many secrets from him,' Alex mumbled, feeling the need to reveal his inner truths. 'I thought all that was starting to come to an end after telling him about you all, but now there's another secret. How many more will there be? And I wonder . . . I worry—'

'Worry about what, dear?'

'I worry that I won't know what to say and what not to say. I think I fear that I'd rather say nothing at all in case one of these secrets just slips out. It's hard to imagine, but—'

'Oh no,' Ambrose said, quickening her pace. 'I can imagine it very well.'

The library was unusually empty when everyone sat down at a table and Arvaeneous unpacked the bundles of paperwork from his briefcase. On the top sheet of each Alex could see that a big knot was printed. Strangely though, the knot was waving slightly, as though the ink hadn't been fully absorbed by the parchment. Alex rubbed his finger over one of the top sheets, but found it to be completely dry.

'The ink is present inside the parchment,' Winton said, having watched Alex in his exploration. 'It never dries, and hence it can continue to change form - look.'

Arvaeneous walked around the table and tapped each springy bundle with his finger, causing the inky knot upon each to unfold and new words to spread to each of the pages in the bundle.

'Single pages can contain encyclopaedias full of information when we are from, all accessible with just a thought.'

At this point Winton rushed off to help Ambrose, who was making her way back to the table with the stack of *Bafflement* books towered in her arms.

Arvaeneous gave a small laugh. 'Those books. Never really give any answers, do they? Always another unsolved mystery at the turn of every page. Alex told me about the letters informing you where you could find them.' Arvaeneous smirked, brushing the top book's golden title and looking at the Evergreens sitting around him. 'My, my, how your mystery deepens. I wouldn't be too surprised to find your names printed in one of these.'

With the consensus being that Alex and Devetta should continue with their chosen *Bafflement* books, to find out why Whitsnare believed they knew about the Heirloom, the others each took a bundle of parchment, and the briefcase was sent refolding away.

Continuing the increasingly strange "Perplexing Prophecies" chapters in his book, Alex turned to a new page of his notebook and picked up his pen, and the words, phrases and ideas of his thoughts flourished into form upon the parchment. After reading about Pricilla Pinkley, the woman who prophesied her years of thievery, subsequent misfortunes and untimely death in outstanding detail, and about a mentally ill boy whose visions of a missing lady from decades before resulted in the discovery of her body, Alex finally entered the next set of chapters. From the secret organisations of Knavesmire and Frideswithe to the Illuminati and the Freemasons, and the theories surrounding their existence, "Sects, Cults and Other Persuasions (Pt. Sixty-Nine through Eighty)" was a deeply intriguing read. *How can the Heirloom possibly fit into any of these tales?* Alex wondered. Moreover, if Winton was correct and it could indeed inflict some degree of control over any living person or persons, just how had something like that come to be wedged so far in the past?

Turning the final page of the mystery he was tiredly reading, Alex looked up to those before him. Of what depraved secrets they were reading about from Whitsnare's darkest collections Alex did not like to think, but no one had spoken a single word in the five hours that had passed. Devotion to their freedom required such dedication.

When Irwin, with Felicity asleep in his arms and her book asleep within hers, noticed the time, they packed up their things and left.

That evening, dinner was still ripe in their stomachs and the deceitful acts of Ingenium, the corporation now spearheaded by Whitsnare, were still fresh in their conversation when to everyone's surprise the doorbell rang. Knowing what this had resulted in last time, Alex placed his eye to one of the peepholes set at various heights upon the door. He sighed with relief—on its other side a lady with frizzy ginger hair was bobbing about excitedly.

'Go on up, it's OK,' Alex said as the doorbell rang three more times, and the group moved up to the attic. As soon as Alex edged open the door, Herga grabbed him in an enthusiastic hug.

'Alex! Ahahaa! It has been so long! How are we?' she shrieked, pulling back to see him before hugging him again. She flicked the door shut behind her. 'Sorry, I forgot my key. Been a long time. How are things, my blossom? Good? Tired? You look tired. Are you eating enough?' She swiftly entered the room as the esteemed guest of the Clockhaus that she was.

'I'm fine, thank you,' Alex replied.

Herga was a short and ample woman, and today she was wearing a black-and-gold leaf-patterned dress beneath a rather clashing cardigan. She always liked to dazzle with some peculiar garment.

Alex blinked in retaliation. 'Abe isn't in—I thought he had headed over to yours?'

'Oh no, I saw him down the high street as I passed,' Herga said dismissively. She sniffed the air before turning back to Alex. 'No, I came to see you! My favourite godson! My only, actually. You have a lot to live up to!'

As they took to the armchairs, Herga inspected the room as though she believed she might just be able to see through its walls. 'Our dear Abraham has told me about some guests you have living with you,' she said with an unusually solemn expression. Then she shrieked, 'I can't wait to meet them!' making Alex feel instantly better. 'Very much looking forward to it—may I?' Alex nodded, and Herga grabbed a handful of grapes from the fruit bowl beside the chair. 'But it seems your guests and your uncle have been a little . . . shall we say distant? It seems? Well, more your uncle, of course.'

Alex wondered whether Abraham had shared with Herga his troubles, but the answer hit him as subtly as the Thunderstruck—of course he had. But Alex thought it rather unlikely she would share them with him.

'I want you all to come over to dinner next week. Everyone, all together,' Herga said assertively, bobbing eagerly in her seat.

Alex tried to picture them all around a table together but it was too difficult to imagine, and the image quickly fell apart in his head. Alex thanked her and commented on the kindness of her gesture.

'Don't worry! We'll be fine!' Herga said reassuringly, leaning in to give him a quick tap on the knee. 'It'll be fun! And we'll get to know these lovely people you have here. Well!' she said, jumping to her feet, 'I'll tell Abe a date and you can all come over. Was only a fleeting visit. I'm off to the school, the kids are doing a show. You should see them all dressed up in their costumes!' She shook her fists, trembling with joy. 'So cute!' After kissing him on each cheek she flailed her hands in the air with a wave and left.

Alex heard a creak and saw small feet at the top of the staircase—Nora, Daniel and Felicity had been watching through a gap in the banisters.

'Is that lady crazy?' Daniel innocently asked.

'Do you know what,' Alex said, climbing up and following the three of them to the attic, 'I think she might be.'

*

With Arvaeneous at the forefront of their search for freedom, the group began to believe that they might just be able to free themselves from Whitsnare's strangling shackles of injustice. The atmosphere grew more intense every time they journeyed to the library, powered by Arvaeneous' infectious determination and his radiating confidence. Despite this, there was an unspoken understanding that it would likely be a great length of time before they were freed. Be it months or years, decades even, they were on this path now, and would stay on it even if it took them forever.

Alex had long accepted this fact. He knew his friends would not be leaving until they arrived in the land of freedom that Arvaeneous had promised. The conditions in which they were living, however, were causing increased concern for Alex; in the days that washed in and washed out with the tides and the unyielding fog, he had barely seen Abraham at the Clockhaus. He now spent as much time as he could at Herga's, or working long days at the shop. The rare times Alex saw him revealed the progression of what appeared to be an illness stirring within his uncle. There was a darkness around his eyes, his lips were cracked and sore and he was slower and stiffer than ever before; he was gradually falling to pieces.

And when they actually spoke, the conversation was lifeless, of the same stunted topics. Abraham consistently sought Alex's promise that he wasn't doing anything to jeopardise his safety. Every conversation would round off with Abraham's reminding his nephew that he mustn't be seen by the window, or leave the Clockhaus, or even entertain the thought of stepping foot outside again in case those who he believed kidnapped his parents would find him.

Not a word had been shared between Abraham and his eight known guests since the awkward introductions. His uncle had shirked every opportunity to join the group for breakfast or dinner, or to sit with them in the evening and discuss suitable topics Alex had pre-arranged, and Alex didn't know what to do. The flinching, faltering smiles Abraham gave whenever he unexpectedly ran into the group made Alex fear his uncle's emotions were becoming as faded as Devetta's. And what was worse, Alex had overheard concern from the Evergreens themselves. Whenever he returned from fetching them all a drink, their whispering would cut itself short.

'Does he not like us?'

'Are we intruding on him?'

'Is it right for us to stay here?'

The topic of Abraham's ambivalence arose when he called Alex up to what was now Winton and Ambrose's bedroom the following Saturday. A sea of trinkets, ornaments and many sentimental things had transformed the room into a memorial of what felt like the distant past. The black chest from which the items had originated had not been opened since Alex moved into the Clockhaus, but Abraham had decided, for some reason, that now was the time to do so. There were boxes of old bottle caps, books filled with treasured stamp collections, bottles of sweet rosé and vintage port from around the world, various ornaments, miniature statues and many things which were once shiny and appealing now aged, dusty and rough to the touch.

Alex often forgot that his uncle had been in an accident some time before he was born when he fell over and struck his head, meaning much of Abraham's memory had been shut off from him, or lost completely. As a result, even the smallest detail or fact unknown to him could cause his uncle great distress.

'I feel a connection to each and every one of these things,' he said as he sat amongst them and picked up a rare medallion, once golden and bright. 'Even if I can't quite remember what that connection is.'

Delving back into the trunk, Abraham pulled out a collection of small photographs and postcards, which slipped from his hands as he sat back down. One of the photographs caught Alex's attention, and he picked it up to study it in more detail.

Standing before his grandparents' house and behind the thick wash of sepia, the bespectacled Abraham stood arm in arm with his brother, William. Both were dressed in their school uniforms, the latter far scruffier than the former, on what was quite possibly their first day of secondary school.

'We must have been about twelve there, I think, but I can't be sure,' Abraham said. Carefully taking the photograph, he ran his finger gently over William's cheeky-grinned face and Alex realised that right in that moment in his uncle's hands, Abraham and William both had their entire lives before them.

Thinking now might be a good time to raise their unspoken troubles, Alex was suddenly beaten to it as Abraham placed the photograph back in its pile and remarked how little he had seen Alex recently.

'Well, you'd see more of me if you didn't lock yourself away all the time,' Alex replied in a dull voice.

Abraham gave him a serious look. He flicked through the postcards, pausing to stroke one or two as though hoping to reignite some form of flashback.

'We've been working very hard. I've been trying to help the Evergreens sort out some issues,' Alex said.

'What *issues*?' Abraham grumbled. 'You know I don't mean this disrespectfully, but what can you possibly help them with?'

'Private matters, for them. It's not my place to say. But everything is all right, we're fine and there's no need to worry,' Alex insisted. 'They needed somewhere to stay, and considering they saved my life that night'—Alex clenched his fists, hating the lie—'saved me from the people who were there for me, I thought what better way to repay them?'

Abraham then asked why they were homeless, but Alex remained ungiving. 'We're getting somewhere now with our efforts, so they probably won't be here for much longer.'

If Alex hadn't felt so disappointed in himself for lying so naturally, he would have been quite impressed with his ability to do so. His final sentence had been the biggest lie of them all. They hadn't gotten anywhere with the contents of the briefcase over the past week, and nothing helpful had made itself known in the books either. 'Don't worry,' Alex said downheartedly, 'I'm sure things will get back to normal soon.'

'Back to normal . . . Good,' Abraham replied, taking a moment to savour his own words before peering back into the chest. After a minute of rummaging around, Abraham let out an almighty gasp. 'Now this! This! How could I forget?' he shrieked, and fell back to the floor with a large book in his lap. He traced his fingers across the title engraved upon its cover: *Ten-Year*.

'What's a ten-year?' Alex asked.

'It's my diary—my ten-year diary!'

Abraham skimmed over its overflowing pages with pure delight. Every few pages he would stop and laugh, or pull an expression of surprise or sadness as he read memories he could not remember living. With renewed strength, he pushed to his feet and raced out of the room, cheering, 'I have to show Herga. She will love this!' A moment later the front door slammed in his wake.

By the time Alex had finished packing away the trunk, Irwin had come looking for him.

'Was that your uncle who just left?' he asked, a thick cloud of peppermint spilling from his mug.

Alex had wanted to wear a positive expression as he nodded, but he knew the muscles in his face had failed him.

'What's wrong? Is your uncle OK?' Irwin asked.

'He is, but . . .' Alex rose to his feet and paused. 'He's just waiting for things to go back to how they were. I have to keep lying, saying that you all won't be here for long and that life will go back to how it was for us.'

There was a faint flash of guilt upon Irwin's face, and Alex instinctively moved in closer to him.

'Please don't feel like that. I don't ever want you to feel like you are intruding on us, on our life here. You have given me a purpose,' Alex said gladly. 'A reason to wake up every day!'

The idea of running away with the Evergreens had never been as lucid as it was now in Alex's imagination. With the Evispen it could very easily be achieved. He could live up to his own reputation of being a ghost and simply drift away one night and be gone. A poisonous guilt then bubbled within Alex's stomach as he pictured Abraham alone, whimpering in the cold and lifeless Clockhaus, and he realised that he could never leave his uncle alone, no matter how far he was pushed.

'I'm sure with time he will get better. It's a huge change in your lives,' Irwin said, moving to lead Alex up to the attic.

'Too much has changed to ever go back now,' Alex said, and closing the lid on their past, he promptly left the room.

— CHAPTER TWELVE —

Herga's Dinner

It was a foggy but otherwise sunny morning when Abraham, to everyone's complete surprise, came to sit amongst Alex, Devetta and the Evergreens in the lounge. Their conversation about the Heirloom and what it could possibly be was cut short by Abraham's shuffling to his armchair and raising his paper shield: that week's over-read *Merlow Messenger*.

Naturally the conversation shifted, into a discussion about the *Precipitous*, but Alex could not take his eyes off his uncle. 'Is he all right?' Ambrose mouthed to Alex as she finished her bowl of strawberry croissants, but he could only shrug.

Barely twenty minutes later, after giving the Evergreens a number of shifty glances over his paper and not turning even one page, Abraham left to his bedroom.

'Maybe it's his way of making the first step to get to know us?' Evie later suggested as Nora expanded the Elongress in the attic and everyone climbed aboard.

'But it shouldn't be like this!' Alex said as he followed everyone inside. 'I know he's grateful to you for supposedly

165

keeping me safe the night we met. But I don't know why he isn't showing it.'

The Elongress closed and Devetta utilised the Evispen, stating that no matter how long they spent at the library, they would return only seconds after departing so that Abraham would not be suspicious.

'What do you think could be holding him back?' Irwin asked.

'I don't know, but it worries me,' Alex said.

*

'Didn't the sign say this room was closed off?' Alex asked as he snuck into the long gallery-like room after Arvaeneous.

'Did it?' Arvaeneous called back over his shoulder. 'I didn't see.'

'You had to pull up the "Do not enter" tape to get in here!'

'So it *did* say the room was off limits.' Arvaeneous glanced back to Alex with a grin. 'I can't for the life of me see why though. Looks perfectly normal, does it not?'

The high-ceilinged room they found themselves in was populated with grand statues and sculptures carved into polished white rock, making it seem as though they had stepped into another building entirely.

Arvaeneous cheered. 'A library, a gallery *and* a museum. How thrilling!'

When Alex caught up to him and joined him in wandering the edge of the room, he asked about the woman from his memory. Arvaeneous studied a series of statues of Greek gods and goddesses before he spoke about Baggie Pertrue, his greatest friend. Baggie was one of the forty-eight people who had been unlawfully locked away, and her fate, along with that of everyone else in the prison apart from Devetta and the Evergreens, was unknown to Arvaeneous.

'With all of me I hope Whitsnare did not find the brothers after they helped everyone to escape,' Arvaeneous said gravely. 'The things he would do to them . . .'

They walked on, their footsteps echoing out over the shiny limestone floor.

'When we broke everyone out we knew we needed to prove that Whitsnare had imprisoned all those people, had caused all of this desolation—and I'm not just talking about the prison,' Arvaeneous continued. 'I ignored my orders to return to the Prisidium with the Haipstring brothers. Instead, they told me where within Ingenium I would be likely to find Whitsnare's most hidden secrets. We didn't know what Whitsnare would do when he found out the prison had been revealed; it was the last chance we had to try to prove his layers of corruption. If Ingenium was suspected and transported for scrutiny and inquisition, we were certain that any evidence that could possibly ensure everyone's freedom would be lost.'

Arvaeneous' jaw clenched; how long it would be before he could accept what Whitsnare had done to those in his prison Alex did not know. Neither did he know how a building could be 'transported' as such.

'There are many things lurking in the long, twisting corridors of Ingenium, and many things that have never seen the light of day, and that never should. Horrific, brilliant, unnatural, fantastical ideas. All kinds of creations between the shallow walls and locked away behind hidden doors,' Arvaeneous said as they passed a series of shiny marble heads.

'I found the place the brothers directed me to, the room of secrets, a room longer than the eyes could see, and there I found the briefcase.'

They slowed to admire another sculpture, this one of three men charging in a chariot, their faces stretched wide with the anger of war.

'You said that Whitsnare caused such desolation in your time—can I ask what else he did?'

'No one believes he has done anything. No one knows he is the one orchestrating everything!' Arvaeneous exclaimed. 'Why would they, a man of his stature?'

Arvaeneous turned away again, calmed himself and then slowly elaborated. 'The time we left was once so pure, a time that truly respected life. But after the Evergreens were framed everything became very dark and disillusioned, Alex. What Whitsnare has done, it is so masterful, so malicious—the perfect way to pull apart the totality of society. On the journey to release everyone from the prison, Lamond told me what he believed had happened, and since then I can't help but see it as the unconquerable truth.'

In short and simple steps Arvaeneous broke down Whitsnare's apparent plan for Alex. First, there was the creation of distrust in authority. Everyone was made to question the resounding faith they'd had in the Prisidium and the Law of the People to serve them and keep them safe. 'That much was easy. It didn't take much to burn that bridge, settle in that layer,' Arvaeneous said with disgust. Next, to further unite people, there were attacks—vicious attacks which served only to emphasise the little the authorities could do to prevent them. The final stage was what brought it all down, everything that people had built since the Crowning.

'And they did it all themselves!' Arvaeneous cried out. 'The complete murder of society.'

Arvaeneous looked at Alex, exploring his eyes. He then asked, like a tutor, 'What is the one thing that can make people do incredible things, things they never knew they had the strength or capability to do, but also the most terrible things?'

The answer came to Alex immediately. 'Fear.'

'Correct.'

'He made everyone fear him?'

'Oh no, something far worse.'

Alex tried to think what could be feared more than Whitsnare, but he was stumped; the answer seemed too vast to fathom.

Sliding his hand through his hair again, as he often did when he was thinking or troubled, Arvaeneous said, 'I . . . do not wish to speak about it anymore, if you would permit, but the Evergreens were right at the centre of it. And that is only the beginning of everything he has done, Alex. There is far too much to speak of. He is a ruthless individual, so calculating and conniving.' Arvaeneous' voice grew fiery. 'Whitsnare walks upon cold corpses, and his shadow is made up of the lifeless minds of those befallen to him.'

The pair had arrived at the end of the room, where upon the thick marble slab spanning at least thirty feet stood the sculpted bodies of twenty men and women draped in fine cloths. Spears pointed, swords sharpened and shields brazened, each side was racing towards the other in a sculptured snapshot of fury and conflict. At its centre, below two male figures swinging weapons at each other's necks, Alex saw a great jewelled crown upon a plinth: the cause of their great war.

'How marvellous!' Arvaeneous said, his rather more jolly charisma returning as they admired the masterpiece.

When Alex finally insisted that they head back to the Clockhaus to get ready for Herga's dinner, they moved back along the other half of the room.

'I do very much wish I could come, I do love a get-together,' Arvaeneous said. 'But I understand it is not easy sharing my presence with your uncle.'

'I will tell him about you soon,' Alex said, knowing it was most unfair to everyone to continue as they were for much longer. 'I promise.'

*

It was just before six o'clock that evening when Alex sorted through his uncle's latest donation of thoroughly washed-out shirts on his bed. The dusty backlog was appreciated, but Alex doubted he would wear any of the items. Upon squeezing them into the chest, he moved aside some old jumpers before stopping. The edge of his father's red diary winked at him from the far back corner of the drawer. With a short shake of his head, he patted a jumper over it, and then another, and pushed the drawer shut.

Forgetting how low the mattress was, Alex fell down awkwardly onto it and recalled the conversation he'd had with his uncle earlier that afternoon. Abraham had said, with immense difficulty, that he was going to let Alex travel to Herga's with 'the others'. It had taken Alex nearly an hour of promising that they would be safe and incredibly careful on their journey, but he knew that if it were not for the suffocating fog, such a gesture would never have been made.

When Alex finished changing and stepped out onto the landing, he heard an odd, screeching sound, like a door handle being slowly turned. Moving to the banister he found Abraham creeping from his bedroom across the lounge. Hair tattered, cardigan creased, he peeled open the front door, snuck out and millimetre by millimetre closed it after him.

So stunned was Alex that he could barely think straight. *Does he really feel so troubled that he has to sneak out to avoid our guests?* Alex thought. *But why did he try to join us this morning?* His uncle's conflicting behaviours were impossible to understand.

Devetta was sitting alone amongst the unfolded Elongress when Alex entered the attic in search of everyone a short while later. Upon noticing him, she folded away the small piece of parchment she was studying and informed him that everyone would soon be returning from the library to get ready.

Planning on telling the group together of what had just happened, Alex thanked her and went to leave.

'Your uncle—he has been heavy on your mind,' Devetta said, causing Alex to turn back and sit down on the closest seat available.

The desire to confess to his uncle the complete truth about his guests lurched through Alex's body. Everyone's secrets, including his own, had caught him in a web from which he could not force himself free. 'I wish I understood why he is being like this, just what is holding him back,' he said.

'There is not something holding your uncle back. He appears to be torn, split in two,' Devetta mystically answered.

'Torn?'

'Something is pulling him apart, that much I see in his recent attempt to join us all before hiding behind his inhibitions. But what is dividing him I could not possibly intuit. We all have our guises, our secrets, Alexander.'

'That we do,' Alex said, eying Devetta curiously. He set his elbows upon his knees and wiped his face. 'Our lives changed again after Maudlyn died. Although Abe can feed himself and take care of himself in that sense, he just doesn't do well on his own. Her death broke his heart and broke him. I'm not sure if anything could fix him.'

Devetta rose to her feet. She linked her hands, keeping her fingers straight. 'I firmly believe all that truly matters in the end is that we have someone, that we are together,' she said peacefully. 'Because only when we are together can anything be accomplished.'

Her dress, which bloomed out around her waist, pulsated from plum into a pleasant shade of green. 'I am ready for this evening,' she calmly announced, and as she stroked the edge of the Elongress, the sets of drawers revolved back like fans, the long golden bar holding many hanging dresses retracted and then the Elongress sealed itself and shrank to a size no bigger than a teacup.

*

The clock struck seven o'clock, and one by one the Evergreens made their way down to the lounge, each dressed in some of the finest clothes they owned. The children were wearing matching jumpers, and Irwin was outfitted in a smart grey blazer, but it was Evie, in a teal dress and with her hair in a fancy updo, who impressed the most. Winton and Ambrose joined them next, hand in hand, before a glow of green brought with it Devetta and then Arvaeneous, who wished them a good evening and waved them off.

The misty halos of street lights and faintly lit windows guided the group down the high street. Barely five minutes later, they arrived at Herga's cottage, close to Markle Woods. Smoke was puffing from its chimney, barely visible amongst the fog, and the front garden was overrun with hundreds of colourful garden gnomes. It was no surprise to Alex that as soon as he knocked on the front door it whipped open and he was pulled inside to his uncle's vigorous inquisition.

'Yes, we're fine, Abe, no one saw us,' Alex said placatingly as he slipped from his restraint. 'You can't see anything in this fog!'

'Come in! Come come!' Herga beckoned as the group amassed in the hallway. 'Coats on the rack, shoes by the door, you know the business. Now'—she lured them into the rosier light of the lounge—'come let me see you all!' The bronze zebra-like pattern of her dress flickered in the fire's glow, and she clicked her heels together. 'Such a pleasure to meet you all at last! My name is Herga, I am a good friend of Abraham and Alex, and any friend of theirs is always welcome here!'

Abraham generously filled two sherry glasses in the kitchen and watched as the children bowed and curtseyed before Herga. She howled with delight. 'Aren't you three the most cutest little bumpkins I have ever seen!' Alex could tell from Evie's expression that she had never heard the word 'bumpkins' before, and he laughed to himself.

After inviting everyone to make themselves at home, Herga waltzed into the small, steamy kitchen and started pouring out drinks.

'Your friend Herga has rather exceptional taste,' Devetta said as her gaze spread to the room and its many queer contents.

'I couldn't agree more,' Alex said.

Herga's house always reminded Alex of a small cabin deep in the woods; its possessions were anything but simple or bland. Anything that could be painted or printed in some kind of startling or colourful pattern always lived up to its fullest potential. Even the fire crackled wildly as though on a high.

'Ah! You have topped up my glass again!' Herga laughed as Abraham attempted to hide the sherry bottle behind him. 'I shall have to keep a closer eye on you!'

'Mummy gets like that when she's had a glass of wine,' Felicity said to her sister as they passed.

'OK, thank you love,' Evie replied, laughing embarrassedly.

'She has a point you know,' Irwin whispered to her.

'Yes, OK! Thank you!'

The appetising smell of basil drifted through the room where everyone was standing and chatting. With it came Herga, who guided Alex over to the window and enquired about how things were going with him and his friends before asking, quite directly, what he was helping them with.

'It's like I told Abraham, it's personal for the family and Devetta, so it's really not my place—'

'Oh you can tell me! I am a very good keeper of people's secrets I'll have you know.'

'I don't doubt that,' Alex replied, glancing at Abraham. 'Well, I'm helping them to find something. It's like they're between lives at the moment, and I offered them help because —'

'They were there that night, yes,' Herga replied. 'He's told me a lot, you know, about them. S'all he speaks about when he visits now.'

'What does he say?'

'It's not anything dangerous that you're up to, is it?' Herga pressed on, almost slurring her words. 'Nothing that could get you . . . found? You know our Abe, he's always thinking like that.'

'Well he needs to stop,' Alex said in a flat voice. Upon finding his arms crossed defensively at his chest, he slowly unfolded them. 'I'm fine!' He tried to laugh. 'He's always worrying about me, probably worrying about everyone else who's living with us too!'

'I can understand why.' Herga smacked her hand loudly over her mouth, and her hazel eyes bulged.

Alex guided Herga further into the corner of the room. 'Do you know why he is acting like he is?' he asked determinedly.

Herga stiffened but finally said, with a duller tongue, 'Try thinking of things from his perspective. Think about what he did that night, the one thing he chose to do, and then everything that has happened since that family returned.'

Alex frowned again but saw Abraham headed in their direction with two full sherry glasses.

'Think about it,' Herga suggested before Abraham arrived within earshot. 'Ah lovely, thank you, my sweet!' She took a hefty swig, swallowed and then pondered for a second. 'I must slow down, yes . . .' she muttered, before shimmying back to the kitchen with a trailing Abraham.

Dinner was soon announced, and everyone took a seat at the rather undersized table in the lounge. Piles of potatoes and mounds of vegetables were built upon plates, followed by scoops of casseroles, fillets of chicken and slices of pies. After everyone congratulated Herga on her generous effort, conversation turned to the impromptu arrival of the *Precipitous* and how, as the *Merlow Messenger* had reported, things had been spotted being removed from the ship in sealed crates. There had also been sketchy reports of presumed passengers being smuggled off the ship and taken away, but the reason it had come crashing into the shore was still unknown.

The topic soon came to a close and, taking everyone by surprise again, Abraham suddenly spoke out.

'So how did you manage to find my nephew again?'

Although Abraham's question was unexpected, the Evergreens responded admirably. After recounting everything that had happened that night as it had taken place, they continued with the fictionalised version of their story: They were evicted from their home over six years later and reunited with Devetta, an old family friend who was now helping them find and hopefully sell a lost family heirloom which had fallen out of traceable records. When no options remained, they'd decided to seek out the boy who had once offered them refuge. The mistruths naturally unfolded. No fascinating time machines, inspiring Ephemors, temporal policemen, disillusioned worlds or elusive evidence. No fun, was how Alex thought of it.

Abraham had eaten barely three forkfuls of food by the time they finished their tale, and Alex could read the signs clearly—his uncle had not fallen for it. Apple yoghurt and cinnamon cake was served for dessert, and thankfully Herga, with a flicker of giddiness still about her, began to talk of her late husband, Terrance, and the tension was safely diffused.

The street was suitably absent of life when thank you's and goodbyes were said at ten o'clock and everyone gathered by the front door. Herga squealed again as the children hugged her, and Alex saw her and Abraham lock eyes for a passing moment before she kissed him on both cheeks and he stepped out to inspect the liveliness of the mist.

'I almost forgot! What's the good news you have to share?' Alex asked, only just remembering as he pulled on his coat.

Herga grinned. 'The next time you all come over I'll tell you. We'll set a date soon, I promise!'

As the group followed Abraham through the fog, Alex felt something tickle his hand. He looked down to find a small hand gripping his, and Daniel looked up at him with a friendly grin.

'You were wrong before,' Daniel said as Herga, waving wildly, was swallowed from sight behind them. 'She is *definitely* crazy.'

*

The *twit-twoo* of owls in the Meadows and Abraham's faint snores below were the only sounds of the sleeping world as Alex lay in bed, staring at the photo of his parents. The printed memory, taken when he was only just a child, always brought him comfort in the darkest hours. It was Christmas morning. His parents were tight within each other's arms and sitting amongst a collection of torn wrapping paper. It was as though they themselves had been unwrapped; they were the best present Alex would ever know and would always hold most dear. The baubles on the Christmas tree glistened and the garlands of tinsel glittered but could not outshine his parents' beautiful smiles.

The sound of voices broke him out of his reverie. Opening his bedroom door, he saw Evie and Irwin's bedroom door slightly ajar; a light was on. Shadows moved through the light, and then suddenly the air was saturated by Evie's sobs.

'I c-can't do this,' she cried. 'I can't k-keep going on like this. God, it eats me alive!'

'Of course it does, my love. It's a burden we all carry,' Winton said soothingly.

Through the thin gap Alex could see the children asleep on the bed by the window. The rest of the family surrounded Evie on the floor. 'It's just too much . . . it's too much.'

Kneeling in front of his wife, Irwin took her hands in his. 'Remember what I said before, the night he told us what happened to him, how his uncle kept him away' he said, seemingly infusing her with his strength. 'Remember what I told you, what I *promised*.'

Evie sniffled again, incapable of speech between her desperate gasps for air.

'Your whole family is here for you. You have to stay strong, my beautiful, loving girl,' Winton said, rubbing her shoulder. 'We all have to stay strong—for him.'

Alex's head twitched and his stomach dropped. *For him? Who?* The answer was obvious. *But why stay strong for me?*

Alex wondered, bouncing the words back and forth in his head.

With no clear answer, he stepped back into his bedroom and closed himself back into the darkness.

— CHAPTER THIRTEEN —

To Lose My Life

It was unmistakable that the spotless epicentre of the Clockhaus was anywhere but Abraham's bedroom beneath the stairs. Abraham's personal space was immaculate. Each book upon every busy bookcase was organised by title and height; ornaments and photo frames were set at perfect angles; the clunky desk facing the side wall was lined with fresh envelopes, pots of colourful inks and formations of stationery. Every thing had its place and every place had its thing—this was the foundation of Abraham's life.

When things were not in order, Abraham would fall into confusion, becoming unsettled and lost, and as much as Alex tried to deny it, he knew that was exactly where his uncle was now. Books lay upon Abraham's bedroom floor. His shirts and jumpers sat crumpled and creased in untidy piles and cold cups of tea drowned his bedside table. To Alex it was an incredibly worrying scene, and although he had been sitting at his uncle's sleeping side for over an hour already, he felt he needed to stay just a little longer.

In line with Alex's predictions, Abraham's attempts to join the group had stopped completely since the dinner at Herga's. He returned to the Clockhaus only at random times late in the day, but when Alex rushed down from the attic to see him, he would already be gone. Now covered in a patchwork blanket, his uncle resembled a broken vase that had been glued back together. Just what had broken him, however, Alex could in no way deduce.

When he finally moved into the lounge later that morning, Alex sat down to pour his devotion into his favourite window. He watched and waited for distant glimpses of people amongst the fog, busying themselves with their lives, oblivious to his watching or even to his existence. It had been almost an hour since everyone had left for the library and he would pause at irregular intervals to appreciate the silence. Then amongst the regular creaks of the Clockhaus Alex heard a noise. He turned at the sound of footsteps on the landing.

'I thought you had gone with everyone?' Alex called up to Evie as she slowly descended the stairs.

'I decided to stay here and do as you asked of me,' she replied, coming to sit next to him. Evie brought her hands out from behind her back to reveal William's diary. Alex looked at it and then up to Evie's sorrowful expression. She shook her head. 'There is nothing in there. Nothing that mentions where they were planning on going the evening they left.'

Knowing he wouldn't be able to read it, Alex had asked Evie to go through the months prior to his parents' vanishing. The diary had weighed increasingly on his mind since its unanticipated introduction into his life; gaining grams, which fortified into kilograms and became a ton—a weight impossible for Alex to bear.

But the diary turned out to be just as ungiving as he had expected.

'Do you mind if I ask why you haven't read it yourself?' Evie asked.

'Well, to me'—Alex turned only slightly in its direction —'it represents everything that has already happened for my parents. It's everything about before, before "that night", before they left. And as much as I want to read it . . . I just can't.'

'But you might find comfort in reading about them?' Evie said as she peeled open the diary. Alex instantly faced away.

'*I can't.* I can't focus on their past when they might have a present, when they could have a future!'

A faint smile of understanding lit up the sadness in Evie's face, and she set the diary aside. 'That's why you look out the window, of course.'

'How can I focus on what happened to them before when they could be right there through that fog, on the other side of this window? Right there!' Alex tapped its unbreakable glass and sighed. 'It's why I always watch. I cannot risk missing them. If I stop watching and start remembering then I fear I'll be so consumed with everything that was before that I'll miss everything that could be . . . and they'll never find me, never come back to me.'

'I know it seems like there must be a reason why we were sent back to you the night they vanished, and maybe there is, sweetie, but we really don't know,' Evie said sympathetically.

'I accept that those pages don't have any entries dated after that night. Some might see that as an end, but I don't—their story isn't finished. Anything could have happened to them. Abe believes Whitsnare's men came after them and then came to take me that night.' Alex let out a huff that could have been a short laugh, but it was in no way funny. He turned back to the foggy window. 'But I've never believed that. I know those men were there for you, and *I believe* that my parents were never involved in any of that. Although I don't know what happened to them'—Alex inhaled warm air into the chambers of his lungs—'I felt such hope for them. *Feel* such hope. I don't know what it is—hope for anything, I suppose, but I feel it so strongly, right here,' he said, placing a hand to his chest.

Evie rubbed his shoulder, pulling him in slightly, and Alex felt immensely thankful.

'I know you're probably wondering why I haven't asked to go back to that night, but although I'm ready here,' Alex tapped his chest, 'I'm not ready here,' and he tapped his temple. 'I'm not strong enough yet.'

'It's ok. Whenever you want to go, we can.'

Alex gave a great sigh of relief. 'Thank you.'

'My granddad always told me that as long as there is light above then there is hope. "Be it in the flare of sunshine, in the lustre of moonlight, in the sea of sky or in the constellation of star, as long as there is light above then there is, and always will be, hope." And when things get difficult, and they often do, I know that any time of day or night I can always look up and find comfort.' Through the window Evie peered up at the sky, which was almost indistinguishable from the bright, thick fog of the foreground. 'In this time, at least.'

Not wanting to pry on her last words and what they meant, Alex instead remained quiet. Together they sat watching the fog whirl and swirl in the breeze until, with a swish of sound, the Elongress returned to the attic. After unsuccessfully trying to persuade him to join her with the others at the library, Evie left and Alex was alone again.

Evie's words about hope stuck firmly in his head, but Alex knew that it was more than simple hope that he possessed; it was a feeling that defined him absolutely. It was the feeling that had pieced him back together after that long snowy drive to the Clockhaus that night. But despite his return to wholeness, he couldn't help but think of that night, Saturday 27 November 1993, as the night he lost his life.

*

'Have you found something, Alex?'

'Is it about the Heirloom?'

'Another clue?'

It was the Friday after Herga's dinner, and following a scrumptious dinner of chicken stuffed with sage and, strangely, tangerine, as per Arvaeneous' request, the group had regathered at the end of the attic to work. No more than fifteen minutes later, Alex's head plunged to within kissing distance of his book. He *had* found something.

'Please share what you have found, Alex,' Ambrose said from across the circle of seats.

As everyone leaned in, Alex said, 'Listen closely. It is reported that after the Battle of Trafalgar was won, and Admiral Lord Nelson, vice admiral of the flagship *Victory*, lay dying from a gunshot wound, he made reference to a certain item of mysterious origin. Alexander Scott, Nelson's chaplain, is claimed to have written a letter to King George III informing him of the black, lidless box to which Nelson had referred, and its location, but it was never known whether the letter, whose existence is often disputed by historians to date, was ever sent.'

Confused glances were exchanged, but one person realised an immediate connection.

'Ah! Black box . . . black box,' Winton mumbled as he picked up *Mysteries of Magnificence*, which he had been reading, and flicked through its chapters.

Alex's finger skimmed the sentences before him. 'It says that King George III eventually went mad, and his son, King George IV, took over his duties.' Alex chuckled. 'One of the theories proposes that it was the contents of the box that caused his madness.'

Winton consulted his notes and hurried to a specific page. 'Now what you just read was from *Mysteries of Cause*, correct?'

Alex nodded.

'Now, you might think that the box was never mentioned again, but listen closely.' Winton went on to read aloud a passage about a historical figure whom Alex had heard of. According to what was written, Sir Winston Churchill had initiated the construction of a number of secretive, wealthy stores to protect items of value or significance during the Second World War. From such vaults a number of seemingly random items were reported missing, including 282 gold-jewelled goblets, 74 silver-encrusted medallions, 40 cases of Heidsieck Monopole & Co 1907 champagne, 18 fine red tapestries, and 1 black box, which was chained in a net of 324 interconnected keyless padlocks.

There was initial silence, followed by Irwin's question. 'Did you say a lidless box, Alex? A black, *lidless* box?'

Alex nodded. 'Why? What's the significance?'

The group turned to face the back corner of the attic, where the Evispen was perched on a rickety old chest.

'The Evispen,' Evie said, her voice faint and distant. 'It was given to us in a white whicker-like cradle that for all purposes was lidless too. It revealed itself to us the day it brought us back to you.'

Winton moved to the balcony doors. 'Just because the two artefacts apparently shared a similar means of preservation doesn't mean that they're the same. We must keep reading.'

Alex flicked back to his page but stopped reading the moment he heard the front door slam. Why was his uncle home, and why was he making so much noise about it?

'How is your uncle?' Arvaeneous asked as he sat down next to Alex.

'I just don't know anymore,' Alex glumly replied. 'He's more distant than ever. I wish he would just tell me what was wrong and we could sort it all out.'

'I hear a noise. It is getting louder,' Devetta declared. As the Elongress she was sitting on shrank at her touch, her feet came back to the floor.

'This place always creaks and whines,' Alex said dismissively.

'No—that noise, it sounds like thumping,' Winton said. He was still at the balcony doors, and turned back to face the room.

'I can't hear anyth—' Alex stopped. He could hear it. It was getting louder and stronger. Just as Devetta enlarged the

Elongress in front of Arvaeneous, large enough to block him from sight, the attic door flew open, producing Abraham.

Alex would have been proud of his uncle's confident entrance if there hadn't been anger scrawled across his face and a glimmer of red in his swinging hand. Abraham thrust his finger towards Alex and then back to the door. 'DOWNSTAIRS. NOW!'

Abraham marched away.

Embarrassment instantly sank beneath rising layers of anxiety within Alex.

'Something tells me this might be the opportunity you've been wishing for,' Arvaeneous said to Alex.

'I think that was your father's diary he had in his hand, Alex. I think he found it,' Evie said nervously.

'It was, yes. He's obviously been searching my bedroom,' Alex replied, knowing he had hidden the diary again that morning. 'But he has finally chosen to discuss what needs to be discussed, so I want you to come down with me, please. You have as much right to hear his explanation as I do.'

Arvaeneous agreed to watch over the children, who hugged their parents as if they were being shipped off to battle. Alex led the remaining four Evergreens and Devetta downstairs.

Abraham was pacing by the front door but stopped upon seeing the group take the sofas behind Alex. 'So you lied about going home,' he said.

'Yes I did,' Alex replied with equal snappiness to his voice.

Abraham began pacing again. His feet smacked the floor as he went.

'It's not as if I could just bring it up in conversation. You'd have hit the roof!'

'But you can't keep doing this, Alex! You have to find another way to remember! You can't go back there. Not ever!' Abraham shouted. 'You know they could easily find you at that house! You're a smart boy, Alex, but that decision could have gotten you killed, or . . . or worse!'

Quite suddenly Alex realised he didn't have a leg to stand on. His decision to return to his childhood home could have easily—and what was worse, nearly had—resulted in either scenario. But words burst from his mouth like the *Precipitous'* foghorn anyway.

'I can't just ignore it like you do! Push away what happened to my parents as though it never happened!'

'How did you get home?' Abraham demanded, slapping the diary on his armchair.

Alex didn't reply.

'I've been locking the doors ever since they arrived. I take the key with me every day. How did you get out?'

'Is that why you tried to sit with us? To make sure we didn't leave?'

'Of course it was! You've been so acting so suspiciously— all of you! I know there are things you haven't been telling me, Alex, and I'll get to that, but there are things they aren't telling *you*. Can't you see that?'

'Like what?'

'Have they not told you the real reason they came back to you?'

Of course they had told him the reason they were back . . . hadn't they?

'Yes, they told me.'

'Would you care to share that answer with me?'

Alex looked over his shoulder, back to the group, to the time-defying family and otherworldly lady, before shaking his head. He turned back to Abraham. 'You're not ready. I will tell you the truth, but I'm not going to tell you like this.'

Abraham gasped. 'Oh, your rules for truth, how charitable they are,' he said, his words dripping with sarcasm. 'Do you not think I deserve an answer? Why else do you think I invited them to stay here in the first place?'

'What?' This time Alex was the one to shout. The skin around his eyes twitched. 'That's why you invited them to stay?'

'It isn't a coincidence that they turn up that same night your parents disappear off the face of the earth, Alex. You said that they don't know anything about what happened to your parents, but they must! And coincidence that they turn up the same night those people came to take you away? You're smarter than this, Alex. Please see the obvious!' Abraham waited for his words to sink in, teeth chattering between his gruff, panting breaths, before posing his final question. 'And how did they find you all these years later?'

'They told you—' Alex started, but Abraham turned his back to the room so Alex immediately stopped.

'If you all moved in here I knew I could keep an eye on you,' Abraham said.

Alex laughed rather rudely. 'But you keep running away at the sight of them!'

'I've tried Alex. I have tried!' Abraham faced him again. 'But how could they possibly know you were here? You've been kept away ever since I took you in! '

'Locked me up,' Alex bitterly corrected.

Things were already at boiling point, but Alex's cold response visibly hurt Abraham.

'You can judge me for what I have done, but I've done it because I love you, Alex, and because I'm keeping you safe. I will never regret what I have done because of those exact reasons.' Abraham's stiff, blunt voice was like a mallet to Alex's chest. 'These people have jeopardised all that I've done to keep you safe and protected.'

Alex wanted nothing more than to spit out the truth—that Abraham had locked him away for nothing, that he was in no danger at all—but his jaw slammed shut and he bit sharply into his tongue. The blood of his unspoken words filled his mouth. Instead, he stepped forward to approach his uncle, and spoke in a calmer voice.

'I know there is more they haven't told me. I worked that out soon after they came back, but I trust they are keeping it from me for a reason: the right reason. I trust that they will tell me when it is right to do so, just as they have trusted me, and now is not the time for the truth to be said. Not to me, and not to you. Not like this. I have to say that I thought you would have been kinder to these people who'—Alex paused, wanting to add 'you believe' to his sentence—'saved my life that night. Aren't you thankful for that?'

'Of course I am, but there are so many questions! I think I have a right to know just who is living under my roof!'

'You do,' Evie said, to Abraham and Alex's surprise, and she entered the arena to stand at Alex's side. 'I very much agree that you deserve to know everything. Involving your nephew in our business should most definitely be your concern, and I am very glad that you have finally decided to act upon that.'

A slight frown rippled upon Abraham's forehead.

'No, don't answer him,' Alex said to Winton, who looked as though he was about to speak, before facing his uncle again. 'It's taken you this long to finally speak up, so let's talk about it. Let's talk about why you've been hiding away behind your newspapers, at Herga's, at the shop?' Alex voice became stronger as he found confidence in his retaliation. 'Locking yourself away, saying barely a word to these lovely people who are only far too kind and willing to be your friend. Let's start there, shall we? We may have kept some things back, Abe, but so have you.'

Alex's leg to stand on was returning. 'Is it because you think they have replaced you?'

Abraham looked shocked, almost devastatingly outraged.

'I've been thinking. Something Herga said,' Alex continued. 'She wouldn't tell me why you've been acting like you have, but she told me to think about things from your point of view and'—Alex swallowed the metallic taste of his blood—'that is the one thing I keep coming back to: that you think I have chosen them over you. Is that it? That I would, what? Completely abandon my uncle who has taken me into his life, completely rewritten his life around me? For me? You think I would do that? That I actually *could*?'

Abraham clutched the back of his armchair. Lines shot across the smooth leather as it creased beneath his fingers.

'Because it is simply not true,' Alex said desperately. 'We have been through everything these years, but always everything together, and I have always followed you. But now I have to make decisions for myself. It hasn't been fair that we all moved in here and expected you to act as if nothing had changed, to just let it be, and for that I am sorry.'

191

He stepped forward and took Abraham's hands, which felt heavy, burdened with secrets—just why was his uncle so ambivalent towards Devetta and the Evergreens?

'But now you have to trust *me* when I say that tomorrow I will be leaving through that door,' Alex said, knowing he had to continue, despite Abraham's tightened grip and frantic fear, evident in his eyes. 'I will be back, but I will be going further than what's on the other side of that window, further than Herga's. Further than home.

'I've decided we are going to visit my grandparents, mum's parents. They deserve to know that I'm alive.'

It took Abraham a long moment to acknowledge this but he finally came around to it. They both then agreed to openly discuss everything upon his return. When they hugged, Abraham held on incredibly tight.

'We'll leave in the morning,' Alex said as they peeled apart. 'I would say try not to worry but . . .' Alex tried to smile but felt it leak from him in a grimace.

'I can stay at Herga's,' Abraham murmured. 'I suppose I've been living with her quite a bit recently.'

'I suppose you have,' Alex said.

He lifted to the full height his toes would allow and kissed his uncle on the forehead. Smearing the trails of tears from his face, Alex led Devetta and the Evergreens upstairs and away, and nothing more needed to be said except 'love you," and finally, 'goodnight.'

— CHAPTER FOURTEEN —

What We Left Behind

At the end of the rolling green field, balanced on the hill overlooking the nearby town, there the small house stood. Several elements were immediately distinguishable, even from a distance. Each of its small square windows was smashed. Large holes were stamped into the cracked slate roof. Even the chimney had collapsed, its toppled head resting in the thick grass to the rear of the house. Apart from such damage, however, the Evergreens' house had survived its formidable journey through time relatively intact.

Having arrived in the Elongress in the neighbouring field, the group made their way rather leisurely towards the house. As they did so, Winton told Alex about how the Evispen had sent them back to this time first, to the summer of 2012, before then whisking them back to the first night they met Alex in 1993. The pit-stop had clearly broken the house's back, meaning it was no longer fit as a conduit of their travel. To a passer by, Alex thought the house must have looked incredibly out of place.

As they neared the broken structure, Winton dived in to telling Alex how all seven of the Evergreens lived together in one household, as most families did in the time they were from. Alex listened intently but with undeniable sadness. There was a hole of seven years in his life—seven whole years of missed opportunities and missed moments that could be as cherished as some of those kept within Winton's Ephemor.

When they arrived in front of the house, Irwin placed his thumb on the doorbell. A shimmery sound rang out through the skeleton, and he forced open the green front door to scout the interior. 'Be careful now. Take only what you need, remember,' he instructed upon returning, gesturing each member of his family, and finally Alex, through. Arvaeneous and Devetta agreed to keep watch outside.

As homey as the living room surely once felt, it now seemed inhospitable and almost lethal. The furniture, all hand carved and skilfully crafted, stood slanted and beaten around the perimeter of the room. Cabinets had blasted out their insides in tiny shards and fragments. The only thing untouched was the wallpaper, which portrayed a tranquil blue sky with drifting white clouds, and Alex noticed, through a hole in the ceiling, twinkling stars shooting upon violet bedroom walls above.

The lounge and the kitchen had seemingly been robbed. Hooks for paintings remained unfulfilled, the shiny worktops in the kitchen were bare and various cupboards were starved of occupants. All that remained in the small dining room were empty cabinets, a dark walnut table with seven chairs and, peculiarly, a slate plaque upon the wall. The various holes carved into the plaque looked as though they might hold the oddly shaped light bulbs Alex had spotted in the

Evergreens' trunk, but why a shrine to such an object existed he had no idea.

The two sisters came down the stairs and into the kitchen. Nora had a stuffed backpack on, and the white rabbit upon Felicity's jumper was running laps around her, causing her to giggle and chase patting hands after it.

'The Law took everything we had for scrutiny,' Nora said, pointing to the holes punched into the walls around them, 'except for the few things we managed to hide.'

'Scrutiny?' Alex asked.

'They had to see if we were hiding anything, didn't they? Like memorandia or secrets about our crime,' Nora said. 'That's where everything's gone, to the Law.'

'I don't think we'll get it back,' Felicity said.

'Oh no, we won't get it back,' Nora said brashly.

For their young age, both Nora and Felicity were incredibly knowledgeable about the dangerous situation they were in. Whereas some parents might shield a child in a cocoon of ignorance, Alex knew that what the Evergreens had been through demanded explanation and honesty for everyone.

'It's pretty boring here,' Nora said, wandering into the lounge. 'You should see Hilloweith Castle. I've seen the paintings. Granddad said it's a place of awe. It's where his family has lived for as far back as he knows!'

'Where's Hill-ow-with Castle?' Alex said.

'Don't know,' Nora replied, 'but the statues of Monty and Martha wander around'—she turned to her sister—'and they have the Great Dance of Garments, the shifting maze gardens and the Hereditree and . . .'

Nora's words continued to rapidly unfurl, just like her mother's often did, until she seemed lost as to what to say next.

'They have everything there,' Felicity said wistfully.

'Do you like things in the age you are from?' Nora asked Alex, folding her arms.

'Things aren't too bad,' Alex said. 'We get along—we have computers.'

'Oh, don't worry, they won't last,' Nora she dismissively, attending to the butterfly pins fluttering in her hair. 'We learned all about the Digital Age some time ago.'

'Oh, right,' Alex said, feeling a bit punctured by the fact that his future was now just history, and not a long-lasting one at that.

'I love doing this!' Nora said as she charged to the wall, and with her playful touch, the calm cloudy sky upon it began to change colour, from rich blue to dark purple. Brooding clouds blew away their lighter cousins, and sketches of lightning ripped across the wall as she caused innocent mayhem.

Evie's and Winton's whispers echoed from the stairs as they came down into the kitchen. 'Can we take this?' Winton asked his daughter, referring to the carved golden frame over his shoulder.

'You can, but not at that size,' Evie replied.

The frame shrank as Winton moved it down his arm until it was the size of a small photo frame, which he tucked in his back pocket. Irwin followed carrying a large red trunk of their belongings, and they all made their way back outside. A resounding, shimmery crackle rang out as Ambrose set her thumb to the doorbell. The clouds upon the wall froze, the lights faded and the various doors and cupboards closed; the broken house had sighed its final farewell.

Alex took control of the Evispen that Arvaeneous passed him, and one by one they stepped into the enlarged Elongress set upon the grass. Reigniting his memories of the barn that he used to play in when he was young, and the sensation of complete freedom it represented in his childhood years, Alex focused on the very spot in which he wished to arrive. With everyone aboard, the lid of the Elongress closed over them. The moment the two halves touched there was a tremendous physical upheaval as the Elongress was sent spiralling towards the sky, and then plummeting back down to the earth. With a great thud they landed on the ground.

Or so they thought.

The top half of the Elongress lifted away above the ten bodies to reveal the wooden beams of a ceiling far closer than Alex had expected. It was only when Arvaeneous went to place a foot outside that the whole Elongress began to shift.

'NOBODY MOVE!' Arvaeneous shouted, barely able to rotate his head back to everyone without the Elongress leaning in his direction. 'We haven't quite landed yet.'

'What do you mean?' Irwin asked

'We're on top of a very large stack of hay. Must be at least twenty-five-feet high.'

'That wasn't there last time!' Alex exclaimed.

'Oh heavens—I hate heights!' Winton squealed.

As Arvaeneous withdrew his outstretched leg, the Elongress tilted dangerously. Alex pushed his feet into the soft padding, wondering whether this was what it felt like to be at the top of a very tall rollercoaster. Arvaeneous edged further back, and suddenly the lid began falling closed over them like a guillotine.

'Arv!' Alex shouted as Irwin yanked him back. The lid slammed shut and the box slipped over the edge. They screamed in the dark as they plummeted. There was a sound like airbags exploding the split second before the Elongress struck solid earth, and with an enormous *CRASH!* its inhabitants were sent flying from its clutch.

Skidding to a halt across the dusty barn floor, Alex peeled open his eyes to find the Evispen safe in his arms.

'Let's do that again!' Daniel exclaimed as he helped Felicity to her feet.

'Please, let's not,' his mother insisted.

While everyone dusted themselves down, the cushioned Elongress slowly deflated. Devetta pocketed it, and they emerged onto a long road and made their way towards the cottage perched upon the sunny horizon. Eagerness and apprehension bickered within Alex's stomach as they walked through the colourful garden, but it was the former that threw his hand to knock on the door. It seemed to take forever, but finally someone answered.

Alex's heart was set to implode as the tall aproned woman looked around at the large group crowding her doorstep. She had coils of fluffy white hair, bunched up cheeks and small but incredibly bright hazel eyes. She was mixing something in a bowl tucked under her arm, but upon spotting Alex she stopped, and her face fell.

'Hi, Nan.'

Her mouth dropped. The bowl skidded away as she crashed to her knees and her trembling hands touched Alex's cheeks. Within seconds her eyes were overflowing with tears.

'Alex? Is that . . . is that you?' she whispered.

'It's me, Nan,' he said. 'It's really me.'

Alex's cheeks rose beneath her touch, and at once he was sucked into her crushing grasp. Cries of happiness blubbered from Geraldine's shaking body until she could finally call out for Horace, who came rushing up behind her.

For as long as Alex could remember, Horace had dressed as though wanting to make the best first impression possible. On this day, in a dusty brown suit, trousers high up around his midriff, his grey hair exemplifying precise brushing, he did not disappoint.

'It's our boy!' Geraldine whimpered. 'It's Alex!'

Horace's heartbreaking smile, unlike Geraldine's chugging sobs, told of a gentle patience, as if he'd known Alex would one day return to them. 'Of course it is,' he said, and he too swamped Alex in a magnificent hug. 'How could it not be you?'

Alex's companions were escorted into the long kitchen, and Horace shook their hands. Geraldine, however, could not keep her eyes off Alex. She seemed almost drunk in her deliriousness. 'You're here . . .' she mumbled over and over.

Before Alex could begin to think about asking if they could stay, Horace began directing his guests into the short hallway and up the stairs to the bedrooms. As they moved away, Alex was able to fully absorb the house that he remembered so well. The kitchen countertops still held familiar jars filled with all kinds of nuts, grains, beans and freshly picked fruits, whilst familiar clay flowerpots, some filled with acorns and others housing scarlet roses, lined the windowsills. The small lounge adjoining the kitchen was just as washed-out as ever with its thin and tired pillows and framed cross-stitches upon the shelves. Even the view out over the golden fields was exactly as he remembered, as though he had just stepped into a memory from an Ephemor.

When Horace returned, Geraldine made a fresh pot of tea and the three of them settled in their usual places in the lounge. During Alex's childhood visits in the summers, after a hard day's work on the farm, his grandparents would sit in the two matching armchairs by the window, and Alex in the settee beside them. Geraldine and Horace would tell stories and tales of the pocket of time before Alex was born, of his mother in her prime years and of his great grandparents, who had grown up during the Second World War.

Hearing these stories was the most enthralling part of Alex's days, but now it was his turn to tell a story, and it would be in no way similar. His grandparents' hands met in the space between them, and so Alex, taking a deep breath, slowly began.

From the near closure of Abraham's shop in the early years to Maudlyn's illness and eventual death in the later, how Abraham had spent his life savings on the lighthouse for him and the pointless, blurry years in between—nothing was held back and no detail left untold.

Alex even told his grandparents things he had not yet shared with Arvaeneous, Devetta and the Evergreens. One such topic was how in the weeks following Alex's settlement at the Clockhaus, Abraham had begun a nationwide campaign to find both him and his truly missing parents. It was told on the evening news, written in newspapers across the country: the Priar family from Merlow was missing, presumed to have been kidnapped. Every time Alex insisted that his grandparents be told the truth, Abraham would cite his aunt, Meredith's sister Lucinda, who worked for a high-status tabloid newspaper, as the reason why he could not risk their ever knowing.

Many visitors had come and gone at the Clockhaus over the wearisome years. So fearful was Abraham that someone would detect the third inhabitant that every room of the Clockhaus was kept spotless, so as to erase any trace of him. 'It's for your own protection,' Abraham would say as he scrubbed out all existence of him. 'It's because I love you.'

The bunker-like room purpose-built for his hiding was dug deep into the rock on which the Clockhaus sat, far down beneath the pantry's false back wall, where the jagged walls steamed with apprehension and the sea air breathed a chill. Any thought of it still sent shivers through Alex. It was where he would spend his hours when he could not be sensed in any way by those who visited. There were the police officers in the first months of his incarceration, the volunteers from far beyond Merlow who devoted their energy to Abraham's cause; and there were also the newspapers who came to lay waste to any truth of Abraham and Maudlyn's ordeal. But it was his grandparents' visits that were the most gut-wrenching to bear whilst he was hidden away.

When Alex told them about the Evergreens, his grandparents were visibly thrown from the path of the story.

'Time travel?' Horace gasped, almost spilling what was his fourth cup of tea down the front of his shirt. 'They're from the future?'

'Yes.'

'What? How is that possible?' Horace said with a laugh.

'I couldn't tell you.'

'But they seem so . . . *normal*,' Geraldine said.

'Wait until you have breakfast with them, that's all I'll say,' Alex said jokingly.

'I still don't believe you! I mean, how can they be from the future?'

'Come on, let me show you,' Alex said, and he led his grandparents upstairs to show them all the amazing things he had witnessed since the Evergreens had come crashing into his life

It was past lunchtime when Geraldine and Horace had finished experiencing the wonders of the Ephemor, the Evispen and everything that could be found in the Evergreen's trunks. After another cup of tea, and some time to digest the overwhelming stories and things they had seen so far, they then took Alex on a walk around the farm, stopping at all the places he used to play when he was young. When they got back it was late afternoon, and so they began to prepare a large pork and vegetable stew for dinner that evening. Sitting at the table in the kitchen skinning vegetables and reflecting on the day thus far, Alex could not have been more overjoyed with his decision to return.

'Do you think Abe will take the news about your guests being from the future very well?' Geraldine asked while lining up carrots and chopping them.

'No, I don't think he will. That's what I'm worried about. It takes him a while to adapt to things.'

'Maybe he's stronger than you think?' Horace said.

'It would take great strength to do the things he has done, all that sacrifice . . .' Geraldine said.

Although Alex had long understood the sacrifices his uncle had made, he only now realised how infrequently he appreciated them. To have had a roof over his head and a mattress beneath him was something to be cherished. He even felt a twinge of appreciation thinking of his uncle's hand-me-downs.

'I don't think anyone would blame you or your uncle if you were to complain,' Horace said after Alex explained how he was thankful. 'You've experienced more in the last few years than most people will in their entire lifetimes.' He stopped wiping dry the chopping board in his hands. 'So have we.'

'And so have Devetta and the Evergreens,' Geraldine added.

*

As the table was filled with both food and guests that evening, Alex could immediately sense that something was different. If he had to place a finger on a defining word it would have been "awkward", but it wasn't awkward in the overt sense. Conversations flowed as everyone tucked into generous helpings of the wholesome stew and Alex sat in the middle of table, trying to juggle the two conversations.

On one side of the table Winton sat amongst Evie and her daughters as he explained in scholarly terms to Geraldine about Ephemorical Legislation. He talked in particular about the common ways in which one would share memorandia from an Ephemor with other people, such as birthdays and Christmases, and always at funerals. It was then revealed that the Ephemor's other primary function was to help people with memory-related illnesses. Winton spoke between eager mouthfuls about the massive recovery patients would make upon seeing beloved memories again—memories that had been stored in Ephemors throughout the decades, and Alex was reminded all over again what an entrancing, magical item it was.

On the other side of the table, Irwin, Daniel, Arvaeneous and Ambrose were sharing with Horace the principal by which the nation from their time lived: 'the omnipotent truth'. After the years of ravaging war, the government, which was subsumed under and held accountable by the Law, was united under one dictating principal: to share the truth from thereon. Only by sharing the utmost truth could the Law of the People be efficiently maintained and could trust flow where it had once broken apart and led the world to almost annihilate itself. A government and therefore a law, as Arvaeneous had put it, based on falseness and lies would not survive again, so the law became the Law of the People, and each and every person of the nation became a pillar of its preservation.

'When there is truth, there is trust,' Ambrose summed up neatly. 'And we wanted to do better, to be better than we were. So there was no violence and there was no murder.'

'That is, until we were framed,' Irwin said as he finally finished his meal and set down his cutlery.

With plates empty, stomachs full and an unusual awkwardness of sorts still lingering, Alex insisted that he take on the washing up that evening. After some convincing, the group trailed away and began filing upstairs.

'Devetta,' Alex said, pulling her aside as everyone left, 'do you know what's wrong with everyone?'

Her eyebrows lifted. 'I am aware of the issue to which you refer. All that I can provide is that a promise is close to being broken. It is nearly time.'

With that, Devetta wished Alex goodnight and glided away.

Irwin and Evie's private conversation at the Clockhaus instantly sprang to Alex's mind. *What did he promise her?* he wondered. And more importantly, *Why is the promise soon going to be broken?*

The second the washing up was complete, Alex and his grandparents assumed their places in the tiny lounge, teacups full once again.

'I thought of this after lunch today,' Geraldine said, taking a sip. 'When your mother was young she had a fondness for dressing up like me. I'm not sure if you knew?' Alex shook his head, beaming. 'Merry used to come down those stairs in one of my old dresses, literally the frumpiest one she could lay her hands on, and would act as if she were me—all day she would!'

Geraldine laughed and giggled as she shared how Meredith would not break character until the following morning. The brief story had brought Meredith fresh and warm into their minds like a blanket placed around their shoulders.

'That reminds me of something else, actually! Back before you were born . . .'

As Geraldine jumped into another delightful story, Alex couldn't help but feel unbelievably content. It was as though everything else had simply eased away, like the beginning of an Ephemor's finest memory. He came to wonder, was this how they had coped over the years? By bestowing incredibly precious memories on each other?

Is this how they survived for all this time?

— CHAPTER FIFTEEN —

The Best Kept Secret

The desire to learn drove Alex to do as much on the farm as his unworked muscles would allow. Milking the cows, feeding the pigs, shearing the sheep, chopping up wood for the log burner in the kitchen, watering the many plants and harvesting Horace's massive collection of fruits and vegetables —Alex had never been so busy nor ached so much at the end of a day. As a result of Evie's insistence that he spend as much time with his grandparents as he possibly could, the five days since their arrival had been some of the most joyful of Alex's life. It had been liberating to be out in the world he had become so shielded and secluded from, and in many effortless images Alex pictured himself living on the farm, with them all, and doing this forever.

After lunch and again just before dinner each day, Alex would sit with Geraldine on the back porch as she knitted, or wander out into the woodlands beyond the fields with her. Every time they would talk, and talk about everything they would. Conversations, however, always returned to familiar ground—to the lives she and Horace had led since Alex's 'kidnapping'.

Unable to fathom what could possibly have happened to Alex and his parents, they sought immediate comfort in the things they could control and hold on to, which for them was Alex, William and Meredith's pasts. 'We were two great black holes, sucking in everything we could, smothering our lives with your parents and you,' Geraldine had said. Eventually though, after years of uselessly sitting and waiting, Geraldine and Horace had dedicated themselves to charitable work. It was a 'natural desperation', Horace explained, to want to make a difference no matter how big or small, no matter for whom or what.

It was on another of his late-evening walks with his grandfather that Alex again thought about his grandparents' struggles through the years. It was a cool evening after a hot, dry day on the fields. Backs still aching, legs feeling ready to give way and bellies full of the enormous steak and ale pie— one of Horace's favourite meals—they waddled slowly along the path through the fields.

'I enjoy walking out at night,' Horace said affably as he lit up his pipe and blew the smoke up to the dark fabric of sky. 'I try to do it as much as I can. Breathe the fresh air and watch the waning moon.' He swivelled around until he found it, burning amongst the prickling gems of starlight. 'Beautiful thing.'

'I've watched it for a long time too,' Alex said, thinking back to the sleepless hours spent on the attic balcony in its company. 'I sometimes forget it's a whole other world up there.'

There was a few seconds' pause, and then Horace, rather out the blue, said, 'Your grandmother and I understand why your uncle did what he did, keeping you away for all those years. By that I mean we find it difficult to blame him, as much as maybe . . . I don't know, maybe we should? We now know he was doing his best to keep you safe, and it feels wrong to blame him for that.'

'But that's the thing, he wasn't,' Alex said tiredly, watching the stems of wheat bend and bow in the late night wind. 'Those men were there for the Evergreens that night, not for me. I was kept away from you and I wasn't even in danger. You went through all that heartache too, and why? Because of what Abraham believed? I know he isn't to blame for everything that's happened, but . . . in some ways, he is.'

'People who have been through the things we have need to be able to see the good amongst the bad or else it all just fades into nothing,' Horace said.

'The thing is, I just don't know if I could ever tell him that he was wrong to do what he did.'

The shadow of the barn was so subtle against the night that Alex and Horace almost walked straight into it. Following the vegetable patches to its west, and passing the sheds stocked full of tools after that, they finally came to the pens of various quietly grunting and snorting animals. Horace fetched a lantern, and as they fed the pigs and goats, they chatted about all Alex's guests' wonderful things: the Elongress, the Evispen, the Ephemor and all the other items and garments that reacted to touch—or could be 'mesmerised', as Winton had titled it. For Horace it was a growing obsession.

'I was thinking about when you told me and your grandmother about that machine of theirs bringing them back to you,' Horace went on to say, before pausing for a great length of time. Finally, he said, 'Are you not intrigued to know just why they came back?'

'I know that the Evispen revealed itself to them the day it decided to bring them back to me. But why, I couldn't say.'

Horace, like Devetta, was looking further into Alex, as though enquiring about an entirely different matter altogether.

'You didn't mean why the Evispen brought them back, did you?'

'I didn't, no,' Horace said, sprinkling out some more pellets to his ecstatic crowd. 'I meant why are they *really* back? Forget about that machine deciding to bring them to you—as mad as that is in itself. Forget everything you know and tell me, why did they come back?'

Scattering out the remnants of his food, Alex let his arms hang over the fence. 'I think I know.'

Horace's long face, shifting in the flickering light from the lantern, wore a curious expression.

'I've always known they turned up to my house that night for a reason, and that reason, for me, has always remained the same. I believe it just as strongly still. The night I met them was the night I lost everything. Although hope has healed me and pieced me back together again, I also feel this great trust in the Evergreens. I like to think that the Evispen, or the person who gave it to them, had the good nature to send them to me so that I wasn't alone when I lost it all.' Alex kept his voice impassive. 'I think that is why they are back, and I take great strength from that.'

'Maybe that is the reason,' Horace said, tilting out one hand, 'or maybe the reason has yet to present itself.' He turned over the other.

Heading back on the road again, with the faint light from the top bedroom window guiding them home, Alex knew what was occupying his grandfather's mind. He'd been wondering the same thing over the past few days, and Horace's expression of deep thinking was so obvious.

'I don't know why everyone has been increasingly "off" since we got here. Maybe they've had an argument, but I haven't spent enough time with them recently to find out.'

'Not to worry,' Horace said with a smile. 'I just wondered whether something was the matter and if I could help at all.'

"Off" was putting it lightly; the behaviour of Arvaeneous, Devetta and the Evergreens had become downright unsettling. Heavy stares across the table at breakfast, short responses to each other during dinner, not to mention heated whispers coming to a sudden end every time Alex went to see them, hidden away in their bedrooms—he didn't know what to make of it. Evie had even stormed out of the cottage a few days previously for what seemed to Alex and his grandparents like no reason at all.

Instead of walking through the woods at lunchtime the next day, Alex and his grandparents got an early start preparing dinner. Having sliced up all the chicken, carrots, broccoli, leeks and parsnips, and skinned and sliced enough potatoes to last a month, he and his grandparents moved on to creating one of Geraldine's favourite apple desserts.

'I do love to cook,' Geraldine said as Alex passed her another red apple from the basket he had stocked full that morning. 'I'm always cooking, aren't I?'

'You always are,' Horace said, 'and all the better we are for it. *A little too better*,' he added sneakily to Alex as he patted his stomach. 'My mother used to cook all the time too. It wasn't so much a chore for her but a passion.'

'Mum was just the same,' Alex said. He stopped. He'd never mentioned his mother in passing like that before, never with his uncle. It felt strange. Emotion warmed his body. 'She liked to cook, especially on Sundays. She would always make a strawberry trifle. It was her favourite.'

Geraldine and Horace set down their utensils to listen to him.

'I remember . . .' Alex said, struggling with the words, 'she always used to sing. Whenever she cooked, she would sing.' Geraldine took Horace's hand. 'She had a beautiful voice. I used to sit and listen to her. She sometimes danced slowly when she thought no one was looking, but I remember. Yes, I remember her always looking peaceful as she sang, like she was content, happy with just how everything was.'

'That she was,' Horace said.

'That's partly why we named her as we did,' Geraldine said. 'The first night after I gave birth to her, I was lying in bed at the hospital, wide awake, trying to think what we should call her. I walked down to the room where she was being kept, and tucked up in all these little blankets was this little bundle, tiny little thing she was. The only bit of her you could see was her face, and'—she gave a small giggle—'she looked like she was smiling.' Geraldine was now smiling too, so much so that her face became briefly unrecognisable. 'I know they say newborns can't smile, but I could have sworn there was this little smile on her face and I knew, I just knew to call her Meredith . . . Merry . . .'

'She was always a joyful person, our Merry, in every way,' Horace said.

'Wherever she is now, I'm sure she is smiling still,' Geraldine added tenderly.

Alex rolled the shiny apple back and forth in his hands. The thought of the only image he had left of his mother, the adored photo of Christmas morning, sent a radiant rush of affection through every swelling vein and vessel. 'I'm sure she is.'

*

Stacks of paperwork in the bedroom where everyone now lived and worked between their trips to the library made it difficult to determine whether the group had finished unpacking or not. So high were the paper towers that Alex didn't notice Winton contained within a fort he had built, nor the children tucked away in the corner of the room reading their books. Alex sat down on the bed beside Ambrose.

As he shared with her some of the sentimental stories of his mother he had heard in the second week of their visit, Ambrose told of their latest theories as to what the Heirloom could possibly be. As he listened to her speak, he could tell that things were still not quite right. It was as if they were in some foreboding recess of a cave. Outside the bubble of their conversation, Alex could see Evie and Irwin. Although sitting next to one another on the parchment-filled bed, each was acting as if the other had no less existed than been revoked of all their parental privileges - it was suddenly *that* serious. Even Daniel and Felicity looked up at their parents with caution.

Dinner that evening, as expected, was a soundless minefield. It was as if the table itself had become no man's land, and the shots of words or the grenades of a cough or even a sneeze would condemn the offender to some ungodly fate. Horace gave Alex a sly, uncertain glance as everyone left after washing up, but worrying as it was, he forgot about it when he sat down with his grandparents and the tales and tea began to flow.

The Christmas when Meredith accidentally pulled down the Christmas tree; the Easter when Aunty Lucinda made a velvet cake filled with so much red wine that it sent the adults into drunken fits of uncontrollable laughter; the trip to the zoo when a young Meredith ran around opening all the pens to set the farmyard animals free, thinking they deserved better. The list went on. The birthdays, family holidays, packed days out and rainy days in; every moment of his mother and father's life was dated, chronicled and shared with resounding pleasure.

The orangey light of the early hours was breathing potential into the day when the stories finally came to a close. Geraldine covered the sleepy Horace with a throw and kissed Alex on the head before wishing him goodnight and heading off to bed. Alex had been so lost in the past that he'd forgotten for a moment about the tense atmosphere he was returning to. Before his foot touched the landing, however, he heard the dull mumbling of voices. Evie's stricken voice became clear, and Alex's hand froze reaching for the door handle.

'We can't tell him, not yet!'

'It isn't fair to ruin his time here with his grandparents!' Winton added tensely.

'We agreed it would be now. We all agreed and it must be so,' Ambrose said. Alex's heart stopped for a second.

Irwin cleared his throat. 'We have dug this far, too deep, and it isn't fair. He is far more involved than he knows, and he ought—wait! Hear me out—he ought to know. We agreed before we came here that this would be the best time to do it, to allow him time to recover!'

'I feel sick,' Evie said as she paced.

'You have to tell him,' Arvaeneous begged.

'We can't,' Winton argued.

'You must!'

Gasps filled the room as Alex entered and closed the door firmly behind him.

'Well you had better get talking,' he said.

*

Every person's face was half lit by the light from the Elongress, but it was the other halves that Alex was now most interested in. One by one they looked everywhere but at him. A minute passed and no words were spoken.

'We'll sit here all night if we have to,' Alex demanded, as though their collective parent.

Evie plunged her head into her hands but it was Irwin who eventually spoke first, with a detectable lack of authority to him.

'You have to understand why . . . why we could not tell you. Please give us an opportunity to explain our reasons. We were scared of how you would react. We couldn't tell you without knowing that you had someone to turn to when you heard—'

'You keep talking, but you're not saying anything,' Alex said disappointedly. 'Just tell me.'

Irwin got shakily to his feet and walked over. Dread crashed down over Alex with each trembling blink. 'The truth is, Alex . . . the real reason we were imprisoned for all that time, was . . . was . . . because of you.'

The last three words were so simple yet preposterously complex. Alex forcibly squeezed them through the struggling, choking machine of his brain. It was only after a minute that Alex remembered that the overall crushing sensation he felt was partly caused by his lack of breathing.

'But Whitsnare imprisoned you because he thought you had the Heirloom. That's what you said! That's what you told me!'

'We were all there because he wants to find you. He thinks you have the Heirloom,' Irwin hesitantly concluded.

There it was again: the unrefined, savage truth. However this one superseded every other in every single way. Jaw shivering, breath ripping in and out of his body now he let it, Alex's heart was racing faster and faster, and felt like it was going to explode.

'You have t-to understand, Alex,' Evie said from the chair beside the Elongress. 'Please see that we could not tell you from the start. We were trying to protect you, to—to keep you safe!' Her father put a hand on her shoulder. 'Th-they-they . . .' She paused and regained control. 'They imprisoned us because they thought w-we could lead them to you. They are certain that you have the Heirloom.'

'But . . . me?'

Devetta, who had been lurking amongst the group, spoke in her typical flat voice that for some reason made Alex want

215

to bellow his frustration at her. 'He knows we are with you. He imprisoned us, to find you, to get the Heirloom. But he framed us before we ever came into contact with you.'

'He must have thought we had already come back and met you before they framed us, but it-it wasn't until *after* Arv and the brothers released us from the prison that the Evispen brought us to you,' Evie said. 'To the night we first met.'

It was the real reason why Thomas and Stephanie had been waiting at his house, he realised. Why they had known that he might be with Devetta and why they had attempted to dispose of her before turning their attention to him. Everything was falling perfectly into place around him.

Why Whitsnare could possibly believe that he had the Heirloom no one in the room could guess. Neither could anyone possibly answer why the other people had been locked away in the prison - with them all being from the same time as the Evergreens there was no chance that Alex could have met any of them.

Alex's trembling legs could only carry him the few steps to the window. He latched on to its edge. The final piece of what this all meant finally become apparent. Alex could have wagered his life that he was going to be violently sick, but he managed to speak the words. 'So th-the the night we first met, those men—they really came to my house for me?'

'Yes, Alex, I'm afraid they did,' Arvaeneous said from behind him. 'Thomas confirmed it when I was tailing him and Stephanie in the weeks before they found you.'

'B-but still . . . my uncle was right?' Alex said between sharp draws of breath. 'They were after me, and he was right to keep me away for all this time?'

In the window, the black reflection of Arvaeneous nodded, and Ambrose said, 'Yes, he was very much right to keep you away.'

Alex began to choke as he sobbed, knocking his head against the window over and over. All his second-guessing, all the arguments with his uncle—each memory took vicious swipes at him. Guilt and regret detonated within him, one after another in an endless chain reaction. He finally managed to formulate words and said in a gasp, 'Don't you blame me? You were put in that prison because of me. If it weren't for me you wouldn't have been put through all the . . . through everything!   They framed you to get you, to find me. *Don't you blame me?*' he shouted before swallowing rather forcefully.

'No, no we don't blame you,' Winton calmly replied.

'WHY NOT?' Alex screamed as he spun around to face them all, now tightly compact around the Elongress. 'How could you not blame me? I am the reason why you suffered all of that! Why countless others went through such pain and misery! Why aren't you angry at me?'

'We don't blame you, love, not a single one of us,' Evie said, and she moved to him, her hands stretching out from behind her cuffs. 'It was Whitsnare who did all of that, all of this.' She hugged him tenderly, pulling him in tight almost as if to prove that he would not break under her caress. 'You are going to get through this. You need to know that we are all here for you. We are all in this, and now'—Evie sighed—'and now you know.'

Alex wiped his face and squinted. 'I need to think,' he said, wriggling free. His mind was already rewriting itself, trying to figure out what all of this meant. He left abruptly and slid shakily onto the sofa in the lounge below. Voices and tiptoeing footsteps continued upstairs for some indiscernible length of time before eventually shrinking away. It was only then that Alex could begin to think straight.

But the only thing he could think about was what would have happened had his uncle not kept him away. Where would he be now? More fittingly, how long would he have lasted? As much as Alex knew there was little use contemplating what could not be changed, the bone-chilling images flooded his tired, weeping mind. Distinctive images of him being locked away in the putrid penitentiary; of being out in the cruel, cold snow that night and vanishing like his parents before his thirteenth birthday.

No, Alex told himself sternly, what had happened had happened, and that was that.

— CHAPTER SIXTEEN —

Only Ever You

Prickles of sunlight pierced the fractured barn roof, causing the dust particles in the air to flame into existence and keeping Alex transfixed for hours. The mask of dried tears upon his face told him that he had been crying, but by some miracle, he had managed to sleep. Now awake, ruined with exhaustion, Alex closed his eyes and breathed in deep.

Up the decaying ladder to the small area above, there lay Alex's past. A shock such as the one he had received the night before had sent him flying up the steps and to giving every toy and game a fresh new purpose. Small cars drove all around him; fields of figurines battled and fought; families of stuffed toys came alive in his hands; pens ran colourful mile upon colourful mile over discoloured and crumpled pages. Everything came back to life, and Alex felt safe in his immaturity, protected in his childishness and ultimately, lost in his past.

When Geraldine's head popped up at the top of the ladder and she came to sit with him, Alex was certain she knew what had happened—no doubt she'd heard the colossal argument the night before. To the least of his expectations, she asked, 'Do you understand much about what Abraham had to do over the years to keep you safe?'

Alex moved to sit on one of the small chairs beside his grandmother. 'All I know is that he kept me hidden away. He never said anything about—'

'He did far more than just keep you hidden and safe,' she replied certainly.

'I don't really know . . .'

Geraldine straightened herself and fiddled with her apron. 'Well, there were the lies to his friends, neighbours—to the whole world—about his missing nephew. And the fear of the repercussions that would ensue if it was discovered his campaign was founded on a lie. And then having to strip his nephew of his life, and the torture of the thought of those men coming after you. All this on top of actually losing his brother and sister-in-law, and then your aunt, while trying to provide for you. Can you see?' she tenderly implored. 'Can you understand just what he has been through?'

Alex now saw his own concerns as infinitesimal in comparison to his uncle's. And to make him feel a hundred times worse, Alex could not recall having ever thanked him once for all that he had done.

'You're right, he has been so strong. And he was right to keep me away,' Alex said, rubbing his drowsy eyes before turning to Geraldine. 'Everything has changed, Nan . . .'

And so, Alex shared the unsettling revelation. The secret was still setting in; it continued to sink through the thick substance of his emotions, through his earlier fling with anger and an evening spent with sadness to the blistering regret with which he would now live, now that he knew he was the reason why everyone had been imprisoned.

As Alex relayed the details, he could see much further into everything. The path ahead remained as fathomless as ever, but that which he had taken was now clearly signposted at every event and intersection. Why Evie had charged ahead to speak with Devetta the night they met her; why Winton had prayed that his daughter have strength for *him*; all the secrets cut short the moment he walked into the room—it was all clear.

Geraldine's cheeks had turned an unsettling colour of purple, and her large hands kept fidgeting in her lap. 'What does this mean with . . .'

'My parents?' Alex said, finishing her question. 'I know it looks like their disappearance is connected to all of this if I'm the one these people wanted all along but'—he placed a hand to his chest—'I have so much hope that it isn't.

'The night the Evergreens returned to me I told them I felt like I had taken the long way around to seeing them again,' Alex said, his voice quivering. 'And all night I've been thinking . . .' He looked to the cracks of light in the roof above and then back to his grandmother again, beaming a sad smile. 'Well, what if it's just that I have to take this long way around to see my parents again?'

*

A small letter left on the kitchen table that morning announced in the tiny squiggles of Winton's handwriting that Arvaeneous, Devetta and the Evergreens had left Alex in the exclusive company of his grandparents. They would return on the eleventh hour seven days later, and so, all over again, Alex gave in to the riches of his grandparents' care.

But the days that followed, though spent on the joyous tasks of the farm, were tough for Alex to bear. The absence of his greatest friends was like a hole punched right through him. As each day drew to an end, he felt as though his newfound purpose—helping Devetta and the Evergreens to freedom—was slowly draining away. Whenever Alex was alone he found himself feeling vulnerable and irritable; the guilt he felt knowing he was the reason everyone had been imprisoned and the relief at knowing Abraham had been right to keep him away continued to tip and sway the scales.

On the first day of their guests' departure, Geraldine and Alex walked to the far edge of the woodlands. Tucked amongst the threadbare bushes was a small alcove that overlooked the undulating fields beyond. The grass stretched down and then swept up far away. It was as though they were standing on the precipice of a long, smooth valley.

A small herd of white horses roamed freely across the plains and Alex paused to admire them. It was the first time he had seen the animals with his own eyes. With their muscular bodies, candyfloss manes and flicking, ropey tails, to watch them was a privilege that he in no way took for granted.

'Do you know what I've realised the most since being here?' Alex asked when Geraldine had finished speaking about how often she'd walk out to this viewpoint over the years. She turned to him. 'I've seen just how much you fill your life with my parents. They are such a big part of your life still, and it makes me realise how much Abraham and I shut them out. It's too painful, so we don't speak about it.'

'Every day I make sure they are with us,' Geraldine replied. 'I see something and I think, "Merry would love that," or "William would find that funny". She lives through us now. They both do. They are a part of us just like you are and will always be a part of them.'

'But you cherish the past, you surround yourself with it. Back home, everything is locked away in a chest and never talked about. It's too difficult to face,' Alex sighed, 'it's too sad to relive.'

Geraldine's head dipped. 'That makes me sad, that really does,' she said. Their eyes met, and within only a second Alex knew exactly what she was going to suggest.

'But I can't look back. I can't . . . And if i'm being honest with myself, I know that it's already started,' he continued, watching the horses walk towards them. 'Here, I've been surrounding myself with their lives, like you both do, and as fantastic as it's been, I mean, truly amazing'—he touched her arm, signalling his profound joy—'it's just—'

'If you begin to remember, then you fear you will forget?' Geraldine finished. 'With hope such as yours, you don't dare to remember the past so as to never risk forgetting about what the future could hold,' she said.

Alex hadn't thought of it like this, but these were the exact words he had been unconsciously working towards.

'It's always there, everything before,' Geraldine said as one of the horses wandered close to them, and she stretched out her hand invitingly. 'If anything, take comfort from that.'

*

The patter of rain on the roof and the song of wind chimes from the porch kept Alex company as he sat beside the small window overlooking the farm. The walls of the bedroom had seemingly crept away over the last seven days, making Alex feel gradually tinier within them as the room became devoid of all purpose. When the twitching hands of his watch reached the eleven o'clock mark there was an abrupt *crack!* and the Elongress appeared in the middle of the room. Evie emerged and then, quite unexpectedly, the doors clamped back together, and with another whoosh of sound, the Elongress disappeared.

'Hello,' Evie whispered.

Wearing a long white gown beneath her coat and wrapped in a scarf with small dots moving upon it like a slow dark rain, she nervously tiptoed to Alex. They hugged for a good long minute before sitting down on the bed. Although Alex had not expected her to explain herself, she immediately did so.

The true reason why their ultimate secret had been kept from Alex was revealed to be twofold. Not only had it spared Alex's feelings, but just as importantly in the Evergreens' eyes, it meant that Alex had not felt obliged to help them as a reflection of his guilt. It was a choice they had wanted him to make for himself before imparting such devastating news, and one that he had undertaken completely of his own accord.

'None of us felt the guilt you likely expected we were feeling after you told us your uncle believed you were in danger,' Evie said, the tight curl of dread in her lips only gradually sinking away. 'Although to you it must have looked like we were to blame for leading those men to your house that night and making Abraham think he needed to keep you safe, we always believed that Whitsnare's men had been there for you. And so when I started crying when you told us about your uncle's keeping you away it was not tears of regret, Alex, as you no doubt imagined,' she said compassionately, 'but tears of relief. *Relief.*' Evie slipped off her scarf and set it beside her. 'Abraham was right to keep you away, and because of that you are safe—have been for all this time.'

Wiping her eyes, Evie then spoke about the promise that Alex had overheard the family secretly discussing back at the Clockhaus. After Alex had revealed his troubled past, Irwin promised that they would tell Alex their secret before the end of the month. Finding the right time, however, had not been easy. Knowing Alex would need someone to fall on when he was told, and discovering when they moved into the Clockhaus that his uncle might not be strong enough to be that person, they knew the time with his grandparents would be the perfect opportunity.

'We always wanted you to know the truth, Alex. It was always our intention.'

Again they hugged, and Alex could feel Evie trembling.

'As much as it pains me to say,' Evie continued, 'there was never any mention of your parents in all the time we were imprisoned. They only ever wanted you, Alex.' She sat back and, for the first time, stared straight into his eyes. 'Only ever you.'

Alex slipped out his most cherished photo from beneath his pillow and passed it to Evie. 'That's them, my parents,' he said proudly.

'I recognise them from the many photos your grandparents have around the house,' Evie said, lifting the photo closer to her.

Alex felt a smile pulling at his mouth. 'I dream of them all the time, what it would be like to see them again, how it will feel. Not when I go to sleep, necessarily. When I close my eyes I often have nightmares of the years since they left.'

'We all have difficulty sleeping with what has been and gone. At the root of every nightmare is a tremendous fear of something,' Evie said quietly. 'I can never escape that prison, that place—for me, it's always there. And I worry about the children too, of course. That I can't keep them safe, that something will happen to them.' Her voice broke off and she cleared her throat. 'That *he* will find them.'

'It may sound strange, but I've grown to fear the Clockhaus,' Alex said with a short laugh. 'Fear that I'll never be able to escape it.'

Evie was still staring at the photograph in her hand. It was as though she was letting the image evolve in her mind, delving into the idea, the possibility, of what it would be like to meet them and what kind of people they were. 'I find that we all dream of a better world in one way or another,' she said. 'We are creatures of ambition, of yearning. We can find it in the darkest moments of our lives, that tiny little light.' She pinched her finger and thumb together. 'Somewhere inside us, it's there. A modicum of hope.'

'Can I ask . . .' Alex paused, wondering whether his question might be too personal. 'What do you feel hope for?'

Over the photograph Evie's eyes shone like sparkling gems. They were vast tunnels within two magnificent glowing rings, drawing Alex in.

'You look so very much like your father,' she finally said, flicking her gaze back and forth between him and the picture. 'But . . . no,' she said politely as she passed the frame back to him. 'That's not who I see when I look at you. Every time I see you I still see him.'

'See who?'

'You're still that little boy under the table, Alex. I can't help but see him the second I meet your eyes.' Evie paused to think. 'It was only when I saw you again, properly saw you in that trench in the woods, that I realised we couldn't tell you our secret, not for some time. As much as I pressed my fingers to my lips for you that night, I was also silencing myself from telling you our secret.'

The light rain above grew louder in Alex's head as the memory of the cold squall made him shudder. It was a moment that now felt like a whole lifetime ago.

'But why does he think that I have the Heirloom? How could I *possibly* have it?' Alex asked.

'We don't know. That is the truth—the absolute.'

A snap in the air signalled the return of the Elongress and everyone Alex had been looking forward to seeing again. Apologies met forgiveness, and things were already back to the strange new normal by the time they'd all moved down to Geraldine and Horace in the kitchen. Rounds of drinks were served for the thirsty travellers, and preparations for dinner quickly began.

Alex was washing his hands at the sink when Ambrose appeared at his side humming a song to herself. She appeared far more free-spirited now that the truth had been declared and the secret no longer held any control over her.

'I wanted to apologise in person for not telling you the truth over these past weeks,' she said in a quiet but more confident voice. A fleeting look of shame dulled her expression for a brief moment. 'I felt very much that we should have told you everything from the start. I vowed to myself that I wouldn't talk about the prison at all,' she said as her fingers studied the velvety roses on the window ledge. 'I decided to remain silent because I feared that the truth would slip out before I could even stop it. It was just like you said yourself about talking to your uncle.'

Again, another piece slotted perfectly into place.

'I don't blame you for the secret,' Alex said. 'None of you. How could I, when I'm keeping the truth about you all from my uncle? You did it to protect me, just like I'm doing for him. Plus I wouldn't have been able to handle the truth from the start, so I am incredibly thankful. I still trust you all, even more than before.'

When their meal lined the table and everyone was ready to tuck in, Alex stood up and announced that it was time for them to return to Abraham, the following morning, and for him to be told the whole truth.

Geraldine then stood and looked around the table at her guests. 'Although there is great sadness in your stories, there is also such wonder, and I feel blessed to have seen some of the things you have shared with us. So very blessed. And of course, you were all a part of bringing our wonderful grandson back to us.'

'And we raise this toast to you,' Arvaeneous said generously, also rising to his feet, 'for your care and your kindness. To it knowing no end!' he cheered and everyone clinked glasses in merriment.

'To it knowing no end!'

Dessert was delivered to the middle of the table in a large glass dish. Geraldine removed its lid to reveal Meredith's favourite course to its salivating audience. 'A little something I made earlier, as they say,' Geraldine said.

'Who says that?' Irwin whispered to Evie at the other end of the table.

'Haven't a clue,' she replied.

The strawberries Alex and Horace had picked and sliced up the day before were fanned out upon the top of the three-tiered cake. Generous slices were passed out around the table, which was met with an overwhelming appreciation from everyone as they tucked in. Alex took a large bite and felt a gush of sweetness flood his mouth.

For one night only, the washing up was left to itself, and as Alex sat down to another feast, this time in the form of his grandparents' tremendous stories, he extended the offer to the remainder of his guests.

'You are more than welcome to join us,' Horace offered to the group, and so Arvaeneous, Devetta and the Evergreens amassed around the two storytellers until the floor was no longer visible. 'Oh, you have to tell them about how Merry used to commandeer that sheep she took a shine to, and how Aunty Hilary chased her all around the pen. Oh! And what about when she—'

Geraldine raised a hand. 'Let's start at the beginning,' she said, with a tempting grin. 'Let's start with how your mother and father first met.'

With a brand new story, and surrounded by his greatest friends again, Alex had never felt so charged before, electrified by his happiness. The more he thought about it, the more he realised that his grandparents' evenings spent in their memories resembled the Evergreens' grouping themselves around an Ephemor, stringing recollections of a more pleasant past together before them. Feeling an odd sense of completion within him, Alex knew that an Ephemor was not required to bring memories back to life again; nights just like this, with an eager voice and a vivid memory, were perfectly sufficient.

*

Their time spent with Alex's grandparents had only truly come to an end when after breakfast the following morning Arvaeneous declared the sad words: 'It's time to say our welfares and farewells.'

'So this is it?' Horace asked as everyone in the bedroom hovered around him and Geraldine. 'It's time?'

'I'm afraid it is,' Alex replied.

One by one everyone stepped forward to say goodbye. Tears were pouring down Geraldine's face before they had even started, but Horace held up relatively well. 'Still got the taste of those honey-whisked eggs,' he said, smacking his lips as he shook Winton's hand.

'They grow on you.' Winton chortled. 'Keep at them.'

Finally, Alex took Grenadine's hand and then Horace's, creating a triangle. Horace squeezed Alex's hand particularly tight, and Alex looked at him.

'You know, watching out that window every day isn't the only way you may see your parents again.'

Alex knew in an instant the point he was making, and he shook his head. 'I can't . . . I can't. I know what you're thinking.'

'I know you can't, not now maybe. But, do you think you ever will? Go back to that night? . . . Find out what happened to them?'

'I don't know, but I have to find them *now*. That's what I have to focus on.'

'Please do one thing for us, Alex,' Geraldine insisted, gripping his other hand. 'Please remember that you are not forgotten. You may have been lost for all this time, but people didn't forget about you or your parents.' She pulled him in one final time before Horace replicated the embrace and Alex lowered into the Elongress packed with trunks and passengers alike.

'You are safe,' Geraldine said quietly. 'And now we know.'

The Evispen was passed along to Arvaeneous, and the lid slowly began to close.

'Safe trip to you all,' Horace said.

'Travel well, my love,' Geraldine added as their tearful faces were shut out. Before Alex could even wipe his eyes, the Elongress lurched upwards, their stomachs plummeted, and they were sent spiralling through the continuum.

— CHAPTER SEVENTEEN —

Another Way to Remember

'You're back!' Abraham cried out. He lunged from his armchair to grab his adored nephew at once. 'You're back, you're back!'

As Alex examined his uncle he could see nothing but a picture of health before him. It was hardly surprising that under Herga's nurturing care his hair was tidily trimmed and combed, the toggles of his fresh brown cardigan were correctly fastened and he was even slightly more rounded at the middle. He smiled crookedly at his guests before asking Alex in a whisper about the new face amongst them.

'He is a friend, but I'm going to introduce him after I've told you what you need to hear,' Alex said, giving Arvaeneous a nod. Abraham gulped.

As Abraham took his seat, Alex, for the first time in his life, walked over to the curtains and dragged them completely shut; knowing he was the one Whitsnare was truly hunting, he knew he had to start taking his own safety seriously. Alex then sat down opposite his uncle, took a deep breath and gradually placed one word before the next to tell the collective story to date.

In the rawest detail the truth was unveiled. Saving nothing but one crucial piece of time-travelling information for later —so as not to completely overwhelm his uncle—Alex told, at last, of the true reason why the forty-eight souls had been buried in the formidable prison.

At once, all colour evacuated Abraham's face. 'They want you?' he stuttered. 'It . . . it's true?'

Alex looked into his uncle's wide, bloodshot eyes. 'Yes,' he regretfully confirmed. 'They've been searching for me all along.'

Two minutes, three; Abraham said nothing. He gripped the sides of the seat as if his whole world were crumbling away around him. The veins in his eyes bulged like hundreds of swelling rivers, and his body shook. Finally, he stuttered, 'Wh-what am I to say to that? . . . You've just confirmed my greatest fear.'

'. . . Yes'

'B-but th-that also means—'

'It means you were right to keep me away for all this time.'

Abraham flew back in his armchair as though he had been hit by a bus. His face flooded with tears and his hands wrung his hair in despair. 'Can you imagine,' he cried, 'just how many times I-I told myself that I was doing the right thing? How many times this stupid old man told h-himself that he was doing the best thing he could do, keeping you away even when there was no sign of danger?' Abraham gave a heavy, shivery sigh. 'I always believed I was right to keep you away, but—but to hear someone agree with me, to say that it was *the right thing to do?'* Abraham shook his head. 'It's just, it means more than I can say.'

'I know,' Alex said consolingly, leaning in to take his hands. 'I know. The only reason I'm here is because of you, and I can only thank you so very much for everything you have done. Please don't feel sorry about what you did,' he said. 'You have been so strong and I am so proud of you—so, *so* proud!' Alex leaned in and hugged his sobbing uncle tight.

When Abraham finally pushed himself to his feet, he hobbled to the group silently gathered on the sofas. 'It makes me so sad that you are here because of such terrible circumstances,' he said. 'And there are no words I could possibly say that would pay you the respect and gratitude that you truly deserve.' In a most uncharacteristic move, Abraham then made his way around the group, reaffirming his gratitude to each of them with a sincere message.

When he finally drew to a halt, Abraham scratched his head. He looked at Alex with a curious expression, and then around at Devetta and the Evergreens. 'Sorry, just a thought —how come I haven't heard about your escape in the news?'

'Well, this is where it gets a bit . . . unusual, a bit tricky,' Alex said, hiding his smirk.

'Tricky?'

'Something marvellous. You see, everyone here, they aren't from around here . . . *now.*'

'Are they from the north?'

At Abraham's remark, even a smile looked as though it might breach Devetta's iron face.

'Not quite,' Irwin chuckled.

'We're from another place, another . . . *time*, far from now,' said Evie. 'We are . . . from the future.'

'Surprise!' Nora shouted, causing a few laughs amongst the group.

Winton brought out the Evispen and explained how it had returned them twice to Alex, seven years apart. It took a few minutes for the realisation to make a home within Abraham, evidenced by his expression, which gradually evolved from a confused frown to an ecstatic smile.

'That's why things have been odd with you all? Because you're from the future?' Abraham gasped as he veered into exhilaration. 'You're all from the bloomin' future?'

'All of us,' Arvaeneous said, and Alex hastened to introduce him.

'Another strange name,' Abraham said. 'It's nice to meet you!'

'And most of all, you.' Arvaeneous swiftly bowed.

'Ah, the bowing game, well you may have one too!' Abraham reciprocated.

'You must have so many questions, and we will answer them,' Winton said to Abraham. 'But let's make tonight a celebration! Let us celebrate the truth and that we are here together. There is always cause for celebration, no matter the size!'

No one could have agreed more than Alex, and after Abraham had made another lap of gratitude, Ambrose politely shooed them away. 'It's a surprise for both of you! Up you go!' she said and they rushed upstairs.

Although birthdays and Christmases had come and gone over the years, they had always been markers of how long it had been since Meredith and William vanished rather than true celebrations. Cards were created, and gifts the other had long since received were rewrapped and re-purposed for the other. *Today will be different*, Alex thought as he buttoned up a smarter shirt and jumped two steps at a time up to the attic. He could feel it: tonight would be the first proper celebration he'd ever had with his uncle.

Something flew past Alex's head as he reached Abraham by the balcony doors, and a small red-breasted robin landed on the Elongress at the end of the room. It fluttered between various cabinets and stools, and then after a few laps of the room it soared up to the small birdhouse at the top of the mountain of furniture.

'We've got a new resident,' Abraham said cheerfully.

'Another one?' Alex replied.

Abraham laughed, an act Alex considered rare. 'Another one, yes.'

The robin, no longer in size than Alex's middle finger and no taller than his smallest, poked its head from the birdhouse, chirped loudly and then scurried back inside. 'Lovely little thing,' Abraham said.

The door opened and Arvaeneous stepped in clutching two scrolls of black parchment under his arm. The discernible grin on his face was justified when he explained that the scrolls had been found amongst the contents of the briefcase.

Alex gasped. 'You found out where the evidence is located?'

'Yes, whilst we were away, but there's a way to go. We still don't know where *exactly*, or *when* these places are, but with time we shall deduce!'

'When?' Abraham said. He had never had to consider such a complexity before.

The white inky knot untied itself from the first parchment, which unrolled before the three of them. A web of lines drew itself into a long, ornate room filled with many peculiar items. Tall windows poured sheaths of light over easels holding lavish paintings, glass boxes of precious jewels, towers of perfectly stacked spheres, covers protecting oddly shaped treasures and hanging tapestries.

Speechless, Abraham leaned in closer to inspect the drawing.

When the second parchment unfurled and drew itself into existence, it revealed a contrasting scene. Lines shimmered across the page one after another, tiny waves rippling around scattered objects and what looked like wreckage of some kind.

'Why would the evidence be in two locations?' Alex asked.

'I couldn't possibly say,' Arvaeneous replied as the parchments became faceless again and rerolled themselves. 'Come on then, they'll be done downstairs by now!'

The turntable was playing Abraham's favourite song, and he conducted an imaginary symphony with his fingers as they descended the final set of stairs. They turned around to find the living room completely transformed.

A great banner with bright, dancing words was draped above the steps to the kitchen: *To Celebrating That We Are Together What We Are Not Apart*. On the side cabinet sat many glass bottles of lucid liquids and jars of colourful sweets. Above them, bright fireworks were exploding, raining down in slow fiery trickles, and red smoke swirled into balloons of various shapes. The children's Halpens flapped down and landed along Abraham's extended arm. Amazed, he stroked their smooth paper bodies before addressing the group.

'Thank you! Thank you so much! We have never had anything like this—ever!'

Nora had in her hand one of the peculiarly shaped light bulbs from the plaque Alex had spotted in their house. It was repeatedly glowing and fading. She held it out to him. 'Here, you try it,' she offered, and as Abraham took it, under her instruction, the bulb followed his commands, turning off and lighting up again.

'But how does it work?' Abraham gasped. 'I mean, how can a thought change something in the physical world?'

Irwin leaned in to answer. 'Our world changes one thought at a time, Abraham. Always has and always will. But in our time, this is quite literally the case.'

Ushered under Winton's wing to the rows of bottles and jars by the front window, Abraham was poured a glass of orange syrupy liquid. Winton also passed Alex a glass. The sweet flavours fizzed and popped on their tongues as though they were swallowing a handful of sparklers.

'That's Cruncrackle—very sweet. A personal favourite,' Winton said, setting the golden bottle back down.

'Let them try Applins!' Daniel squealed as he picked up one of the jars rattling on the side bench. The contents of the jar were whizzing around in a blur of green and yellow. Prising it open, Daniel managed to grab two sweets that shot out, and passed them in a closed fist to Alex and Abraham.

'Go on, quick! Before you lose them!' Winton said.

The sweets hopped from their hands to their tongues and then stopped moving, cracked open and released a burst of what tasted to Alex like apple.

Abraham gave a contended sigh. 'Custard!'

'Apple or custard, you get one or the other!' Daniel said.

'So, Abraham, I have to ask you about your vinyl collection over here,' Winton said, and they walked over to the bookshelf talking animatedly.

'You must be most delighted that Abraham now knows the truth,' Devetta said, appearing at Alex's side as he sat down on the staircase. Alex turned and studied her face, as he found himself doing from time to time, in search of her feelings. As far as he could deduce, Devetta appeared peaceful, possibly content, but he could only as much as guess at her ungiving expression.

'I am, yes. Very happy. This day is long overdue.'

There were already signs of a solid friendship forming between Winton and Abraham as they chatted by the bookcase, but the latter looked most confused by their conversation.

'You just made that up didn't you?' Alex heard his uncle say.

Winton set down his handful of vinyls. 'What? *Collywibbles*?'

'Yes!'

'No, I didn't! It's the feeling of hundreds of excited butterflies in your stomach!'

'You mean *collywobbles*,' Abraham said, tutting.

'No, collywobbles are when you feel queasy or nervous. Colly*wibbles* are when you feel rather exhilarated.'

'Come on you're making up words.' Abraham chuckled. 'You're pulling my leg!'

'I am not being contrafibulous!'

'See! Right there!' Abraham looked around to anyone who would listen. 'Making up words!' They broke into a fit of laughter.

'They will get along swimmingly,' Devetta said.

That much was true, for as the sun slowly sank away and evening dawned, the Clockhaus did not darken. The bonds between Abraham and his guests grew only stronger as they had their first unrestrained conversations. The Evergreens talked of their ambitious search through history for the Heirloom, and their discoveries to date. After Felicity displayed her *Big Book of Butterflies* and Ambrose showed Abraham the printed chrysanthemums upon her dress, which were beginning to bloom, Abraham took a seat on the sofa appearing rather astonished. The Evergreens then made their way into the middle of the room and, as Alex expected was customary in their time, offered to share their memories with him.

'Think of it like hearing a story but actually getting to live the moment itself,' Evie said, glancing at Alex; they both knew how much Abraham was going to enjoy this.

'It's another way to remember,' Alex told his uncle.

'Well in that case it would be an absolute honour,' Abraham replied, and so the memorandia began by generous donation.

Abraham found himself in a memory of London at night. As per Winton's magnificent remembrance, the marble winged horses of Westminster soared about a black wet sky. A sunrise over the snow-capped Fortuna-Lysia mountains, a memory from the group's recent days away, was bestowed by Ambrose. Evie's memory of the painted cliffs of Dover followed, to Abraham's ecstatic applause.

Then, with a serving of cherry tea from the Quottle, Abraham spotted an empty golden frame leaning by his bedroom door and cocked his head.

'Ah, good thinking! We only picked that up recently,' Winton said, 'shall we get a canvas of us all?'

Arvaeneous offered to do it for them, and the rest of the group merged in the middle of the lounge and organised themselves for a portrait. The frame shrunk to fit comfortably within Arvaeneous' hands, and Alex snuggled into Evie at the edge of the jovial gathering. As she pulled him in closer, he caught a glimpse of something white in her opposite hand. It was her Ephemor: a white metallic-looking feather. Its soft tips began to glow.

Alex's insides tingled as he stared at it. Arvaeneous manoeuvred the frame about in an unintentionally comedic way, and the young girls' uncontrolled giggles filled the air— Evie had chosen this very moment to remember, to return to and to cherish for the rest of her life. As thousands of tiny threads began to weave from the four walls of the frame into its centre, creating the picture, Alex realised just how precious moments like this were, and gave the biggest and brightest smile possible.

*

The landing was unusually populated with people when Alex left his bedroom the following morning. Devetta and the Evergreens were huddled together at the top of the stairs, peering down through the banister at the scene unfolding in the lounge. Curious as to what was happening, Alex sat down amongst them.

'Abraham's been there since five o'clock this morning, when Arv made the mistake of fetching a drink,' Irwin said. Alex spotted the two men sitting by the bookcase, Abraham asking excited questions about the future whilst Arvaeneous struggled to keep his eyes open. 'What number are we on now?'

'Eighty-six,' Daniel said, quickly tallying up the scribbles in his notebook.

'Eighty-six what?' Alex said.

'That's the number of questions Abraham's asked so far this morning,' Nora said.

'I don't know how Arvaeneous has kept going,' Ambrose said.

'Poor bugger,' Winton mumbled. 'Although I'm surprised you weren't the same, Alex!'

At these words Arvaeneous spotted the crowd on the stairs and snapped awake. 'Oh look, everyone is up—come down! *Please . . .*' he begged, and so the group descended.

Abraham still hadn't finished sharing with Alex all the wonders he'd been made privy to even after everyone was dressed and ready to leave for the library. Shortly before Devetta removed the Elongress from a pocket in her dress, Abraham appeared troubled; he wandered around the lounge, occasionally glancing at the bookcase.

'Everything all right?' Alex asked,

His words instigated his uncle's next action right away; Abraham instantly retrieved a small, recognisable book from the tallest shelf of the bookcase. It was William's diary.

'I found something when you were gone, in your father's diary. A name, and an address,' Abraham said, flicking to a later page.

'Whose?' Alex rushed over to him.

Abraham held out the open book for him to see:

Phillip Trefew,
Twenty-Three Filibaur Way
Magralow
Cornwall
27.11.93

Alex read it again, this time aloud for everyone to hear.

'Phillip was a colleague and friend of your grandparents.' Abraham removed his glasses and folded them over the collar of his jumper. 'It seems your parents visited him that night, the night they left.'

Taking back the diary, Abraham flicked through the pages. 'There is hope for them,' he said conclusively.

'Yes, exactly!' Alex said.

'I know the address. Do you think—'

'We could visit him today? See if your parents went to see him?' Irwin said, completing Abraham's suggestion.

Devetta strolled forward and expanded their tiny carriage to a reputable size.

'My giddy aunt!' Abraham gasped, and he moved at once to explore the Elongress' gorgeous interior.

Once Arvaeneous had finished explaining to Abraham the basic principles of how the Evispen worked, and donated a weapon from his briefcase to Devetta, they all climbed aboard.

'Alex?' Abraham said as he slotted in amongst the group.

'Yes?'

'Alex, we're standing in a box.'

'Yes, but it's how we travel from one place to another,' he laughed.

'Oh, right, OK then . . .'

With Winton, Ambrose and the children remaining behind, they waved goodbye and the doors of the Elongress sealed shut. Abraham took the Evispen and as he fixed his thoughts it flurried with life, sending shudders up the walls of the Elongress. Then with an almighty lurch they were whisked away.

Suddenly a bellowing screech split the air, and the Elongress was flung into a deathly spin. The bodies within were crushed into the walls, the ruthless force rinsing their lungs and draining their heads.

Abraham's concentration slipped away entirely. 'What is happening!'

'Keep your mind on the destination!' Arvaeneous shouted.

The screeching stabbed Alex's ears, and he felt an unbearable sickness mounting. He clawed at the walls until—

CRASH!

The doors swept open and Devetta stepped out into an alleyway lined with trees. As everyone stumbled out after her, another high-pitched scream shrieked through the air.

'Is that normal?' Abraham shouted over the ringing in his ears.

'Oh no—it's doing it again!' Evie cried out as she snatched the Evispen from Abraham; it jackhammered in her hands.

'What does it mean?' Abraham said.

With a finger Arvaeneous drew everyone's attention to the numbers across the Evispen's clockwork face. The final tile of the current date, 29 07 2001, was twitching. It suddenly flipped backwards, and then again and again, as though counting down, until one by one, the tiles began to spin in and out of numbers and odd symbols.

'It was doing that the night we met!' Irwin exclaimed to Alex before withdrawing his weapon and scanning the pathway behind them.

The spinning cogs and intricate vessels within the Evispen hissed in rising fury, and the dull humming noise Alex recalled from the night he first met the Evergreens sounded around them. Devetta immediately shrunk the Elongress to a size just big enough to hold the Evispen. She clamped the doors shut and it was silenced, but still it shook like an overly frustrated jack-in-the-box.

'If we cannot set a date, we will be unable to leave,' Devetta concluded.

'Why is it doing this? What does it mean?' Abraham asked again.

Irwin looked to Evie and they both turned to Alex. 'It means . . . they are coming,' Irwin said.

'Just like that? We were home barely a minute ago!' Abraham shrieked.

'We need to go, come on!'

Following Arvaeneous, they charged out into the street, after which Abraham led the way down the road. Either side of them, magnificent houses and trimmed gardens rushed by until their path sloped downwards and they skidded into a crossroads. Everyone stopped except for Abraham, who bolted ahead, down the hill and up the steps to the front door of a large wood-panelled house. Arvaeneous joined him, scanning the garden for intruders, his hand hovering over the trigger-less handle of the Thunderstruck saddled beneath his cloak. Evie and Irwin were at the door seconds later, rapping the brass handle in desperation.

It was whisked open a few seconds later to reveal a short man in a dressing gown who had white hair and a matching beard. His small face scrunched up, inspecting his guests, until he slipped on his glasses to examine them in more clarity.

'Phillip!' Abraham panted.

'Abraham?' Phillip squeaked.

With no time for introduction, everyone hurried past the stunned man and into the house.

'Wh—Hey—Hello? *Hello?*' Phillip called out, but the group ignored him.

Irwin closed the door behind them. Phillip scanned his breathless guests before his gaze rested on the only face he recognised.

'Abraham, what are you doing here? What is going on?'

'We need your help. We don't have long and we can't explain,' Abraham said in a scared but firm voice. Everyone huddled in the hallway. 'I'm sorry to ask you like this, but my brother, William, and his wife, Meredith, did they come to see you? The night they vanished?'

Phillip's small face twitched. 'The night they vanished? . . . Yes, they saw me. But why? What's wrong?'

'Do you know where they went? What happened to them?' Alex asked.

Phillip laid his eyes on him properly, and instantly they flew open. 'Alex, is that—?'

'It's me, yes, but we really don't have—'

'What happened to you? I mean . . . it's you! You're alive!'

'We won't be for long unless you please answer our questions!' Evie said.

'Don't worry about me,' Alex said. 'I just need to know, my parents—do you know where they went?'

Phillip opened his mouth, but upon seeing Devetta in the neighbouring room, peeking between the plush curtains, he immediately moved to confront her. Before he could take a single step in her direction, however, Arvaeneous strode forward to block his path. 'There are people coming here who wish to do us, and possibly you, harm,' he said sharply. 'If you know anything relevant I suggest you speak right away, sir! *What* did Alex's parents come to see you about, please?'

'You mean, you aren't with them?' Phillip said, gawking at Alex.

Alex shook his head.

Phillip scratched his face. 'Well, they came to tell me about your grandparents. They said that they had passed away a few weeks before. I wasn't in the country at the time of their funeral, and so they had come to tell me about the service. I'm sorry for your loss,' Phillip said. 'But they did say that—'

'There are people entering the street,' Devetta said, stealing the moment. She moved back over to them, her vacant expression making her words more chilling: 'It is them. We must act now.'

— CHAPTER EIGHTEEN —

Unplanned Destinations

Shadows were amassing from the alcoves in the street and between the trees of the surrounding woodlands as the group flew up the stairs of the stately house, searching for a place to hide. Upon reaching the top floor, Phillip hurried everyone into the corner bedroom. He locked the door behind them and gave a short nod, as if this action had secured their safety.

'I'm afraid that really won't do a thing,' Arvaeneous said, and Phillip instantly distanced himself from the door.

Irwin peered into the miniature Elongress. 'We can't go, we can't jump—it's not doing anything!' he said and instantly everyone set to action.

Arvaeneous formed a barricade against the door using the expensive furniture in the room. Devetta helped Evie drag the large bed out from against the wall whilst Abraham darted to and fro, uncertain where to lend his aid.

Alex moved to the nearby window. Far below, men, like ghosts, were drifting into the scene.

'You too, Alex,' Evie commanded. Hastily guiding Alex over to the gully between the bed and the back wall, she positioned him between Phillip and Abraham. 'I'm not losing you, not now.'

'What else did my parents say? You were going to say something else!' Alex said, pressing Phillip for an answer as they crouched down low.

'They were seeing some old friends that night, and before you ask, they didn't say whom,' Phillip insisted. He went on to ask about who was chasing them, but Alex wasn't listening.

Visiting friends? Could that be all it was? It must be, Alex thought, clinging to the constant comfort of hope.

'Ssshhhh!'

Everyone abided Evie's command and froze, not daring to move or breathe. Footsteps were moving far below, like whispers echoing up through the floors. However unrelenting they were, no orders were shouted and no voices were heard.

Devetta leaned over the bed to the three of them and spoke her orders with volition. 'When they open that door, there will be not a single sound cast. At the moment that will announce itself, follow my actions, no questions contended.'

Her words, as ever, were a riddle, and she immediately claimed a vantage point far back in the room and withdrew her unfolding weapon. Evie squeezed in beside Abraham, and Arvaeneous positioned himself beneath the bed with the Thunderstruck primed in his arms. The door handle twitched, just before -

BOOM!

The stack of furniture exploded across the room, and three oppressors entered with fire. Red and green pulsing shots blinded their audience, punching the walls and detonating the room's costly items. Irwin and Devetta fired back, and Arvaeneous sent repercussions from the Thunderstruck, blasting in retaliation. Abraham pushed Alex down to the floor, but through the explosions Alex could see the man Devetta had referred to as Digwitch, and another whose eyes flickered in an animalistic glow. The third assailant was shot and sent flying into the hallway, and in a swift movement Alex pulled Phillip to the floor to prevent the buckling bed frame from ripping his head clean off.

Now centimetres apart, Phillip spoke directly into Alex's ear. 'Your parents said they were seeing someone not far from here!' he shouted, 'Down Hickory Lane!'

'What were they doing there?' Alex screamed back.

'I don't know!'

The Thunderstruck beneath the bed choked again, and a shockwave ripped through the air, sending the remaining attackers and the nearby piano crashing into the far wall. It was as the piano's musical screams died away that Alex caught a glimpse of Devetta reaching into a slit in her purple dress. She retrieved a glass ball, squeezed it tightly in her palm and then bowled it across the wooden floor. It rolled across the landing and disappeared through a gap in the banister.

Devetta plunged her fingers into her ears, and at once everyone followed suit. In the ghostly quietness seconds melted into minutes, but all around them things were coming to life. First twitching, and then shaking uncontrollably, it was as though the quaking Elongress in Evie's hands had infected everything around it. Pictures fell from the cracking walls as rich, broken objects quivered and rattled across the floor. The bed trembled forward, and Alex and the others behind it raced out of the bedroom, into the fracturing hallway and down the splitting stairs.

Dodging a plume of debris on the penultimate floor, Alex spotted the glass ball suspended in midair, shaking intensely, and he pushed his fingers deeper into his ears. The screams on their attackers' faces were acutely more terrifying in the absence of sound. When Arvaeneous had finished tackling a man about to attack Evie, the group rushed down into the darkened street.

'Go! Keep running!' Arvaeneous shouted as everyone unplugged their ears and set their sights for the peak of the hill.

Onwards they ran, back up the steep slope. With the sound of a thousand tree trunks snapping like toothpicks, Phillip's house came crashing down behind them. A number of bodies emerged from the debris, and upon spotting the group, began firing again. Remorseless explosions tore up the road after them, and Irwin and Arvaeneous made no hesitations in firing back.

'Alex . . .' Phillip panted, running at his side. 'Alex you need to know . . .'

'Know what?'

'Alex, your parents, what they had with them—'

'The night they saw you?'

'It was with them, it never left their side.' Phillip wheezed. 'Your father, he . . . he didn't take his eyes off it the entire time.'

'Phillip, what was it!'

'It was . . . a box!' Phillip gasped, his slippers tumbling from his feet as he struggled to keep up. 'A box, with, with no way in!'

'Watch out!' Irwin shrieked, pushing Phillip aside as a scorching red shot headed right for him. Arvaeneous delivered revengeful fire, striking one of the men to the ground.

'No,' Alex begged, his chest tightening. 'Please . . .'

'No lid to open. It was black—'

'Don't tell me this! Please don't tell me this!' Alex screamed, for it meant only one thing.

A shot narrowly missed Abraham, causing his glasses to fly from his face. Another dark, static-like pulse fizzled past Irwin and struck the upcoming wall. A split second later a third shot was fired, but there was no destruction and no sound of impact.

Phillip was suddenly ripped from Alex's hand, and slammed to the ground. Something was not right; Phillip was convulsing rapidly, terrifyingly. Their oppressors, doused in black, stopped as though to watch their victory from afar, and as Alex threw himself down to Phillip and rolled him over, the man's face began to change. His thick skin constricted, as though life were draining out of it. He was ageing before Alex's very eyes. He stretched his ghost-white hand up to Alex.

'I . . . always remembered . . .' Philip wheezed, and then he fell back lifelessly to the ground. The life force of Philip's body left with but only a sigh; he simply eased through the limits of life like breaking the ribbon at the end of a long race, and he had won. And he was gone.

'We have to go. Alex, we have to go.' Arvaeneous' demeanour was incredibly calm in the face of such disgrace.

Alex was dragged to his feet and away, wishing with all of his being that he would find before him the courage to carry on.

*

Waves of tears blurred image and colour as Alex raced on with the group, beyond the black railings they had been following and into the small park contained within them. The distress of Phillip's slipping away so suddenly, along with the revelation that his parents had the Heirloom with them the night they vanished, had brought Alex the closest he had ever been to giving up. Only the watery outline of Arvaeneous, charging beside him, made him feel safer despite his deliriousness.

The pond next to them erupted, drenching them with water grenades. They were under attack once again. Arvaeneous whisked the Thunderstruck from his holster and returned fire upon the three relentless pursuers. His colossal shots flattened hedges and carved trenches through the grassy banks before striking one of the men, sending him crashing over a nearby bench.

Trees withered black as they were hit by Digwitch's raging shots. The fleeing group charged out of the other side of the park and into Hickory Lane thereafter. When they reached a sign which read *You are now leaving Magralow*, Abraham diverted into an alleyway between the houses opposite. Up the steps into the back garden of the last house in the county, they all came skidding to a halt, too breathless to speak. By the time Alex arrived, Arvaeneous had managed to unlock the back door, and they made their way in, uninvited, to the second house of the evening.

They tiptoed through the dark, cluttered kitchen trying to block the prominent smell of gone-off fruit and withering flowers. The house reminded Alex distinctly of the gloom

Abraham's bedroom had slumped into, but the littered counters and messy floors distinguished the area as one that his uncle would never be able to tolerate.

A man dressed in a knitted jumper and holding a large goldfish bowl strolled into the dim hallway in front of the group. Immediately noticing the six bodies huddled in the dark, he scrambled backwards. A surge of water slopped over his arms. 'Please don't hurt me,' he squealed. He raised the bowl before him and its small orange occupant swam to his defence.

'Robert, it's Abraham—Abraham and Alex Priar.'

Robert set down the bowl, and his face revealed the same shock as Phillip's had upon seeing the boy who had been missing seven years. Without hesitation Abraham set about asking where William and Meredith had visited him the night they vanished. Introductions overlooked, the group was invited into the equally lightless lounge at the front of the house. When Robert flicked on a small lamp, the room was revealed to be cluttered with stacks of newspapers dating back to 1993.

'Your parents did come to me that night,' Robert said, watching Arvaeneous peer out into the street, which was filling with anxious neighbours. 'And I know where you're going with this, but I moved it a long time ago now. I did what he asked—'

'The Heirloom?' Irwin said.

'Yes, the Heirloom.'

A cracking noise from somewhere nearby made the hairs on Alex's arms spike. He snapped his head around. 'Did you hear that?'

'Hear what?' Abraham replied.

'You moved it to where?' Evie pressed on.

'I hid it far away from here.'

The lamp suddenly went out. There were shrieks from the crowd outside.

'The whole street's gone dark. I can't see where they are,' Arvaeneous said. 'We have to move.'

Alex rushed to Robert. 'Where did you move it to? I need to know where you hid the Heirloom!'

'It's hundreds of miles away from here!'

'That's not a problem,' Arvaeneous replied.

Evie opened the Elongress; the Evispen's numbers were stuttering, and occasionally stopping before rolling on again. 'The further away we get from them the better the Evispen works,' she said before passing it to Arvaeneous, who inspected it as well. With the Elongress fully expanded, Abraham, Evie, Irwin and Arvaeneous climbed inside, but stretching out his arms, Alex blocked Robert and Devetta from boarding.

'Get them back, get them safe. Right now,' Alex said to Arvaeneous.

Arvaeneous did not question him.

'Alex?' Abraham said from the back of the Elongress. 'What's going on?'

'Arv is taking you home.'

'Wait!' cried Irwin and Abraham, but at Alex's touch the Elongress snapped shut, and a second later it had vanished with a loud *crack!*

Alex hurried Robert and Devetta through the kitchen and back into the alleyway. 'I had to get them away, get them safe, but I need you, Robert, to take us to where the Heirloom is,' Alex said, relieved that he had managed to send the rest of the group to safety. 'And I need you, Devetta, to . . .' He looked at her, and she looked at him. 'Just be prepared to do something like you did back at the Phillip's house again.'

They paused at the edge of the alleyway and took a moment to catch their breath before Devetta motioned them out into the street.

'MARONE! DIGWITCH! THEY'RE OVER HERE!' yelled a voice from further up the street.

'Go! Now!' Alex shouted, and they quickly crossed the border into Merlow and raced on up the road. An army of wicked pulses flickered around them. Devetta, now the most trusted to get the three of them out alive, sent shots flying back over her shoulder.

With a glance back Alex saw that Marone, the man with the animalistic eyes, had a face filled with explosive anger. His arms swung like clubs and his feet trampled like sledgehammers. He was thickset but most agile, dodging Devetta's brutal shots one after another. 'HE WANTS YOU, ALEX!' he shouted with a cackle. 'YOU CANNOT HIDE.'

Suddenly Arvaeneous reappeared ahead, and Alex breathed a sigh of relief. He tucked the shrunken Elongress under one arm and whipped out the Thunderstruck, pointing it firmly in Marone's direction. 'You dare speak to him,' he said, his words hot with disgust. A deep grumbling creaked through his weapon followed by an enormous pounding explosion which swept Marone from the ground and crushed the abandoned cars behind him in a single swoop.

'Alex!' Evie hollered as she emerged beside Arvaeneous, and they charged onwards down one of the narrowing streets.

'I tried to tell her to stay but she wouldn't let me leave without her!' Arvaeneous said.

In a corner of the road ahead a small alleyway led the group out into a large ploughed field. Arvaeneous shot-put the Elongress a phenomenal distance, and when it tumbled upon the dirt the box expanded, throwing its light out and becoming their beacon of escape. Pulses of weapons deafened their ears and eruptions of soil showered them in dirt as they raced aboard. Evie lovingly pushed everyone inside, and the doors clamped shut. The numbers upon the Evispen had barely stopped spinning before there was a trio of explosions and a prompt *crack!*

*

The Elongress parted and the chase was afoot; Digwitch could be only seconds behind. Bitter-cold air stung their skin as they charged across the field of snow and past the farmyard pens to the village down the road. Leading them down zigzagging alleyways between houses, twice Robert paused to listen for their oppressors and get his bearings before silently proceeding. But the thick snowfall and the houses castled in white led him to misguide the group, and so they were forced to hide in a small alcove out of sight whilst he determined which way to go next.

Feeling as though cracks were etching themselves all over his skin, Alex rubbed his arms and watched as Devetta peeled open the Elongress in the crook of her arm. The numbers upon the Evispen tucked within it trembled and flickered again, resulting in anxious glances between the group. The sound of crunching footsteps closed in.

'Where is the little scubberut?' Marone called out as he appeared. His black clothing was a stark contrast to the white ice of the road. He scowled, almost salivating in the frosty air. Digwitch strolled to his side. His loyal machine was clutched in the crook of his arm, the rows of digits and shapes spinning furiously.

As Alex stood, eyes closed and breathing low, the undeniable truth of Phillip's final words pervaded him. A short shiver shot through him like a bullet, and he could have sworn that the cracks in his skin were cutting into him, through him. The pieces which had slowly reconnected over the years suddenly began to pull apart, and Alex pictured his body falling away from him. It shattered in absolute perfection, into a million pieces of glass upon the ground.

'Don't follow me.'

The words were devoid of emotion as Alex walked through the huddled group and towards the street.

'Alex? Alex what—'

'Let me go now, Evie.'

A strong grip squeezed Alex's arm; Arvaeneous had seen his intention. But in some miracle of strength, Alex tore away from him.

'Alex? ALEX! No! NO!' Evie lunged at him, careless of revealing where they hid for it was too late; Marone and Digwitch had turned towards an emerging Alex.

'Get Robert safe. Don't worry about me.'

Forcing away the many loving hand was without doubt the hardest action Alex had ever achieved. And as he dragged up his head to Marone's cackling and Digwitch's gladiatorial stance, Alex knew that this time, he was saving them all.

*

'There he is! There he is!'

Alex had only taken a few steps when the woman's voice scratched like jagged nails on a chalkboard from further down the road. She thrust a long finger at Alex and screeched, 'Bind him!'

Marone grabbed Alex and wound a thick rope around his wrists in a figure of eight. The rope then continued to move on its own, slithering like a snake and burning into his skin. Alex could not find it in him to wince or flicker with feeling.

'Did we gets him? Is he ours is he?'

'Yes, Orvitica!' Marone retorted.

Wearing a tattered black dress, which bunched heavily around her shoulders, the scrawny woman twitched and snapped her head at every small sound with short, seething breaths. Her crooked fingers rhythmically flexed and then curled up into fists. She giggled fanatically, before screeching obscenely, and Alex looked to the ground; clearly she was deranged in some peculiar way.

Before Digwitch could address Alex, a deep revving sound grumbled from the alleyway, and inch by inch the tip of the Thunderstruck triumphantly emerged. At its other end stood Arvaeneous, the evening light emphasising the contours of his drained, discoloured face.

'I cannot let Alex leave with you,' he said, wrestling to control the weapon. 'He is *not* going.'

Digwitch scrutinised the man standing defiant before him, and stepped forward. 'You were the one,' he quietly said. 'The one who set them all free.'

Arvaeneous smirked. 'That's right. You didn't get him then, and you aren't getting him now.'

'You? YOU!' Orvitica howled, her thin nostrils flaring as she scrunched up her hideous pale face. 'Kill him, Dig! I want you to kill him!'

'Do you know what a disgrace you are?' Marone said, charging forward, feasting his livid eyes upon Arvaeneous. 'What made you think you have the right to interfere with *his* plans?' He stood at the very end of the Thunderstruck, and Alex knew that if it weren't for Digwitch's presence, the man would have lunged at Arvaeneous like a savage dog.

'This man will get his day before Whitsnare,' Digwitch said, contemplating Arvaeneous' every weakness, every point of attack. 'He will feel the plight of Whitsnare's magnificent mind, rest assured.'

The Thunderstruck dipped in and out of disgruntled groans, waiting to blow down its opponents the moment its commander told it to.

Snarling at Arvaeneous, Marone finally retreated. As he turned around, Alex saw him properly for the first time and took a sharp breath. Marone's face was most terrifying; his skin was covered with tattoos that resembled a haunting white skull. The ghostly tattoos were moving; the teeth stretching high up into his cheeks were grinding; his jawbone, like a thick tree trunk, was shifting, and the thick veins weaving down his neck were pulsing and wriggling.

In a sudden and unprovoked attack, Marone punched a blistering red pulse from his weapon into Arvaeneous' chest. As Arvaeneous flew backwards, the blast from Thunderstruck shot out, wailing over plunging heads before it and chopping the crooked barn behind them right through its middle.

Alex collided with the snowy ground under Digwitch's brute force as debris came crashing down around them.

Seeing Orvitica lying only feet from him, Alex kept completely motionless.

'We have the reason for why we are here. Pick up the boy,' Digwitch ordered in a cruel and raspy voice.

With a swift yank Marone pulled Alex to his feet and dragged him away through the streets to the sound of Evie's agonising, pleading calls.

— CHAPTER NINETEEN —

Falling Through the Sky

The sunset spilled out ruby red over the town as Alex's captors escorted him through the maze of snow-drenched alleyways. He tried to look over his shoulder, to those he had left behind, but Orvitica pierced his eardrums as she screamed, 'DON'T LOOK BACK AT THEM!' and promptly shoved him to the ground. 'GET! UP! GET UP!' she then howled, and Alex clambered back to his feet. He did not look back again.

They crossed a dozen parallel streets before reaching the thick bed of woodlands bordering the southwest of the tiny village. The pain in Alex's wrists was becoming increasingly prominent. When Digwitch noticed the trail of blood in the snow, he ordered that Alex's hands be covered. Marone immobilised the handcuffs and sent a piece of material spinning around Alex's wrists to constrict the flow.

Orvitica screeched some semblance of a song as they waded their way through the frozen woodland. When she skipped past Alex, he saw that, like Marone, she too had a face resembling a skull. Although her face was half hidden by a black netted veil, Alex could clearly see the deep dark pits around her eyes, her craggy cheekbones and jagged teeth. With a twirl she raced to Marone's side.

'Hows did you know about Arvy being one who released those?'

With a disgusted glance towards her, Digwitch coolly replied, 'Whitsnare informed me.'

'And you didn't think to tell us? You didn't think to share that?' Marone retorted.

'He did not want it clouding what we are really here for.'

'Be damned what we are here for! I want to crunch that man's little neck right in my hands!'

Orvitica's face, like Marone's, twitched with madness, as though there was some sinister connection between them.

'Whitsnare charged me with the responsibility of delivering the boy to him,' Digwitch said. 'I would say that devouring that man is also one of Whitsnare's greatest fantasies.' Digwitch's head revolved almost all the way around, to look at the chained Alex. 'But I know very well how it falls second capturing you.'

Despite his dread, Alex felt a glimmer of smugness knowing how Arvaeneous had angered his captors. An opening broke free inside, allowing this feeling to spread through him.

'He showed us that day, you know, how he set them all free,' Alex said with a smirk.

'Don't you dare talk about him—' Marone began.

'You know he works for the Pr—'

'Dare speak over mine!' Orvitica shrieked, and she struck him down again with the back of her skeletal hand. Still being dragged by Marone, Alex finally got back to his feet just as the quartet arrived at the edge of a circular opening.

Digwitch stopped to assess the area. 'Get the door,' he ordered, crossing his arms behind his back. He watched as Marone moved to the roots of the gigantic fallen tree trunk which halved the enclosure and lifted up from them a gilded black door.

Digwitch then produced a clunky key, which he at once saw to fitting into the lock. He turned it three times one way and then four times the other before stepping aside.

This time Marone didn't have to be told what to do; he removed the key, turned the handle and forcefully pushed on the door. It swung open to reveal a scene identical to the one already before them, the only difference being that it was entirely snowless—a different time of the same place. Digwitch marched through the doorway and out of sight. To Alex's despair, he returned a minute later with the loathsome Thomas and Stephanie.

'So, they got you then,' Thomas said with his spiteful charm.

'I am surprised these two could pull their empty heads together,' Stephanie said, glancing disparagingly at Marone and Orvitica.

'I was here to push them into form,' Digwitch said. He turned an evil look to Marone. 'Am I going to have to drag him through myself?'

Orvitica grabbed Alex and flung him through the doorway.

Coming dangerously close to Stephanie, whose stomach was still bulging and who did little to hide the fact that she truly despised him, Alex swerved away and steadied himself.

Upon straightening up, he found that it was spring in their enclosure; there were birds singing in the branches above, and the earth flourished with tall grass and thick bushes.

With a different combination of turns, Marone locked the door behind them. Using this distraction, Stephanie placed a hand on Alex's shoulder. It was very warm, somehow verging on hot, and it gripped him tighter as it slid up towards his squirming neck. It was only when Digwitch turned faintly in their direction that she whipped her hand away.

The second Marone removed the key, vines began to grow out of the keyhole. Slithering across the door, in all directions they extended out creating the structural outline of a large square room. Leaves and petals flourished from the thick stems as they entwined around each other, and within less than a minute, a solid, unbreachable fortress stood before them. The overgrowth flexed and hardened, and as the petals fell away the thick, thorny walls—twisted like barbed wire—were revealed.

Foreseeing his master's orders, Marone unlocked the door again—this time turning it six times to the left and four times to the right—and slung Alex through into his newly crafted prison.

Stephanie strolled into the dark room, but Thomas stopped beside Marone, looking to pick a fight. 'You know what, I am losing the little patience I have for you, Marone. Tell me, will Whitsnare appreciate the state of him when he arrives? Have you *seen* his wrists? His face? I presume it was you and'—he scowled at Orvitica beside him—'this batty woman who did this? Who else.' He tutted, and the skull that was Marone's face growled. 'Don't you give me that sickening look,' Thomas spat.

Following Thomas inside, Digwitch didn't bother turning towards Marone or Orvitica as he said, 'Do not follow,' and slammed the door in their faces.

How the room had grown before his eyes was another mystery to Alex, although in the company of his captors, he was rapidly coming to expect the unexpected.

From the bulb in Stephanie's hand an electric blue light lit up the room revealing a variety of doors around Alex. Some were leaning against the spiky walls whilst others were stacked in tall piles. There were thick, wooden doors; small attic hatches; locked cupboard doors and glass windows of all varieties; doors that looked fitting as entrances to palaces and those that clearly belonged to far less grander venues. Each was encased in the four borders of a thick frame, meaning that all around Alex stood hundreds of different entrances and exits to daresay thousands of different times and locations.

With the entrance sealing behind him, Digwitch moved through the room. He placed the time machine in a metallic pouch and set it on the stack of doors, before moving to the door that all others in the room faced. It stood at the other end of the cramped room to Alex and was made of a distinguished dark wood. 'Whitsnare will knock when he is ready,' Digwitch said, stroking the carved piece.

'So where did they hide you? That family?' Thomas said as he circled Alex, his fingers long and curled like a vulture's claws.

Not knowing what Thomas was referring to, Alex remained quiet.

Thomas' top lip curled. 'We know they took you the first night you met, back to our time, their time—that's where you vanished to for all those years. We know they hid you when they turned themselves in to the Law.' He leaned down to Alex. 'I know they think they got free when they were released from that prison, but do you know what, Alex? Look at me.'

In a swift motion Thomas seized Alex's head so that his jaw sat in his palm. The four spindly fingers and the thumb opposite pressed into Alex's cheeks, and Alex knew that with a simple twist of his hand, Thomas could break his neck like a twig. Thomas' gaze drilled into Alex's. 'They will never be free.'

With a dismissive fling of his hand Thomas threw Alex to the floor and strode away.

Alex understood. Whitsnare had imprisoned the Evergreens in their time because he thought the Evergreens had in fact kidnapped him and hidden him in their time, when in fact he had never left the twentieth century. *What a distorted understanding of things*, Alex thought. He went to smile, to let the feeling conquer him, but instantly decided against it. This still did not explain why Whitsnare had imprisoned the additional forty-one people, nor just how he had known that the Evergreens had returned to Alex's time in the first place.

BANG! BANG! BANG!

Alex gasped. This was it. He was here.

Digwitch pressed his ear against the door. Thomas stepped over to him.

'Stephanie should not be here. Whitsnare may not be best pleased that she is,' Thomas said, his voice now dry and cautious.

'No, he would not like it,' Digwitch agreed, and he held out a key for Thomas to collect.

BANG! BANG! BANG!

With a passing grin at Alex, Stephanie kissed her hand, pressed it to Thomas' cheek and waddled through the door he unlocked and pushed open for her. Thomas then closed, locked and tested the door as the knocking rang out one final time.

BOOM! BOOM! BOOM!

Following a series of metallic clicks, the blue door closest to Alex unexpectedly burst open, and the bodies of three men flew upwards in their momentum and then fell, crashing to the floor.

'Mog! You're on my arm, brother! My arm!'

'I can't move, you gargantuan twit!'

Digwitch huffed as he turned his back on the unwelcome guests, but Thomas strutted over to them at once.

'I ask the heavens,' he said in a voice like grit, flinging Lamond aside. 'Every single time I see one of you'—he threw Filligus into a stack of green doors—'I wonder how the hell you are worthy, in *any way* of Whitsnare!' He heaved Mogum up to his feet and shoved him back to the floor.

'I don't know how you can say their names, Thomas,' Digwitch said impassively. 'Makes my lungs bleed.'

Alex found himself on his feet searching the men's faces, knowing they had to be the three brave brothers from Arvaeneous' memory. Evidently Whitsnare had not found out about their involvement in releasing everyone from his most adored prison.

'Well a very good, er . . . morning, is it? to you too!' Mogum replied, brushing himself down.

The eldest of the three, Lamond, like a shepherd, led his brothers to their feet and straightened the lapels of his fitted green morning coat. 'Whitsnare sent for us. There is something here that he needs.'

'We have him!' Thomas shouted.

'Whitsnare needs many things,' Lamond replied, running his hands over the surfaces of the many doors he passed as he walked through the room. 'Yes, *he* is the one he wants above all'—Lamond gave Alex only a brief look—'but Whitsnare wants many other things too.'

'Get on with it then!' Thomas ordered, glancing at Digwitch, who nodded his approval.

With dipped heads the three men began to search the room. Alex noticed that the specific doors they located had anything up to four locks built into them. In order to successfully unlock each, a number of turns one way, and then a number of turns the other way, of specific keys was required. When a door was unlocked and the passageway between two different times and two different places was made, there was a series of loud clicks and swords of light shone through the keyholes.

Alex watched as Filligus stepped through into a large courtroom whilst Lamond poked his head into what appeared to be a long chamber filled with sealed vaults. Seeing Mogum step onto the soft sands of a black beach, Alex wondered whether, if he was forced to do so, he could possibly escape through one of the doors to safety.

Thomas forced his eyes shut to contain his frustration as Mogum tripped over his own feet. 'So are you going to answer my question at last?' he said upon facing Alex again.

'Would help if you actually asked me something?' Alex replied, daring to bite back.

'Before the now late Arvaeneous came to your rescue, I asked you a question. Answer it.'

Alex was too focused on wishing that Arvaeneous had somehow survived Marone's scathing attack to give a reply.

'Do you even know why the Evergreens came back to you?'

'Why should I tell you?'

Thomas gave a twisted smirk. 'It was easy to break into their minds, you know, all those people we imprisoned. Such shallow skulls … but they told of very little about you,' he said. 'You must have had to plunge your hands so very deep into their heads to purge their memories of you. How telling that is of you, Alex, to murder their memories.' He took his time circling him once before continuing. 'So where is it, Alex? Everything that Whitsnare desires?'

'I don't know.'

'I know that you know.'

Alex watched Thomas make another lap around him.

'The problem is, Alex, that I do not believe you. Whitsnare knows you have what he so desires, and he will scour your mind until he gets what is—'

'OW!' Mogum screeched as he clasped his face. The key, having shot from the keyhole of the door that Filligus had just gone to unlock, jangled around on the floor. Alex would have found Mogum's outburst funny if a jet of water hadn't suddenly shot from the unlit keyhole.

'What the—' Lamond gasped.

'Oh, that's bad, that's rather not good,' Filligus mumbled. He immediately covered the keyhole, but the water responded unforgivingly by seeping beneath the door.

Lamond charged to the door to stop it from bursting open, but the instant he collided with it the lock and handle blew off, and then the whole door burst apart. A wall of stormy water cascaded into the room, sweeping the brothers clean off their feet as stacks of doors came falling down around them.

The icy water rose at an alarming rate, drowning Alex's ankles and crawling up to his waist within only a minute as his captors split off around him. Digwitch moved from one end of the room to the other, slicing through the water like a knife as he searched for the only machine that could grant his escape, whilst Thomas shot aggressively at their sealed entrance. Filligus fumbled to slot a key into a door floating at his waist. The door swung open, creating a floating rectangular hole. The water began surging through the hole, and Alex felt himself suddenly pulled forward. He tipped headfirst through the opening.

'Alex!' Lamond gargled, clamping onto his ankle. As Alex plunged through the opening, he found himself suspended over a stampede raging across dusty African plains. He screamed, but the rushing wind and sloshing water quite literally drowned it out. As Alex hung defencelessly over the deafening trampling of wildebeest and elephants, a hungry leopard suddenly leapt up from the valley below. Alex flung his arms upwards. 'Pull me up! Pull me up!' he screamed. The giant paws reached for him again, and Alex squirmed as the leopard's vicious jaw snapped at his ear.

As Lamond dragged him back up and into the still rising pool, a golden glint caught Alex's eye. The pouch Digwitch had retrieved opened like an oyster and he took out the device that was similar, if not identical, to the Evispen. As he utilised its power, Thomas' chaotic firing ceased and the woven floor beneath them dropped away completely. The water hurled upwards before crashing down again as they landed, apparently, somewhere entirely different.

The room flexed and creaked around them, seconds before cracks burst across the prison's walls. Lamond linked his arm through Alex's and clamped it tight to his side just in time; in a mass exodus of unstoppable power, the wall opposite the door they had entered crumbled away. Lamond, Filligus, Mogum and Alex, clinging to each other, could do nothing to stop themselves being swept away, screaming, over the edge.

The thick water dissipated into fine mist, and Alex lost his grip on the men. Tumbling free, the rotating world spinning a sickness within him, he caught sight of his broken prison perched above on a rocky mountain edge; below, a chasm of pure emptiness dragged him down with eager gravity.

Spotting Filligus beneath him, Alex pulled in his arms to descend more quickly. A violently spinning door ahead burst apart, and Alex shielded his face. Regaining his formation, he made it down to Filligus and grabbed his arm to balance out alongside him.

'What is he doing?' Alex called out, having spotted Lamond dive down and land upon a yellow door below.

'Finding a way out. Ahhh!'

'Watch out!' Mogum shouted as he flew down to them. He latched onto Filligus' other trusted hand, and they were sent tailspinning. 'Has he got anywhere yet? We haven't got long!'

A fire burst from the door Lamond had managed to unlock, instantly igniting his cloak before the ruthless updraft just as quickly extinguished it. He cast aside the door, and as Alex flew past he caught a glimpse of the vast burning city contained within it. Lamond rocketed to another door with elegant swiftness, but before he had even removed his key the door tore open, spewing a flock of black eagles into the air. They weaved and cut around them in a contagious panic.

Lush forestry and a large lake zoomed into intimidating clarity; individual trees could now be identified, and ripples upon the lake waved invitingly. Yet as Lamond soared down, he unlocked and threw forward a final door to find no immediate threat.

'That's the one! Quick, down you go, Alex!' Filligus shouted as Lamond beckoned to them.

At terminal velocity, Alex seized the door frame and pulled himself through. Gravity instantly slammed him to the ground, and he landed awkwardly on his shoulder. A second later the other bodies came crashing down around him.

'Is that it? Are we safe here?' Alex said, panting wildly.

Although they were in a dark corridor, through the doorway before them the mountains and forest continued to spin. A few seconds later, the door finally collided with the ground splicing the connection between the two locations. The mountains and the forest instantly vanished, and in their place sat the small bedroom of the house they now found themselves within.

Lamond sprang to his feet and began to search the other rooms off the corridor.

'Nothing like a good jump!' Filligus said, taking off after his brother.

'It was more like falling, wasn't it?' Mogum replied. Upon standing he bumped off the wall to follow Filligus.

'All men who jump will fall, but not all men who fall have made the jump,' Filligus called out from the study a few doors down. 'If you're going to fall you might as well jump, brother!'

As Alex got steadily to his feet and walked along the corridor, he emerged into a small living room filled with comfy-looking armchairs and bookcases that stretched across the ceiling. He watched as the patterns upon the cushions moved in a kaleidoscope of alluring shapes; as the colourful hot-air balloons upon the wallpaper floated around each other, and the authentic-looking parrot shook out its wooden wings in a dangling cage beside him. A sense of disbelief drew Alex over to window nearby as he realised the time he was now standing in.

'We're alone. Alex, are you ready? Got to get you home, haven't we?' Filligus said, poking his head into the lounge from the neighbouring room with a friendly grin.

'. . . Be right there . . .' Alex said. Stepping over to the window, he slowly cast apart the flowering curtains.

A city bathed in sunlight greeted him. Raising its many celestial, sky-scraping hands to caress the fluffy clouds, the metropolis was the most sensational view that Alex had ever seen. He felt the awesome wave of its magnificence knock him back a step.

'Hello to you too, London,' Alex said, before dashing to make its acquaintance far more personally.

— CHAPTER TWENTY —

An Empire of Dreams

The silvery hares, prancing through the shrubberies upon the hallway walls, followed Alex as he was steered by the Haipstring brothers out into the street. Stepping down to the narrow road, Alex admired the row of smooth terraced houses spreading to the skies above, each pinned by thick stone pillars and pointed black railings. Great chandeliers hung from the bridges which connected the houses high above, illuminating the thin mist clinging to the air.

'This is Old Ampleton, the edge of the Earlinfude District,' Filligus said, opening the door of a familiar metallic vehicle which was parked, floating, at the edge of the street. 'We are talking *old* old London.'

Filligus and Mogum jumped in either side of Lamond in the front seat as Alex climbed in the back, and the doors closed automatically. Alex could see that the dashboard contained many bright dials and lights. The second Lamond placed his hands upon the steering wheel, the car rumbled to life and they glided away.

The front headlights clicked on, and their journey through the crooked street became illuminated. Alex glimpsed families in the houses they passed. Two children in pyjamas joyfully chased Halpens in one room, a family sat around a table with small platefuls of food at their reach in another, and in a house on the corner of a street, the sphere of a memory encapsulated numerous generations as one.

It had taken some time for feeling to return to Alex since he had felt himself come crashing apart again, but the tips of his limbs were beginning to twitch with each revitalising pulse. When he asked just 'when' they were, Filligus explained that they had arrived in a time that the Evergreens' and Whitsnare's past selves were already in. It was the time before the Evergreens had even been framed for their crime.

When Lamond asked Alex how Whitsnare's followers, his 'malice', as they were referred to, had found him, Alex reluctantly explained his surrender, and the car shuddered.

'You surrendered to them?' Filligus gasped as he turned back to Alex. 'Why?'

'I did it because . . .' Alex turned to stare out the window, losing focus in a sleepy haze. 'Because I was broken. I found out something and it broke me. It pulled me apart again.'

'I can't believe you gave in to them. You're brave, I'll give you that!'

'It wasn't bravery,' Alex said sorrowfully. 'It was desperation.'

Evie's calls came crying through his head. To keep himself distracted, Alex changed the subject, asking the Haipstring brothers what time they were from. He was quickly assured that they were from the same time as the Evergreens: the brothers too had experienced their framing, capture, escape and subsequent journey back to Alex, just as Whitsnare and his followers had.

'Whitsnare has everything wrong, though,' Alex said. 'He thinks the Evergreens kidnapped me, took me back to their time the first night I met them, and that that's where I vanished to for all those years, but it was my uncle who kept me away! But they only met me for the first time *after* they escaped the prison!'

'Oh, we know,' Mogum said.

'Whitsnare must know he was wrong,' said Mogum, 'but he has not shared this fact with anyone.'

The car emerged into a large roundabout with a tall stone column at its centre. Alex sank low in his seat, and he could see on top of the plinth a bronze statue of a man holding out a top hat in one hand and swinging around a cane in the other. He kicked his legs about and gave a spin as the car sailed off down one of the many side streets.

Unknowing when, or even if, he might see his three saviours again, Alex took the opportunity to thank them for rescuing all those who had been left for dead in the prison. This then prompted Alex to ask how they had uncovered the prison in the first place, and as the car swung like a hammock through the twisting streets, Filligus told the tale.

To Alex's great surprise, the rescue had begun with a Halpen that had visited Filligus on no fewer than six occasions. 'It was waiting on my bedside table one morning when I awoke; it was at my window the next day; in the carriage on my way to work the morning after that,' Filligus said to Alex, who found himself in a spell of disbelief. 'It looked, mad though this may sound, as if it wanted me to follow it. So follow it I did.' Out of the city, through Rewley and even as far as Enwauld and Wyndenhame, Filligus travelled until he came to an old, derelict building that held no obvious purpose. But then he discovered what lay buried deep beneath it.

'The Halpen must have been trying to get back to its owner, one of the prisoners. Who knows whom it belonged to, but it was because of that Halpen that we were able to rescue all of those people,' Mogum said.

'We thought at first that releasing everyone would reveal Whitsnare in his entirety; we were certain! However, upon investigation, there was no incriminating connection between him and that prison,' Lamond said with a tight clench in his jaw. 'But it was undoubtedly his creation.'

When Alex wiped the condensation from the window he saw unsettling behaviour in the people they sailed past. An elderly woman hustled her two grandchildren along the road, peering around corners as she went. In alleyways, stalls and markets were closing up in a hurry. Within a dozen blocks, every window had been blacked out and the streets were completely deserted. The dark clouds above threatened thunder and Alex couldn't help but feel incredibly concerned.

'The times that we are in now are very dark times, Alex,' Lamond said in a grave voice. 'The darkest ages there have been for a long time, ever since the height of the Crowning. Mistruths and mistrusts have been uncovered in the Prisidium. There have been savage attacks. Fear is rife throughout the country, and it is about to be topped by the news that the Evergreens are vicious murderers, the first people to murder in a century of humanity's purest, most golden ages.'

'What did Whitsnare make people fear?' Alex asked. 'Arvaeneous said he made them fear something, but that's what I don't understand—what could possibly be worse than Whitsnare?'

'They fear each other,' Filligus reluctantly answered, his eyes catching Alex's in the rear-view mirror. Even Mogum, seemingly the most lighthearted of the group and twirling a small stone in his hand, turned a nauseating shade, as if he had been struck down by a gruelling sickness. 'Imagine a whole nation where you can trust no one. Your neighbour, your friend . . . your mother or your son. You fear yourself, even. Trust in nothing leads to fear of everything.'

A burst of light from the distant sunset drew the car out amongst a patchwork of colourful, seemingly endless fields. From the tallest building of the skyline, the light spread out in all directions, creating the illusion of drifting spotlights.

'Welcome, Alex, to the Illustrious City of London,' Lamond declared as the car finally glided down into the glowing city.

The buildings all around them were white, silver and cyan, like towering, sculpted mirrors. Amongst the many billboards blushing with exuberant colours, a large sign stood ahead: LONDON: POWERED BY PEOPLE. It showed a picture of a hand tipping a finger down to the tallest skyscraper, and then at once, the building and all those around it lit up in a lustre of light. Flocks of birds came shooting from the red letter boxes along the streets, and magnificent murmurations wove in and out of shapes overhead. It all felt so alive, and again, what was now on the other side of the window had been re-envisioned beyond Alex's wildest, most jubilant imagination.

Their ride through the elaborate streets of London passed timelessly. Night started upon them, and the low clouds above were injected with illumination, sending light crawling down the streets. After passing through a long tunnel of hawthorn trees, they emerged amongst the princely stone buildings of a place once referred to as Kensington. White marble horses strolled majestically in the parks. Posters upon walls flashed amber and red, but the only signs that Alex could clearly make out were the ones decreeing that all purchases made must be *Lawfully Approved for Truth*. This made Alex wonder just how an object could possibly be "untruthful" in any given way.

Leaving the eye of the city, or 'the Concourse' as it was known, they took off towards a part of the metropolis that was, in stark contrast, barely lit. Darkness painted everything, but a bright sign for *The Emeraldias* showed that they were travelling along the bottom of a large slate-rock wall. It was half as tall as the buildings they had left behind but the most distinct shape amongst the pinnacles of the city skyline.

The car swayed beneath an archway engraved with the words *THE ROCKY CAVERN* and floated progressively deeper into the great emerald rock. When the path widened far enough, Lamond pulled the car over and parked, and the four passengers exited. Lamond drew them into a thin furrowed tunnel nearby, but as Alex felt along the craggy wall, the image of Abraham burst into his head. He stopped in his tracks. *I am going to get back to him, back to them all*, he told himself, and as if following the rocky path back to the Clockhaus, he pushed onwards until they came out into the wide crevice which ran through the rock's centre.

A dim cloud above brightened and followed them, introducing detail to the archaic shoppes in the walls either side of them. A dark shoppe with a large curved front window, *Rotundas Ripley's*, housed hundreds of jars filled with brightly coloured sweets, many of which were jumping, sliming or otherwise fizzing in some delicious capacity. *Gildrick's Gloves* was overrun with hundreds of gloves jumping between cabinets and pulling down tapestries, and slithering scarves tangling themselves in knots upon the floor, as though they had escaped in the night for a secret, wild party. They walked onwards, past *The Revelry*, a shoppe that contained many elaborate frames and exploding fireworks. Passing a cafe built into a corner of rock, Alex's footsteps dwindled to a halt. The small table he could see inside was where Ambrose and Winton first met. He was certain that it wasn't only because it was late in the day that *Hurlock's Bistro* was now cold and deserted.

The scuffles of Lamond's feet ahead and Filligus' hushed warning to move up the stairwell beside them told Alex that they were not as alone as they had thought. With their breaths held, they watched as a couple dressed in long robes hurried past talking in quiet voices to one another.

'Just up here,' Lamond whispered as he began to ascend the steps. 'We are nearly there.'

From every landing small alleyways were carved deeper into the rock, each lined with avenues of shoppes, ateliers and cafes to explore. Most of them, Alex realised, were shut down or boarded up. Upon reaching the very top of the stairwell, the four hurried to the end of an alleyway called Cityscape Watch. With its cracking ruby panels and large circular window, Alex thought the final shoppe, *The Auspicioustry*, wouldn't have looked too out of place along Merlow's high street.

Lamond stroked a thin burned line upon the handleless door, gaining them entry, and the three brothers surveyed the murky interior before bringing Alex inside. Moving between the floating shelves stacked with hundreds of wrapped parcels, Alex came to the tall windows at the far end of the room. Overlooking the crevice they had walked through only minutes before, Alex spotted various vintage-looking shoppes embedded in the rocky face opposite. In the distance, the glassy capital continued to shine as the sun sat just above the horizon.

Lamond came to Alex's side with a tiny piece of parchment unfolding in his hand. 'There is something I must show you,' he said, his tone void of any particular emotion.

Upon seeing a news article shimmer into formation upon the parchment, Alex crept closer.

'You may have wondered how Whitsnare knew the Evergreens were back in your time,' Lamond said whilst moving to hold the parchment against the nearby wall. 'The thing is, he never knew they were there.' The ink from the clipping began to seep out over the wall. 'He only knew you were.'

Before them, a startling title came to spell out:

Ship Crashes into Merlow's Shores!

Columns of text dripped beneath the headline picture slithering into print, the silky liquid making the moment look alive. Alex stepped closer to inspect the picture but he needn't have, for he easily spotted the cause of concern: a young-looking boy huddled on the shoreline amongst a group of people dressed in their nightclothes. Alex gasped.

'Once the Evergreens escaped, Whitsnare was lost as to where they, and therefore for you, had gone. But through his fastidious exploration of the past he found this,' Lamond explained. 'A great ship crashing in the tiny town of Merlow - the place where you had vanished, never to be seen again? It did just beg to be found. And there you were.'

'Why didn't he go to that moment to get me? I could have been snatched! I was defenceless!'

Lamond looked back to the parchment and the ink slowly drained back into it. 'He tried, trust me, but his time machine, his Pivense, as he calls it, wouldn't let him. It is just as much a mystery to him as it is to you, I avow.'

A canvas leaning against the shelves suddenly flashed and sparked with colour, drawing Alex over as Lamond shielded his face. He turned it upright, and a rush of bold reds and deep blacks came to spell out an alarming message:

THE WANTED OF THE LAW.

THE UNWANTED OF THE PEOPLE.

The words floated above seven faces. The black-and-white portraits of the Evergreen family flashed as though they were being photographed in slow, blinding punches. Beneath their names sat the terrifying warning:

THE EVERGREEN FAMILY: ARRAIGNED ON THE INJUSTICE OF THE PEOPLE AND ITS LAW IN THE FIRST DEGREE OF MURDER.

IF WITNESSED, SUMMON THE LAW.

GIVE MIND TO YOUR VIGILANCE.

'But'—Alex shook his head—'how can the whole world just believe that these people are cold-hearted killers? How can people just believe that?'

'There is a reason, Alex,' Lamond said sombrely, facing the window again. 'A simple but incredibly dark reason, but it is not our truth to share.'

The canvas conjured such sadness in Alex; the loving Evergreen family, so innocent and pure, painted with such disgrace. Trying to focus on returning to them, Alex joined Lamond at the tall window, where he found that half of the setting sun had been blacked out.

'Wow, is that an eclipse? I've never seen one before,' Alex said.

Lamond's eyes were open wide, absorbing the remaining life-giving light. It was only after a moment's silence that he spoke. 'Did the Evergreens tell you about what happened over a century ago, when we almost managed to wipe ourselves off the face of the earth?'

'You mean the Crowning?'

Lamond nodded rhythmically. 'After we finally brought it to an end, after the bloodshed drained away through the streets, they called this country many names. So many! Valour Victorious. The Great Kingdom. But the one that they still call it to this day? The one that is scribed into the walls of all the temples and cenotaphs—do you know?'

Alex could only shake his head.

'An Empire of Dreams,' Lamond said. 'An *Empire* . . . of *Dreams*. Conjures up quite the image, doesn't it? An endless landscape of everything you ever imagined, ever hoped would be. This title is the most recognised in our time, but it wasn't bestowed upon our country because we ended the war. Oh no, it was in the Crowning's haunting shadow that we received such a title. An Empire of Dreams refers to the world that was envisioned *after* the world had ended. The title refers to how this nation persevered and rebuilt itself a thousand times stronger, into everything you saw on your way here. It became everything that people had dreamt of for their world.'

For a long minute Lamond closed his eyes before reopening them and fixing them solidly on the shrinking sun. 'You would never know looking at this city that one hundred ages ago this land was in ruins, desolate and poisoned. Barely a single structure stood upon these plains. But now, the commonwealth, look at it. The glass stretches as far and as high as you can see. And somewhere out there, Whitsnare is slowly pulling it all apart again. Gathering the crowds, churning the masses. Brewing the revolution. He is like a great swathing hammer slowly gliding through this city. Nothing stands in his way.'

The grief upon Lamond's face was painful for Alex to watch, and he felt almost as though he could relive the losses Lamond talked about through his expression alone. 'Today is the last day that people in this country will ever see sunlight,' Lamond said. 'This is the day that night will never end.'

'What could possibly do that?' Alex said.

'No one knows. We can only presume it was Whitsnare, but how he did it . . .' Lamond shook his head. 'In the coming times, the nation, the world, will come to believe that it was a result of the Evergreens' depravity, that it happened because they killed again. The world will come to call these final days the "Eve of Eternal Night".'

Together they stood, watching as the eclipse became total and a shadowy blanket descended over the noiseless city. Only a circular slither of light remained, although faint, in the sky. Lamond's fingers brushed the glass as longingly as Alex's had over the years. 'And there is it . . .' he said, his sentence wilting as the ring of light faded, stripping all windows of their final, distant shine; the halo of the Evergreens had been extinguished. Staring up at the bottomless black above, Alex noticed that there were no stars. All light had somehow been scrubbed from the sky.

In the centre of the adjoining room, which was stacked with wrapped boxes and heavy crates, Alex found a white door standing by itself. It was contained within a thick frame, which Mogum was leaning against. The bulky black key in his hand had a shimmery yellow thread wrapped around its shaft, and as he unlocked the door with six turns of the key one way and two the other, a number of clicks echoed through the room.

A light shone through the keyhole and the gap underneath the door, which Mogum then pushed open.

'There you are, home. Just a step away,' Filligus said.

Alex walked over to the frame. Through the passageway, on the other side of the street, stood his childhood home. A familiar cold sea air rushed through the opening, igniting goosebumps upon Alex's arms.

'May be a little out, I'm afraid,' Mogum said. 'Whitsnare made lots of passages back to your time, storing them here, but this one is the closest we have to when you likely left Merlow.'

A hand fell on Alex's shoulder, and he turned around to Lamond. 'The times that are coming for you, Alex, for you and the Evergreens and Devetta and Arvaeneous, they are not going to be easy.' He moved closer. 'But if you are strong, I know you can do it. You can free them. It is a very noble thing, Alex, to try and save them all. Very noble indeed.'

After shaking Lamond's hand firmly, Alex looked to his brothers. 'None of you deserve to be treated as you are by those monsters. You rescued everyone in that prison, and you rescued me. You are brilliant, brave people who we all owe our lives to. Please don't ever forget that.'

Lamond bowed. 'Thank you, Alex. Please give my greetings to them all. I hope to see them again very soon.'

'We will do our utmost to keep you hidden,' Mogum said, as he too bent over one arm.

'But I have no doubt that we will meet again,' Filligus said, also bowing his respects and giving Alex a wink. 'In fact, I must insist upon it.'

Wishing them goodbye, Alex took a single step through the frame and the door to the future closed behind him.

Over the road and into the shrouded alleyway Alex raced, his sights set on the meadows. He would often pause, throwing himself against a tree just to listen, to determine if the wind carried danger. Upon finally reaching the Clockhaus, his fingers had barely slipped over the handle when the back door flew open and he collapsed into many outstretched hands.

His ears deaf, his eyes blind, Alex could only feel himself lifted to land in the bathroom off the landing.

'You're OK, you are fine, just fine!' Abraham's brittle voice tried to convince itself. Assessing Alex's wrists, he threw the medicine cabinet's contents into the sink to find bandages before crashing to his nephew's side. Try though they might, his shaking hands were unable to open the packet. 'Patch you right up . . .' he said in an attempt at overthrowing his failing abilities, but within a second he had slowed to a halt and fell into Alex's side, sobbing.

'Oh Alex . . . Alex . . .'

'It's all right, I'm home now. I'm here,' Alex mumbled.

'We thought you had gone, we thought that was it, we . . . we just . . .'

Abraham's voice dissolved and together they sat, becoming redundant to one another.

Feeling his body shudder with the desperate need for sleep, and knowing that two beds were waiting nearby, Alex painfully replaced the bandages around his wrists, and pushed back to his feet. He scooped his uncle up into his arms and carried him into the first floor bedroom. After tucking in the corners of a blanket around his uncle, Alex found it far too easy to collapse into the adjacent bed and leave everything behind.

— CHAPTER TWENTY-ONE —

Hope of Glass, Guilt of Stone

The rush of the sea carried Alex through the thinning barrier between sleep and wakefulness some indiscernible length of time later. His ears trembled as the waves crashed over the rocks below the open window, and as he steadily sat up and peeled back the covers, he found the room to be astonishingly bright. His wet eyes swam with pain. Everything was being experienced through a newly cleansed filter; it was as if someone had tilted his head and puffed sharply into his ear, blowing the dust and cobwebbed fragments out through the other.

The bed beside him had been well slept in; its blankets were ruffled and the pillow was dented. A set of clothes hung over the backs of the chairs set at the end of his bed. Alex climbed to his feet and began to change. As he removed his layers, the marks of his surrender became more evident. Long cuts were scratched into his arms, and throbbing bruises, already an unhealthy shade of purple, stained his sides and legs. He carefully pulled on a clean T-shirt, and his own face, red and beaten, startled him in the mirror.

Abraham was standing alone by the balcony doors when Alex finally made his way up to the attic. Dressed in a lumpy black jumper that in no way suited him, Abraham had his hands over his face and was whispering to himself. Upon seeing his nephew he rushed over to him and pulled him into his carefully aimed embrace. The contact was painful, but Alex held on to his uncle with all his might. Together they sat down by the mountain of furniture, still stunned beyond words.

When Abraham did eventually speak, it was revealed that Alex had been asleep for two days but missing since surrendering to Whitsnare's malicious followers for over ten.

'After you . . . went, Robert led us to the Heirloom, to where the black box locked in hundreds of unbreakable padlocks was buried,' Abraham explained in a dry voice. 'He had hidden it amongst hundreds of acres of fields, somewhere so specific that you would just *have* to know where it was to find it. But someone had found it—it was gone,' he finished dispiritedly. 'We took him home—Robert is safe—but the Heirloom . . . it's gone, Alex.'

A hot rush of frustration came over Alex and he sat back in his chair. The more he thought about it the quicker he realised that even if they had found the Heirloom, it wouldn't have changed a thing. Whitsnare still believed he was in possession of it even when he wasn't, and he would not stop hunting down Alex, Devetta and the Evergreens until he had it.

Abraham's mouth creased, and then he spoke the words Alex had known were coming next.

'Can you tell me . . . why you did it? Why you gave yourself up?'

Faced with explaining what felt like a crime of abandonment, Alex understood that his act of surrender had had consequences far more severe than he could have anticipated.

'When Phillip said that Mum and Dad had the Heirloom with them that night, it made me realise that Whitsnare would have gone after them too,' Alex said. 'Arv told me what Whitsnare had done to find the Heirloom, the people, the minds he tortured, and I knew my parents wouldn't be exempt from him . . . I felt it.'

'Felt what?'

'I felt the hope I have for them come crashing down around me,' Alex said, admitting his most powerful drive to his uncle for the first time. 'I have held on to that feeling of hope for them ever since they left.'

Abraham's mouth opened and his eyebrows pulled together.

'After I found out that I'm the one Whitsnare wants, I held on to that hope more and more. I was blind to everything else but that hope, nothing would shake it,' Alex said, knowing how very stubborn he could be. 'And then Phillip said that my parents had with them what Whitsnare wanted and, all of a sudden, it was like there was no chance they could have escaped him.'

'You've been holding on for all this time?'

Alex did not respond immediately. 'I never stopped,' he finally admitted. 'I didn't believe those men were there for me or my parents like you did, and that allowed me to *hope*,' Alex said with one of Evie's sympathetic smiles. 'It allowed me to *dream*.'

When Alex noticed the Evispen on the cabinet over Abraham's shoulder he realised that his hope was not only rebuilding following its recent and spectacular destruction, but also becoming a hundred times stronger. *Who knows what happened to them?* Alex thought, thinking solely of his parents and where they went that cold November night. *How can I say that I won't ever see them again?*

After some reflection, Abraham mumbled that he too now understood his own feelings, in particular his earlier ambivalence towards the Evergreens. He had only gotten as far as the word 'guilt', however, when Alex immediately sought clarification.

'You felt guilt? What for?'

'That night,' Abraham said, his eyes looking set to weep. 'Guilt that I left you. The night I left you alone was the night you were almost killed. Your parents charged me with caring for you and I just . . . just *abandoned* you, Alex,' he said, his voice strained. 'I never tackled those feelings over the years. I didn't even realise what I felt that night. There was so much going on and so much that had to be done.'

It was such guilt that had fuelled Abraham's vow to never leave his nephew again and, by extension, his belief that Alex was in danger. It was only when Alex had told him about the Evergreens' protecting him the night they met, at a time when Abraham could not, that the guilt had exploded into his life.

'I knew I couldn't risk your being found, so I invited them all to stay here. But my guilt was reflected in their faces every time I saw them. *They kept him safe. Why didn't you? You weren't there,*' Abraham revealed, giving his feelings a harsh and ruthless voice.

'You should have told me, I wouldn't have brought them —'

'But you had to. And I offered, remember?' Abraham said. He removed his glasses and began to clean them on his jumper. 'I had to know why they had protected you, why they had been there. I never should have left you alone that night. I never should have stepped out into the snow.' Abraham paused and hung his head for a moment. 'And then when you came back from your grandparents and told me the Evergreens' story and their secrets, it suddenly clicked.'

'What? What clicked?'

Abraham put his glasses back on. 'I finally saw that although they saved you that night, knowing what we do now and what Whitsnare wants . . . well, I'd like to think that I've kept you safe each and every night since.'

His uncle's words were verbal euphoria for Alex. 'You did, every day.' Alex beamed, and kissed him on the top of his head. 'Every single day, and I cannot thank you nor love you enough for it.'

They hugged tightly; at last, the gap of secrets and misunderstanding between them had closed.

'That's what everyone has been telling me since you left,' Abraham cried. 'Oh Alex, they've been so kind.'

All the care in the world couldn't have been more than that which the Evergreens were capable of giving, evidenced when Alex came downstairs to a standing ovation that afternoon. They clamoured to his assistance with antidotes of handshakes and medicines of heartwarming hugs. But it was only as Arvaeneous emerged on a pair of Abraham's old crutches that Alex received an infusion of fluid relief, like an IV drip straight into the valves of his heart, and he set about patching Arvaeneous up with the same remedies he had received.

'Look at us,' Arvaeneous said with a chuckle. 'What a right old pair!' A prominent cut across his temple had yet to heal, and he hobbled to keep the weight off his right foot. Despite his friend's injuries, however, Alex saw only his strengths.

'I knew you would be all right. You are very brave,' Daniel said to Alex.

The gurgling hunger within Alex was quelled with three gigantic sandwiches and copious amounts of tea—Abraham's best and sworn-by medicine—before he shared his story. From the snow to the woods, the brothers, the flood and the fall into the future; so much had happened and somehow a week and a half had been misplaced in the process, as simply as pocketed change is lost between the sofa cushions.

'I can't believe they thought we kidnapped you,' Evie said. Her mouth gaped open. 'How very wrong they were.'

'Did they say how Whitsnare knew your parents had the Heirloom?' Irwin asked.

Alex shook his head.

'How—*why* did your parents have it in the first place?' Winton said next. 'That's what I'm most stumped about!'

'As I've told everyone, I never knew they had it either,' Abraham said.

'But you were right all along, Abe. My parents have always been a part of this,' Alex concluded.

Dinner was cooking when Alex sat down beside Winton by his favourite window, which was clamped with new, thicker curtains.

'I mean, who writes half in English and half in French?' Winton exclaimed as though continuing some earlier conversation with Alex. His hands were filled with the group's notes and he dropped them, lost for words. 'It just flits between the two languages as if she isn't even aware she's doing it! How is that supposed to help us?'

'Whose is it?'

'Devetta's, I reckon.'

'So, still no ideas on what the Heirloom could be?'

Winton huffed as he drew the papers back to him and said that nothing more than their earlier ideas about the Heirloom's possible ability to control or possess people had developed. When Irwin and Ambrose joined them, Alex took the opportunity to ask how his uncle had fared during the days he was absent. Spotting the man in question singing along to the radio in the kitchen with a conductive spatula in hand, Alex felt grateful for how rapidly things had improved between them all.

'It hit him hard, your not being here,' Irwin said before taking a long sip from his glass of wine. 'If someone hadn't been here for him I don't know how he would have fared. You have always been the supporting bridge between your uncle and us, and without you we crashed together. Though we were with him when he wanted us to be.'

Knowing how in debt he was to them for their kindness, Alex tried to express his gratitude. Unfortunately, however, only guilt shone from his face, and Ambrose reached for his hand.

'Don't beat yourself up about the choice you made,' she said in her caring way. 'You were doing a brave thing—the best thing you could in a situation that I cannot begin to imagine. Don't judge yourself for the decision you made to turn yourself, in dear.'

Alex gave a rather thin smile.

'Promise me now, no more feeling bad,' she said.

'I promise,' Alex said, and he excused himself to the kitchen.

*

Watching Alex leave, Winton set aside his readings and leaned in to his wife and son-in-law, appearing rather concerned. 'When are we going to tell him the truth?' he whispered, inadvertently catching Evie's attention with the hook of his words.

'No, we can't—not yet!' Evie whispered, moving in closer. She checked behind her before saying, 'You heard what he just went through. We can't tell him now!'

'I must agree,' Irwin said.

'It could shatter him all over again,' Ambrose said.

'But surely he should know that the Evispen didn't bring us back, that we *chose* to come back!'

'*Shhhh!*' Evie hissed. 'Not here!'

'He cannot know yet, he must be stronger for this,' Irwin insisted. 'He just needs time.'

'Even with a time machine we never seem to have enough of it,' Winton mumbled, sitting back.

The four Evergreens each finally committed to keeping the secret a little longer. They watched Alex, now dancing about the kitchen with his uncle.

'He really is only just starting to realise how involved in everything he is,' Evie said with a crestfallen edge to her voice.

'Ah, to be young,' Winton said. He shook out his pages and resumed his reading.

'I can help, I want to help!' Alex insisted as he pulled up a chair in the circle and sat down decisively. 'Helping you all will make me better! Trust me!'

It was very early on Saturday morning, and the sun was burning prominently on the horizon, unhampered by the thick mist blowing in like foggy tidal waves. Everyone had enjoyed a delicious fruit porridge, courtesy of Ambrose, before heading up to the attic to begin the day's work. As they all found their seats and were delegated fresh stacks of paperwork from the briefcase, Alex excitedly opened *Mysteries of Cause* from where he had left off.

Setting down his crutches, Arvaeneous slowly lowered and then fell onto the chair beside Alex with a moan of pain. He pulled out his notebook and it flicked open for him.

'So, have you found anything more from the—'

'Oh yes!' Arvaeneous shrieked before Alex could finish. 'We have found a map, the third location!' He pulled out a black scroll from the inside of his blue cloak and straightened it out before passing it to Alex. 'This one will be more difficult to infiltrate. I think it speaks for itself as to why.'

The floor plan in Alex's lap detailed a series of various-shaped rooms in constant motion. It was quite literally like an endlessly shifting jigsaw puzzle. Alex watched as over and over the individual rooms came together, interconnected, changed shape and then drifted away to refit again. Whole corridors opened into existence and then on the next rotation were crushed out of it. Determining a channel for entrance or escape would be problematic to say the least.

'This one concerns me the most,' Arvaeneous said with an uncommon hint of apprehension, and he rolled up the parchment. 'Finding these locations is the first step to proving Whitsnare's guilt and the Evergreens' innocence.'

Alex studied Arvaeneous, his eyes pausing at the cuts and colourful bruises that decorated his face. 'Do you mind if I ask you something that's been playing on my mind recently?' Alex asked.

'Well we can't have that. Please, I invite it.'

'Can I ask what you meant when we met, in the field? You said that you had to be sure of me?'

Arvaeneous' finger tapped against his pointed chin. 'I had to be certain that you hadn't been turned by Whitsnare. I wouldn't put it past Whitsnare to employ and delude a young child for his dark work.' Arvaeneous turned his head slightly as though to gain an entirely different viewpoint. 'But that's not all I was checking for,' he said. 'I had to see that you would fight for the Evergreens, that you would not give them up. I knew that this would be a long road, that we would have to fight for everyone's freedom. I knew from the very start that I needed to be certain of you as someone I could place my utmost faith in. My utmost,' he repeated.

'And . . . I passed?'

Arvaeneous gave a small laugh and clapped Alex on the back. 'You passed,' he said with a wink.

Following the flutter of Nora's hare Halpen through the room, Alex's gaze fell naturally on Devetta, who was sitting upon the Elongress. Although he could not see specifically what she was reading, he noticed the thick black book open in her lap as being the one she had packed when she left the cabin.

Alex watched as her eyes swept back and forth across the pages she flicked past, absorbing their contents. There was something about studying her that was so mesmerising; a trance he couldn't help but be pulled in to as he wondered, again, just how she came to be sitting amongst them. Her past itself was a book, its contents steeped in mystery. *Just who is she?* Alex wondered to himself.

For a long minute Alex stared at her until, to his surprise, he witnessed something he never thought he would see. He gave a short inhale and leaned in closer. Devetta had turned to study the very final page of the book, but it was in her expression that Alex was now lost. No longer was her face a blank canvas. No more was it unpopulated by any evidence of feeling.

He felt great relief at knowing an earlier thought about her was now confirmed to be wrong: Whitsnare had not scrubbed all emotion from her in the prison, for as she closed the book and looked up at him, brandished upon her face was a timid, mischievous smile.

*

The attic was warmer now that all eleven of the Clockhaus' inhabitants spent every day within it, progressing through the remainder of the briefcase's contents and the *Bafflement* series' cosmic span of history. Abraham had been assigned *Collection VIII: Beginnings of Our Ends*, and during every break, he would spill its stories: crop circles, flocks of birds dying, schools of fish falling from the sky—signs of the impending apocalypse or some equally thrilling end of all things.

Having departed from his cocoon of guilt, Abraham had emerged as a new person into the group. Like Alex, Abraham now had a purpose, and just as Alex's life had been enriched by his guests, so had his uncle's. Winton and Abraham were often seen chatting and snickering like a couple of schoolboys in the lounge or a corner of the attic. When he heard his uncle laugh, Alex found himself pausing to marvel. The release from his anchor of guilt had never let Abraham fly so high.

One day, when the Evergreens were seeking comfort in their memories, Abraham shared with Alex his greatest fear. It was something that had also kept Alex awake at night since escaping the future: that those searching for him would blow down the Clockhaus' walls at any given moment. Alex was rather overjoyed, however, when he heard his uncle say, 'We will get through it, all of us together, because we are all each other has now.'

Abraham then told his nephew of the joyful wonders he had been shown recently, including Ambrose's herd of gloves which would run all over the lounge on the tips of their fingers, and Daniel's book *A Fantastical Flock of Frogs*, which had sent hundreds of the tiny crafted creatures leaping all around the Clockhaus. They had been found in all manner of hiding places, including coat pockets, the sought-after biscuit tin and even the drawers of the Elongress. Abraham was laughing about how he had found three hiding in his pillowcase as Alex glanced, again, to the memory shielding the Evergreens.

From what he could make out they were standing upon a white sandy beach below a luscious, cloudless sky. Quite unexpectedly Irwin stepped out of the sphere and then, at the extension of his hand, Evie. Alex watched as they moved aside and began to talk in quiet, covert tongues. It was the third time Alex had seen this happen since returning, and although they did not concern him—for what was their business was theirs—he did begin to wonder about these conversations.

The Evispen, the most mystifying object in the room, possibly in the whole century, then caught Alex's gaze. He had found himself thinking about it every so often over the past week. He let it tow his mind over and over to his grandparents' final question. When Abraham followed his gaze to the time machine, Alex knew he should elaborate on his feelings.

'I keep thinking—how do we know what happened to Mum and Dad? How can we say that they are gone when we haven't been back, when we could be the ones to rescue them? When I could be the one to save them?'

'Save them?' Abraham said, a recognisable worry returning to his demeanour.

'Ever since I got back all I've been thinking of is how the brothers rescued me from those horrible people. I was whisked away to a completely different time. I, too, had vanished. I realise now that with the Evispen anything, *anything* is possible. Who knows what could have happened to them? Maybe Whitsnare never got to them, maybe my parents are waiting for me to come back to them.' Alex's heart was pounding. His mind was warm and cosy with loving, tender images of them. 'What if I just haven't gone back *yet*?'

'Alex . . .' Abraham said delicately.

'There is hope for them. You said it yourself before we went to see Phillip. The Evispen is hope, and the feeling in here'—he touched his chest—'it will only get stronger.'

'Hope for what?' Abraham asked.

'The three brothers saved me, just as I tried to save everyone by surrendering. That hope for Mum and Dad, I feel it now for all of them. It is a hope for everyone who needs my help,' Alex said with a smile. Taking a gradual intake of cool air to his hot heart, he concluded, 'I can save them all.'

At that moment the Elongress appeared with the sound of a cracked whip, and Arvaeneous and Devetta stepped out.

'Good afternoon,' Arvaeneous said, removing his shrinking top hat. 'Devetta and I have been searching for any material that might help in our quest for the evidence.' Arvaeneous showed them the book tucked under his arm: *Famously Unfamous Wreckages, Ruins and Devastations*. As he began to explain how Whitsnare had likely hidden the evidence in a highly perilous location, the Evergreens' memory began to fade.

The family was misty eyed, and explained they had just relived their journey to Calistow and the great cathedrals built into its white-rock mountains. Irwin then shuffled forward and declared that they had an announcement to make, seemingly to everyone's surprise but Evie's.

'You said, Alex, when you described your journey back to us that you returned by a door, and that there were doors that led to all kinds of places?' Irwin began.

'I encountered a few, yes,' Alex said, recalling the roar of the hungry leopard. 'Why? Have you got one?'

'When the Evispen was bestowed to us, with it there were a number of other items, none of which have made sense, up until now. Amongst those items was a key,' Evie said.

'This key,' Irwin said. He held up a long black key with a yellow ribbon twisted along its neck. Daniel lifted Felicity up to see it more clearly.

'That's just like one of the keys the brothers had. It can unlock any door to a specific time and place,' Alex said.

Abraham stroked the tag tied to its end. 'Home,' he read aloud. 'Does that mean your time?'

'It was the only home we knew of until now,' Evie said, prompting smiles from uncle and nephew alike.

Irwin gripped the key decisively, and with Arvaeneous' assistance, shifted one of the faded doors out from the mountain of furniture into the middle of the room.

'We've already been to your home—is that where this leads?' Alex asked Ambrose, who was standing near him at the back of the group.

'Where we went before was only our house. There is an important difference. Our true home is something far greater —the home of our family, back when we are from: Hilloweith Castle.'

The eleven of them clustered tightly together around the now free-standing door. Nora stood with her brother and sister at her sides, and Winton and Ambrose put their arms around each other. As Arvaeneous and Devetta flanked the group, Irwin took hold of the key and turned it. A number of loud clicks rang out, like tens of different locks unlocking, and a light glowered through the lock and beneath the door. The room held its breath as Irwin opened the door only a millimetre, letting a sheet of light slip into the attic.

'Can I just ask—has anyone else got the collywibbles?' Winton said, glancing around. Abraham looked to Alex, and taking each other's hands, they nodded.

'Oh yes,' Abraham said excitedly.

Irwin looked around at them all. 'Ready?' he said teasingly, and as he pushed open the door, and as the air of another time swept into the room, they stepped forward into somewhere, somewhen, as one.

THE END

HOW DID YOU ENJOY THE STORY?

Firstly, I would like to thank you for taking the time to read *An Empire of Dreams*. It has taken over six years of hard work and dedication to write this book and get the sequels planned and prepared.

Keep up to date with the latest developments, get sneak peeks of the story to come and be involved in free giveaways by following me on social media:

Facebook - www.facebook.com/LewisJJones8
Instagram - www.instagram.com/lewisjjones8

Gaining exposure as an independent author relies mostly on word-of-mouth, so if you have the time and inclination, please consider leaving a review.

The easiest way to share you thoughts on the book is to search for 'An Empire of Dreams' on **Amazon** or **Goodreads** to quickly and easily find the book page.

Every review really does make a difference.

Thank you.

ABOUT THE AUTHOR

Lewis J Jones is a twenty-five-year-old author who lives in South-East London, England.

Following a dream he had at the age of 19, Lewis began to write what has transformed into a ambitious time-travel adventure series called:

Of Hearts & Minds

An admirer of encapsulating stories with multi-layered characters and interconnected storylines, and a devoted fan of time-travel, Lewis seeks to share a story that explores not only our hearts and minds, but also our strongest hopes and our most daring dreams.

Lewis would love to hear what you thought of the book - he is contactable by email at: **lewisjjones8@gmail.com**